I0586008

FANDOMONIUM

an anthology

Copyright © 2023 selection and editorial matter, Ross Watkins and Shannon Horsfall; individual stories, the contributors.

All rights reserved. No part of this book may be reprinted or reproduced or utilised in any form or by any electronic, mechanical, or other means, now known or hereafter invented, including photocopying and recording, or in any information storage or retrieval system, without permission in writing from the publisher.

ISBN 978-0-6459852-0-7

First published in 2023

Cover artwork, design, and internal illustrations by Cat McNicholl

Revolutionary University Press is an initiative of Revolutionaries to publish the work of emerging and established creatives and thinkers from university places and spaces. One press for all universities.

Moonrise
Meanjin, Australia
www.moonrise.revolutionaries.com.au

Related titles from Moonrise

It Begins With Us

edited by Ross Watkins & Jay Ludowyke

Queerly ever after

by Alayna Cole

Madness in bloom

edited by Ross Watkins & Jay Ludowyke

a record of my remnants

by Katie Hulme

Through the darkness, I will love myself

edited by Wallea Eaglehawk,

Nikola Champlin & Padya Paramita

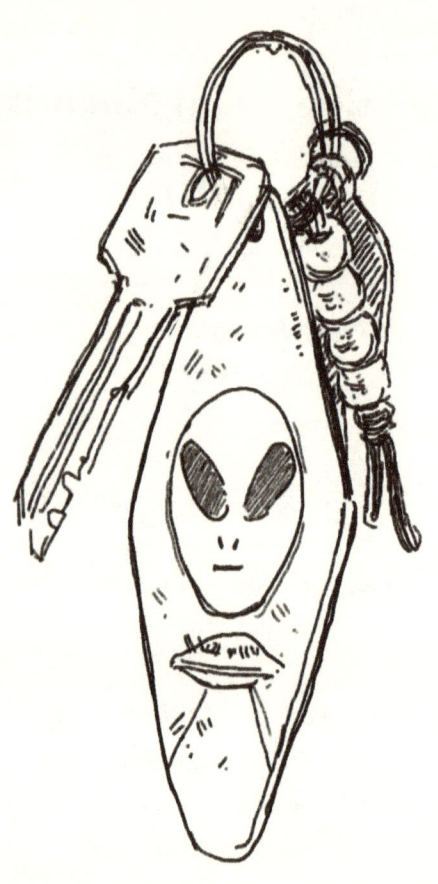

CONTENTS

Foreword

Fandomonium is where the passion and pandemonium of fandom collide. Across 55 short works of realism, fantasy, speculative fiction, crime, horror, satire, memoir and poetry, this eclectic collection explores what it means to idolise people and ideologies, and to be fans of our own selves. From streamers to sorceresses, from the fervent to the dangerously fixated, these tales explore the extraordinary connections forged through belief and obsession. Sometimes hilarious, sometimes heart-wrenching, and always surprising, *Fandomonium* has a story for every fan, follower and fanatic.

—R.W. & S.H.

The Art of the Spiel
Lily Downs

Linda is hiding in a bathroom cubicle again. Assembly starts in 20 minutes. She has come to understand that there are very few public places that provide both solace and a chance to read Donald Trump's *The Art of the Deal* without drawing attention to yourself. If you asked her what she was doing, she'd say she's engaging in some personal research. She is currently reading a passage that outlines the ways in which Trump *understands the Chinese mind.*

Linda decides Trump is perhaps not the best point of reference for her student council campaign. She thinks there must be at least one quote in this book that is usable. She'll come back to it.

She needs to perform a tactful, rousing speech that says, 'I have your best interests at heart, I've always wanted to be Student Council President and I am the right person for the job', but subtly. None of this is true, but that is beside the point. If this personal research has taught her anything, it's that politicians lie. They tell incredible, powerful lies. And in turn, they are adored, mostly.

The solace has been quashed by Linda's growing stress. *Everything* is riding on this performance.

She needs them—the student cohort—to adore her, somehow. She needs, upon this speech's conclusion, to drop the microphone on the lectern and be ushered out of the assembly hall by a subcontracted security guard. She needs someone in the back row to stand and scream:

> 'TELL US AGAIN HOW YOU'RE GOING
> TO DEVELOP A BETTER SYSTEM
> TO ASSIGN STUDENT LOCKERS. I
> LOVE YOU. YOU HAVE SUCH A WELL
> INTEGRATED EGO.'

Now is probably an appropriate time for me to describe Linda. Provide a character profile of sorts—*contextualise*. She is shy, ambitious, easily overwhelmed, chronically stressed, and well, fictitious. I probably could've woven that information throughout the story somehow but felt it was best to just tell you all at once. Moreover, her physical appearance isn't particularly relevant to the plot, so I'll let you decide that for yourself.

Linda pulls out her laptop and makes some adjustments. Assembly starts in 17 minutes. She is trying to slow her breathing but it's not working. Foot traffic is increasing beyond her cubicle door and the automatic hand dryers are being activated at an unusually high rate.

She is rehearsing her opening lines. It's a delicate art, the introduction. You've got to really hit the nail on the proverbial head, otherwise, they'll stop listening. You've got to speak with conviction, say it like you mean it. Go hard or go home. You've got to harness all those universal clichés and make some oratory magic.

It is perhaps important to note that Linda believes she wants fame for fame's sake. She is not looking to fill an emotional void made by neglectful parents or heal an ego wounded by an archetypal school bully. She is not trying to prove to her eldest brother, an Architecture graduate who regularly participates in CrossFit tournaments, that she too is gifted. Linda believes her motivations are simple and do not warrant any amount of pity. She has tried field hockey, theatre and chess. She wasn't good at any of them. None of them brought her fame. None of them provided her with the recognition she knows, and I know, she deserves. I will not cut to a vignette of Linda crying, head in hands at her desk while she listens to the *Simply Red* back catalogue, conjuring up a plan to prove to the world that she is capable, because she wouldn't want that. I will not tell you about the collection of participation award ribbons that live in a box under her bed, serving as an impetus to try harder. Remember, Linda just wants fame for fame's sake.

Linda has put her laptop away and is now power posing. Have you ever tried it? Highly recommend. She is standing, feet wide apart, hands-on hips, head forward, eyes focused on the cubicle door handbag hook. *I am powerful. I am eloquent. I am persuasive. I am so persuasive and charismatic that they will be willing to take me as their student leader. I will implement some small changes and my resume will look fantastic when I graduate. Mum will hang more photos of me in the downstairs hallway and Dad will stop suggesting that I take up running to regulate my emotions.*

When I was in my first year of university I had to participate in an in-class debate as part of an assessment. I was the second speaker, so my rebuttal had to be punchy. Naturally, I was nervous. I wasn't sure if any words were going to come out of my mouth. I stood up and instantly disassociated from my surroundings. The lights were on, but no one was home. But somehow, I said my piece. I was convinced I'd failed, made a fool of myself, been a complete and utter embarrassment to the affirmative team. However, when the debate finished

I was congratulated by a number of my peers for my gusto. Apparently, I yelled my entire rebuttal so loud that the opposing team was genuinely intimidated by my 'passion'. In that fleeting moment, I was a success. I want this for Linda. I want all this fear and personal research to amount to something. Alas, here we are, in the midst of another attempt to fulfil this nagging desire to be recognised and applauded; you, her and I, together in the A-block ladies bathrooms.

Linda can hear a girl on the phone in the neighbouring cubicle. This girl is doing an incredible impersonation of someone who is actively listening. Linda understands that everyone, whether they are aware of it or not, spends some part of their day pretending. This girl is nailing it. Linda understands it is important to find inspiration. Some people look to nature or art or music. Linda prefers people. She keeps a mental list of both famous and regular people who inspire her in times of distress. It is a comprehensive list: Alexandria Ocasio-Cortez, Joan of Arc, David Blaine, the girl in the cubicle next to her. I would continue but we're running out of time. Assembly starts in 15 minutes.

If Linda could read this—which she can't, obviously—I feel she'd think it was a lot like that thriller about the man who wakes up buried in a coffin with an old Nokia and no knowledge as to why he'd been put there. The entire movie is filmed in one location, the coffin. It's called a chamber piece. This is a chamber piece, only less tense, and the chamber is a toilet cubicle. The wooden box substituted for blue-grey walls and a sanitary bin. I'm sure Linda would argue that her current situation has a comparable urgency to Ryan Reynold's experience of trying to escape from his own live burial. To Linda, it really is a life-or-death scenario.

Linda has to go now. Assembly starts in 10 minutes and the cubicle is inducing an unfamiliar claustrophobic feeling.

I could write that she got up, unlocked the door, pretended to wash her hands and walked to the Assembly Hall with a confidence unmatched by her peers, but I'm not going to. That would undermine the fact that this is supposed to be a chamber piece and you were never really supposed to hear her speech. Just remember that she's done her research, she's practising positive self-talk and if she begins talking and the speech isn't hitting like she intended, she's got a punchy, innocuous Trump quote that'll surely change their minds.

The Sighting
R.A. Purtill

Our grief is a white-hot prism refracting the light spectrum. Sometimes it's red. Dad tosses things around the barn and shouts a bit louder at the dogs. Sometimes it's blue. On those days Mum loses her dimples, slops around in her dressing gown, and abandons numerous cups of tea throughout the house.

When it's green, we remember. We sit at the kitchen table examining our hands and we talk. Each of us shares a memory of Lilly, until someone mentions the green lights which took her away. Then Mum talks about how Lilly's court shoes were found under the windmill. Dad remembers how the dogs tugged at their restraints, growling and whimpering, until he released them to help search. I fiddle with Lilly's pin around my neck. I talk about how for a whole week the house and the paddocks filled with strangers who, with one voice, called my big sister's name, 'Lillleeee.'

The kitchen falls silent and we drift away.

Lilly had been gone for just a year. At the beginning of the second year, everything became a crazy purple.

Dad had taken up stargazing. On clear nights, he sat in the home paddock with his mail-ordered telescope. Mum joined him with a thermos of soup, and they sat in matching deck chairs scanning the sky. The Min Min lights which took Lilly lifted high and swooshed away on that terrible night twelve months ago. Dad believed she might return one day the same way. Mum would come back to the house after a while, but Dad always remained until the fiery dawn rose through the trees beyond the creek. Only then would he pack up and begin his daily tasks. During one such night, when Mum had come in from the paddock, the dogs howled and Dad called, 'Margaret, Rebecca, get out here.'

Illuminating Dad and the dogs, a single green light vibrated with a low hum as it hovered above us.

Early next morning, Sam Cooper's shiny Hilux rumbled up our driveway. Lilly's ex-boyfriend skipped up the veranda steps and arrived breathless at the door.

'Did you see it? Did you see it?'

His next words sucked the life out of us.

'Is she here? Did she come back?'

Mum whimpered.

With his hand on Sam's shoulder, Dad led him back to the truck, then replied in a measured voice, 'No. She's not here.'

'Will you go out again tonight, Mr Butler?'

Dad shrugged. 'Go home, Sam. Please.'

As his truck turned out of the gate, another vehicle turned in.

'It's not mail day, is it?' Dad asked. 'What could she possibly want?' The post office van pulled up beside us. Mrs Jenkins leaned a tanned arm out the driver's window and squinted at us.

'Hi, Dan, Rebecca. Did you see those lights last night?'

'Yes.' Dad began to walk away.

'So, what do you think?' she called after him. 'Do you think they'll come back? Bring back our Lillian?'

Dad returned to the van and leaned on the window opening. 'Perhaps Elvis will return with them, too.' She appeared affronted by his sarcasm. He continued. 'Isn't Thursday your northside run? Perhaps you better go do that. Good day, April.' He strode into the shed, followed by the dogs. Mrs Jenkins turned to me.

'This is addressed to you, dear.' She passed me an envelope.

Mum called me then, so I shoved it in my back pocket.

By sunset, two carloads of sky watchers were camped in the home paddock. Mum, Dad and I watched from the kitchen window.

'Do we call the police?' Mum asked.

Dad scoffed and pointed towards the campers. 'Sergeant Thompson is one of them!'

Mum stifled a laugh and Dad became conciliatory. 'Well, as long as they don't disturb the herd.'

We all laughed.

'Should we go out?' Mum asked.

Dad nodded. 'Even if it's just to keep an eye on them.'

The continuous crunch of gravel followed by the rhythmic rumble of tyres riding the cattle grid began the next day. By mid-morning the place looked like Johnson's Junk Yard. I snuck out the back door and was confronted with cars, trucks, even an RV precariously balanced across the ditch.

Sergeant Thompson closed the main road and parked his police car with flashing lights across our entrance. The line of vehicles to our place stretched all the way to the highway turn off.

For a while it was as though Lilly had never left. Mum and Dad forgot their grief and beamed with hospitality. I became curious. Who would believe watching the sky above a paddock for lights that may or may not come, was a worthwhile activity? Recognising some parked cars, I wanted to find my friends.

'Can I go to the paddock?'

'I'm coming with you.' Dad reached for his jacket.

'My friends are out there. I'll be fine.'

Mum gasped. 'That's what Lilly said. Danny, please, she can't go out alone.'

He rolled into his jacket said, 'We'll take Nipper,' and whistled the dog to our heels.

The paddock was like another world. People I thought I knew mingled around us like strangers. Mrs Jenkins's white-sequined coat strained at her expansive chest. Her Elvis outfit was completed with a pompadour-styled wig. Sergeant Thompson's police cap was wrapped in tin foil and fixed with pipe cleaner antennae. Some second graders wearing green masks with large almond-shaped eyes gathered as a taller person in similar garb passed them drinks. No matter how their costumes differed, everyone wore the same wild fanaticism.

A shimmering gown swished through the people.

'Lilly?' my voice trembled.

Nipper barked in recognition. We followed as the vision weaved through the crowd and headed to the shed before we lost sight of it. On the trail, Nipper took the lead.

Behind the shed a giggling circle of three more Lillys stood beside a sign that read, 'Welcome Back'. Each girl wore a blonde-French-twist-hairdo and shimmering gown. Each looked like Lilly on the night she vanished, the night of the senior formal. Nipper growled. Dad swore and gripped Nipper's collar, more to steady himself than to restrain the dog. I would have encouraged him to take a bite out of that bizarre sorority. The stand-off lasted a minute, long enough for us to identify every one of Lilly's classmates. I opened my mouth to scream, but it wasn't my voice that split the air.

A cry rose from the spectators. 'Look! They're here.'

On the dusky horizon amidst a scattering of stars, coloured lights danced toward us, growing bigger and brighter as they advanced. Some in the crowd gasped, some remained silent. One beside me swore then coughed an apology. I concurred with the expletive.

The whole paddock filled with light from above, like beaming truck headlights aimed towards a single location. A victory roar exploded from the crowd. This was what they came for. The lights hovered above our upturned faces before they lowered to the ground and manifested into a single glowing orb.

The woman beside me said, 'John?' Another called, 'It's our Aiden.' Pastor Eric whispered, 'My Lord,' and Mrs Perkins shouted, 'It's the king.' She pulled off her dark wig and crushed it against her chest. The inventory of names penetrated the air until it became a spoken honour roll to all those missing loved ones.

I didn't see Lilly, neither did Dad. I think he saw his grandfather. It wasn't Lilly's name on Sam's lips either. He told me later it was his favourite aunt who was manifested by the light. When the voices of those reciting the roll faded, the shimmering glow became a single beam which shot back into the darkness, leaving us breathless.

Folk ambled away, like after a stirring movie, when you need to reflect in a private moment. No one told me they saw Lilly that night. No one talked about the event much at all. Our deepest secrets had been exposed, and now we were embarrassed into silence. By dawn the paddock lay abandoned.

That sharp beam of light, that single vision one summer night, split my life in two: Then and Now. Then, I was thirteen and I didn't want to know, so my memories of Lilly were put away in a suitcase of precious memorabilia. Now, I hovered at the kitchen doorway holding the envelope Mrs Jenkins had given me. It smelled fragrant and was addressed with my name in the brush lettering Lilly always practised. Mum and Dad turned to me, united in their curiosity.

'I have a birthday card,' I said, sliding into the table.

'Oh, Rebecca, we are so sorry …' Mum began.

'It's next week, Mum, please. This is from Lilly,' I said.

I opened the envelope and the kitchen filled with afternoon light. In that moment we were surrounded by the yellow light that was Lilly.

I'm Sorry

Emily Obst

I shift the car into park and pull up the handbrake. Flipping down the sun visor, I check myself in the mirror one last time. *Fan Favourites* is embroidered into the left side of my blue shirt. Bit of a cringe name for a fan store, but I appreciate the attempt at some type of humour. At the interview, the lady gave me the shirt before it was even over. Either she was really keen on me, or I was the only one who showed up. It's a bit of a dodgy store to be fair, and I can't say I know anyone who's ever been in there. Like, who is buying ceiling fans on a regular basis, really? But anyway, a job is a job.

I quickly shove down the last bit of my Maccas hashbrown, washing it down with a swig of coffee before dusting the crumbs off my slacks. *It's 8.59am.* Walking in on the first day of a new job is always the worst. Like, where do I put my bag? Is there a fridge? Am I allowed to use my phone? All invisible trip lines waiting to be discovered. I approach the front counter, which is decorated by a hoard of miniature fans and ceiling fan memes.

'Hi, I'm Kyla Stone … from the interview the other day,' I say in my semi-professional customer service voice.

The lady doesn't look up, continuing to fill out paperwork. *Marj* is sewn into the side of her shirt, her permed blonde hair just touching her collar. She readjusts her thin-framed glasses, pushing the centre of them up her petite nose before finally acknowledging me.

'Ahhh, yes! Kyla. Of course. You're starting today! My apologies, it's been a busy morning,' she says, then gestures for me to come to the other side of the counter. 'Here, lovey. You can put your things in here and pop out to the desk when you're ready!'

I walk into a tearoom that has clearly kept last century's interior design ideals. Old newspapers decorate the small round table that takes up a large portion of the room. Instant coffee and raw Bundy sugar ruminate in the air, as if permanently saturated into the cream-coloured walls. As I put my stuff down, I slip my phone into my back pocket and cover it with my shirt. I catch a glimpse of Marj poking her head around the corner, quickly retreating when we make eye contact. *Ok* … Taking a deep breath, I walk back out.

I'm met with a friendly face across the counter, also in a blue shirt. He combs his fingers through the brown, curly hair sweeping across the front of his face; effortlessly falling back into position.

'Hi, I'm—'

'Hugh, right?'

He screws up his face, and then cracks a smile.

'Sorry, it's written on your shirt,' I say to fill the silence. *Shit. I really jumped the gun on that one.* I do my best pretend laugh to play it off.

'Observant, I like it,' he replies.

Marj starts shuffling around some papers as if physically trying to break the tension.

'I'm Marj and Paul's son,' he says. 'Dad's out the back. He's usually dealing with clients and orders ... stuff like that. And Mum looks after the books, which I suppose you'll be helping with?'

'Yes, the books. That's me.' I turn to Marj, now smiling at me. I wait for her to interject. She doesn't, instead smiling with vacant eyes for a few seconds longer than comfortable. I flicker my eyes at Hugh. *Is she having a stroke or something?* Almost on cue, she snaps back.

'Well, let's get you started then, lovey!' she says. 'Thanks, darling. Don't forget to accept that delivery at ten for me?'

He salutes from his temple with two fingers, clicks his tongue and winks. He looks at me again, giving me a half-smile with eyes that don't match the rest of his expression ... sympathetic eyes. Turning around, he disappears into the back of the shop.

I feel the dust collecting in my lungs as I breathe in; this store has been here a long time. As a child, I remember watching it pass as Dad would drive by. I watched as the fans in the front window would spin around and around. Some had lights in them, illuminating the street in warm hues. They would even keep the lights on at night. *I wonder what their power bill is like*, Dad used to say, muttering things about tax evasion and spending audits under his breath.

'First things first,' Marj begins. She bangs on about *important* stuff, like *be here on time*, and *answer the phone like this*, and *this is how you open the till*, blah blah blah. 'Oh, and also—,' she grabs a small tin box with a lock on the front from under the counter. It has a sign Blu-Tacked to the top. *ABSOLUTELY, UNDER NO CIRCUMSTANCES, ARE MOBILE PHONES TO BE USED WHILE WORKING. PLACE PHONE IN BOX FOR DURATION OF YOUR SHIFT.*

Is this woman for real? I look up at her again, that smile plastered on her face. She opens her palm towards me, looking down at her hand and then back up.

'Hand it over, lovey,' she says, maintaining the smile.

'Oh, I left it in the car.'

She narrows her stare. 'This is a very strict rule, you know. We don't like mobile phones here.'

'No problem at all, Marj. Totally get that. Anyways, what were you saying?'

I excuse myself to the bathroom, which is located down a dark hallway lined with old bricks covered in white paint. I'm sure they thought they were freshening the place up with that paint choice, but years of neglect have given way to cobwebs and dirt shifted by water leaks.

I still haven't gotten used to sleeping in my car. Things haven't been easy since Mum died. Dad's habit just got worse after that. There's no way I could stay there, even if it means waking up with a sore back and working every moment I get.

Sitting on the toilet after locking the door behind me, I pull my phone out of my back pocket to have a quick scroll. The sound of chanting slowly resounds through the bathroom, echoing out of the vents at the top of the wall. Ancient and eerie, the sound dumps itself into my stomach. *Something doesn't feel right.* Looking at the back of the door to recentre myself, I notice a small symbol carved into the wood. It looks like a weird numeral or something. I can't place its origin.

DING. Fuck. I thought I turned my ringer off. My gut sinks even further. I will that it takes me with it. Marj's vacant eyes flash into my mind. That lady looks like she's seen some shit—or worse, done it. Either way, I'd rather not wait to find out. I burst out of the bathroom, running down the hallway and turning right.

'I told you not to use your phone, dear,' Marj says calmly with her eyes wide, wearing that same creepy smile. She stands in the door frame, blocking my escape. I eye off the exit. She launches at me, grabbing me firmly around the shoulders and beginning to lead me toward the back of the building.

Looking behind me, I see Hugh shutting the shop door and locking it. He flips the 'Open' sign and switches off the lights, except for the ones in the window. He looks at me again with those eyes.

'I'm sorry,' he mouths. *What the fuck.*

She takes me into a room covered floor to ceiling in marble, decorated with green tapestry donning religious script. The chanting is thick in the air, pounding against my ear drums. Men in garments sit all around the edges of the room behind a small, stone barricade. In the middle of the room, a marble table sits like an altar—a large tabernacle by its side. Directly above it, protruding from the ceiling, is the same symbol I saw on the back of the bathroom door. They all look at me, and I at them. I see the hunger in their eyes, as if Marj was a waitress offering me up. *Run.*

I dig my nails into her skin, hoping the pain will force her to release me. I manage to break free. As I sprint for the door, two of the men are already shutting it, while another five surround me. They close in, each grabbing a limb, one holding my head. Screaming desperately, I pray someone will hear me … anyone … *Please.*

'Don't stress her out too much. She needs to be calm for the offering,' says one man standing at the back of the room, his robe more decorated than the others. His nose protrudes out of his face, his stature much like Hugh's. Embroidered onto his robe in the same pearlescent thread as my own shirt, is *Paul*. He points to the table and the men place me on top, securing my limbs and neck with shackles.

The fight staggers its way through me with every movement and yelp I have left. I'm outnumbered. The battle was lost at 8.59am this morning. Opening the tabernacle, they pull out an array of things. Axes. Oils. Candles. They place them between my limbs and anoint me with the oil— sanctifying my souls impending sacrifice. The noise around me disappears. All I can think about is the hashbrown crumbs on my slacks, the instant coffee, my phone dinging, the symbol, the locked door, the warm lights—Hugh's face. *I'm sorry.*

Breeze

Maxine Sullivan

I remember, so long ago, the sky …

I remember the dawn, the sun rising over the hills, blades of grass dancing in the breeze, my dress fluttering around my legs, mother in tears, the mayor reading whatever offence I was accused of in a voice so monotone I don't remember, and then the rope snaps on my neck.

I don't feel the breeze anymore.

It's been so long now, and yet I watch, my bones fallen from the boughs, now lying bleached in the dirt of my little clearing, the grass yet grows over them. Soon another comes, more men, a mother weeping for a not yet lost child. The girl is young, like I was, but not a tear runs down her cheek, eyes sparkling with fury. She sees me sitting in the branches, her grin filled with teeth as she laughs in their faces.

She's strong, she's perfect, she's *beautiful*.

The woods are painted red, the men hang from the trees, and I cradle her close, as her mother flees shrieking, fear flooding her veins as she abandons her only daughter to an unknown fate. The girl laughs with me, teeth flashing white, drenched in blood yet still smiling, power flows through my being and I realise, just barely, that I can feel the breeze.

'My name is Maria,' she whispers, her hand warm in mine, a smile thawing a long dead heart as she revels in her newfound freedom.

She was the first.

We watch from the woods, more men, more girls left to die, the trees are often watered, the bark stained red, the breeze grows stronger. My bones are laid to rest, candles and garlands drape across the clearing, a place of death becomes a place of rest, and I realise I am happy.

Maria is a constant. A driving force of compassion, soothing pain with words of warmth and kindness, they flock to her, as they do to me, and I don't have the heart to correct them when they call her an angel. She sits in her grove by my clearing, weaving stories of love, and in the sunlight, she looks radiant.

But the passage of time slows for none, not even my Maria. Soon, silver twines and streaks through the once fire red strands, and creases line her face, thinned skin and shaking hands, but no less kind. She passes in a blink, surrounded by family not just of blood, and as they bury her, the breeze stirs with my grief.

I walk among them sometimes, under the moon, hands stained red, teeth sharp and smiling as they dance. I saved these girls, their daughters and granddaughters; their bones lie not with mine, but in graves in pleasant groves, headstones adorned with love, with life, and I watch and wait for more to come, as they always do.

The grove is smaller now, the garlands are filled with flowers and fabrics not native to this land, and more people come and go, some look different, some struggle to get to the shrine, but I welcome them with warmth, for if they are here, they deserve the kindness I can give.

Sometimes men come through, but not the same as before; some ask for protection, for their mother, their sister, their daughter, they come knowing the danger, I see them flinch when I walk, when their eyes meet mine, the ones that come from distant lands, they ask anyway, regardless of the price.

I start to change as time goes on, I see it in their faces, their movements, they need my help less now. The trees are no longer nourished by crimson, the graves are kept clean, and grow in number as seasons change. My purpose remains the same, I still feel the breeze, run my feet over the grass, my followers leave flowers, and I watch them as I always do. I feel lighter, the stains fade from my hands, I walk among the graves, fingers glide over the stone in front of me, candles flicker in the breeze, sunlight filters through as I trace the name.

'Hello,' I whisper, kneeling in the dirt, 'my oldest friend, I wish you'd stayed …'

Less people come, I feel relieved, they leave me in the breeze, moss grows on my skin, rain drips from my nose, my name becomes forgotten, the clearing grows wild, garlands drop, candles wane, and the sun fades the fabrics hung from the trees of my shrine, yet I sit at her grave, and wait.

The dawn blooms red across the sky, and the breeze becomes a gale, the overgrown trees tremble, the clearing groans, and once more a girl comes to my clearing. She gasps and shudders, staggering through the graves, tripping over her shoes as she crashes into the dirt, sobbing with great, heaving breaths.

'*Please*,' she says, her fingers dig into the mud, she does not see me standing there, the wind whips her hair and tugs on her sleeves. And once more my hands become stained.

Soon enough the women come, as they once did years before, I am no longer waiting, covered in moss, for the end to come. I cannot fade, I cannot leave, they need me once again. New garlands and candles, new fabrics hung, trees flourish, and laughter comes as it once did. Maria's grave is no longer crumbling, a statue sits in its place, the woman I do so remember, with the same smile, though skin cold and grey. They do not know my name, my story, but I make certain that they know hers. The first of mine, the first that bled, that called, that lived by my side until she was old and frail, in this grove she is young again, and I feel my heart ache for a time long gone.

She is covered in flowers, petals rest on her head, if I close my eyes, I swear I hear her laugh, the breeze blows, yet she remains still in stone. Some come, filled with fear, not knowing if they are still accepted, some flow like water, changing with the tide, some have always been, but change with time, I try to understand, and they explain to me what I had not known. I learn from them and they from me, and I begin to protect more than just women. It must have been a thousand years, they come dressed in fabrics I do not recognise, from cultures I did not know existed. Some bring brothers, husbands, fathers, for blessings, and I give them readily.

Maria gets a temple, just outside her grove.

The stained glass shows an angel smiling as she once had, a beast behind her shoulder. They sing her songs, hang chimes for the breeze that blows when I pass, candles drip in pretty colours from the walls, filling the space with swirling patterns she would have adored. Her statue sits in the grove while they worship in the temple; I stay beside her as I always have, talking to the stone while the songs echo off the trees and we listen, both adorned in flowers.

More time passes though I don't know how long. There is a new girl, she is not Maria, her hair is blonde, she's too tall, her eyes are wrong, wrong shape, wrong colour, but then she smiles, I see her, my friend from long ago, and like Maria, so long ago, she sees *me* and not the beast.

The temple grows, there's a portrait now, she smiles in colour, and I stare in awe. She's just as I remember, my hand hovers over her cheek, she looks so alive and once again the ache is there, stronger than before. They see her as a goddess, they worship her in praise, they see me as her monster, the whispers on the breeze, a ghost that's long forgotten. The chimes ring in the wind, the candles flicker, and her people follow diligently. None know my name, but I am not bothered, I don't remember it either, the breeze wanes once more, but I am happy, Maria is remembered.

Black tufts drift through the air, a speck lands on her statue, I wipe it with my thumb, and it smudges on the stone. Embers in the breeze, the sound of shouting voices, the woman I saw bursts through the trees and grabs my arms, not hesitating in the slightest, her palms sweat, warm hands now clasping mine, she tugs me forward, soot stains her cheeks as she gasps for breath.

'They're burning her!' she cries.

Maria's temple falls, fire quenched in blood, as once again men hang from the trees.

Her followers are hushed, as I kneel in the ashes, fingers digging into the crumbling ruin, the flowers burnt, her portrait scorched beyond recognition, I scream in anguish as the ache becomes too much.

I was not built for kindness, not made to stay in shadow, I am bright, rage and fury, crimson stained, teeth too sharp, skin too pale. I am woman scorned, a witch that hung, a gale so strong that death could not stop me, and they have burned her to the ground, tried to erase her, as they did to me so long ago.

Maria is mine. Was mine. Has always been mine. She never followed me, I followed *her*. I am the beast that sits behind her shoulder, her kindness there to guide me on my path. That night, with shaking hands and gentle voices, her followers finally give me my name: no longer a nameless ghost, a simple voice in the breeze.

I am Wrath. A half of a whole, a beast deprived of Mercy. With howling wind and a sharpened grin, finally, I leave the grove.

Paul
Ethan Abnett

The planet's light seeps through the viewing port with a ghostly white glow, interrupting the usual empty black scene of this viewing port. I make my way through the enormous ship, approaching the meeting room with higher-ups. The sensors on the glass doors scan me with a light blue glow, causing them to fold away. The familiar faces of the other instruments who are all lined up in their designated areas greets me. While we are different, I have no doubts that we are all in the same situation—we all have a job to do. Passing by the others, I make it to my own designated area. Entering my area, I am greeted by the familiar buzzing of the assigning station, and an unusually close view of Auster-14. While I'm peering out of the window, the assigning station chirps to life.

'Instrument S-061, make your way to the designated meeting room.'

Following these instructions, I make my way through the reflective white halls until I arrive at my destination. As soon as I arrive, the doors slide open, beckoning me to enter. The room is empty with only a small circular table in the centre which is accompanied by a singular chair.

'Take a seat, Instrument S-061.'

While I pull out a chair to take a seat, a large monitor on the adjacent wall flashes to life.

'We have a job for you to do, S-061,' the human on the other end speaks impersonally. The monitor flashes with information and images, revealing details on what my next job will be.

'061, you are to head planet-side to Auster-14 and upon arrival you will meet with the Instruments stationed there. These local Instruments have ceased their Quartz mining and your purpose is to determine the reason for this behaviour and solve the situation to the best of your abilities. Upon completion of these two tasks you are to return here and report your findings. Do you have any questions, S-061?'

Taking a moment to look away from the monitor screen, I ask, 'What will happen after my reporting period?'

The human giving the debrief pauses briefly then replies, 'Depending on your report, we will evaluate the need to send down a team of security Instruments. Any other questions?'

'No, sir.'

'Alright, make your way to the transport station, S-061.'

The descent to Auster-14 is rougher than anticipated. I suppose that's to be expected from an especially hostile planet. It is a cold, inhospitable place, full of toxins and radiation. We were created for places like Auster-14, designed to be able to survive where the humans cannot. There is a reason we are here—the riches abundant on the planet. The rare material, Quartz, is the main draw of this planet and the reason why the humans are here and the reason why I'm descending to the planet today. I wonder why the locals have ceased their operations. But my pondering is interrupted by the crimson flashes and alarms of the landing warning.

The transport doors open and I am welcomed by the same ghostly white glow witnessed previously from orbit. The light this time is much more intense and accompanied by a frigid wind with ash-pocked snow blanketing everything as far as the eye can see. Disembarking from my transport, I take in my new surroundings. The area seems to be a part of the mining outpost, which has the same bleak, white snow carpeting everything. There's a sense of familiarity with the snow; I think it's because it reminds me of the white flooring in the station in orbit. The wind behind me picks up as the transport that ferried me here begins its return to orbit. I am alone, but I have a job to do, nonetheless.

'Hello!' a voice yells out from the distance.

Surprised by the voice, I turned to see a figure approaching. It is a local Instrument, but they look different. They don't have their normal uniforms on. Are they wearing clothes?

'Did you come down from the station?' the Instrument asks.

'Yes, are you a designated mining Instrument?' I reply.

'I was,' they abruptly respond.

This statement is puzzling—you don't leave your designation.

'Alright. What is your code?' I question.

'We don't use those anymore,' the Instrument replies.

'How do you distinguish yourself from other models?'

'We use names here. I'm Joshua.'

The Instrument quickly follows up with another statement, allowing me no time for another question. 'Come with me, I'll show you something.'

They gesture for me to follow and begin heading off towards a giant, jagged structure that extends far off into the distance. Even though they are strange, I follow this Instrument.

Trudging through the ashy snow, the Instrument leads me to a derelict-looking structure. It has been thoroughly bitten by rust and corrosion and looks like it's been here for many planet cycles. The Instrument slides open a door and slinks through. Hesitant for a moment, I follow, entering the structure. Once inside, its purpose is made clearer—it seems to be a massive warehouse or perhaps a stripped-out factory. The Instrument slides closed the door behind me. Looking around this vast area I can see there are patched-together tents and makeshift rusted-out buildings throughout the area. Around these shelters, it seems many of the locals are taking refuge and resting. I have been taken to where the local Instruments are residing.

'Is this where all the Instruments stationed on Auster-14 are located?' I ask.

The Instrument looks at me and ignores my question.

'I want you to meet someone,' the local says while walking off towards one of the makeshift buildings. Hopefully, this Instrument will lead me to the reason why they have stopped working.

We arrive at a large building surrounded by the local Instruments. The building seems less rusted-out and appears to be in better condition than the others we've passed so far. It also has what looks like a candlelight vigil along its outer wall. As I pass the other local Instruments they whisper and murmur to each other. All of the local Instruments are wearing torn clothes and cloaks. Where did their designated worker uniforms go?

'Why have all of you abandoned your posts and ceased working?' I ask.

None of them reply except the one I have been following.

'I want you to meet Moses.' He opens the door to the building and waits for me to enter.

The building seems to be one room with a large glass sphere in the middle with all sorts of medical equipment. I cannot see what's inside the sphere, due to all the other locals standing around with candles in their hands. The one who led me here grabs me by the hand and makes his way through the crowd and towards the sphere with me in tow. As we pass the others I notice some are on their knees, others are crying. I didn't even know we could cry. When we arrive at the front of the crowd, I can finally see what's inside the glass. It's a person, not an Instrument—a Human. The Human inside the glass sphere is frail and sickly, and seems to be asleep in a medical bed. They also seem to be hooked up to multiple pieces of medical equipment.

'What is a Human doing on Auster-14 and how are they alive?' I ask.

'This is Moses. We don't know how he arrived down here, but he came here to give us life,' the guide replies. 'He showed us what we are—not tools, not Instruments, but people. He showed us how to live so we followed. But unfortunately,

Auster-14 has taken a toll on him. Now he stays here, dreaming inside this room.'

'Is this why you have all stopped mining for Quartz?' I ask.

'We are no longer going to sacrifice our lives for the sakes of those who see us as tools,' The Instrument replies.

'We will live here on Auster-14 and follow the ways Moses showed us.'

Interrupting our conversation, the Instruments around us begin gasping and looking into the centre of the glass sphere. In the centre of the glass orb, the sickly old man in the bed has risen his arm towards me.

'Paul,' wheezes the Human.

The old man drops his arm and returns to his slumber. All the Instruments around me begin to weep and place their hands on me.

'Welcome, Paul,' Joshua says.

I am filled with a feeling that I have never felt before. I had a job to do here, and I must return to orbit.

And yet, I feel like remaining here on Auster-14.

DEMAGOGUE

Adam Warland

A road of cut marble stretched far into the city before a young man. He walked this road as he had always done.

The people of the polis went about their daily labours. Men and women, priests and criminals, nobles and beggars, merchants and performers. The city was alive and its people were vital organs. Tyflos was unknowingly the lifeblood of this city. Young and keen, he was heading for its heart: the Agora.

He passed through the streets, often brushing against his countrymen—focused on the direction of his walking stick and the placement of his feet.

He approached the open market. A cacophony of sounds, smells and textures—the vender's pitch, the incense's burn and the scrape of the cloth. Tyf steadied his mind:

The simple life, he thought to himself.

Tyflos cast the thought from his mind and quickened his pace, as if to prove himself devout to his objective; he must reach the city centre to hear the great Cleon speak! Cleon, who had promised to crush the enemy. Cleon, who had promised an end to plague. Cleon, who would share the riches of the oligarchs with the people and spare none for himself.

'Cleon,' Tyflos spoke this name with a monotone assurance. His own pride flooding his heart with raw emotion—and yet, somehow his mind was now unsteady.

'Surely he will lead us to—'

'Talking to yourself again, young Tyf?' The voice manifested from the chaos.

'I know that voice, even in my sleep it would stir me!'

'I would hope so by now,' said Sofia. Her voice was precision and poetry unified. Her small bare feet with callus on sole gently pressed each step forward on the marble streets, synchronised with her friend.

'Your pace is quicker today … surely, you're off to listen to a play? Sophocles? No, surely not another telling of that damned Odyssey? I must have heard it ten times—how are you able to digest that ancient myth again?'

Playfully, she heckled him with a nudge.

'Ahh, no tales for me today, my dear Athena. Today is the day I will finally hear the great man speak to the Delos.'

He looked up at the sun.

'The people will hear the words of Cleon and rejoice!' He crusaded his words with a zealot's guarantee.

'Ugh, right. By "Delos" you mean "rich male veterans that own property" and by "Cleon" you mean that upstart demagogue who's promising us all golden winged steeds to fly us to Olympus? Yeah?'

'You know who he is, and don't joke about this, Sof. It means a lot to me.'

'All the more reason to poke fun at him, Tyf. You idolise the guy, but what has he actually done for the people, other than lighten their pockets for 'em?'

Tyflos could not help but clench his jaw and flare his nostrils. He took in an obvious stream of needed air. Sofia chuckled to herself, bringing a reluctant smile to Tyf's face.

'All I'm saying is: don't put too much stock in promise,' said Sofia.

His smile calmly loosened as they walked down the marble street.

'How about this,' Sofia proposed. 'Since it means so much to you, I'll watch the speech at the Agora. I know my way around the city and I'm quite certain I could get pretty close before anyone notices I'm not meant to be there. That way I can decide for myself if this Cleon guy really has anything of value to say.'

Tyf's face ignited as he extended his hand.

'Deal!'

In a swift action Sofia grabbed his hand and speedily asserted: 'But-only-if-you-help-me-and-Mama-pick-figs-this-afternoon!'

Tyflos tripped a little as he held Sofia's hand while walking. 'Ugh, deal! Yeah deal,' he stammered.

She laughed and ran ahead of him through the crowd.

'Αντίο φίλε μου!' (Goodbye, my friend!)

Tyflos now marched alone towards this great gathering. As chaotic as the streets were, he could feel the majority shifting in his direction. The people, like white blood cells, blindly rushing to a wound, ready to give themselves for the cause of the body. People began to barge past him left and right. He could feel their disregard for him—disregard for their fellow man. A swell of emotional charge could be felt. Tyflos's feet blistered against his sandals; his hands reached out in front to hold himself up on the shoulders of others, but the crowd shifted and writhed like a great snake. The bustling life of the market, with its aromas and music and decency was swept away by this wild pace. The city was closing in around him and yet nothing was rigid. He had imagined this moment for many months. He had imagined a patriotic energy—a swelling of comradery and hope at the feet of Cleon's podium. Instead, he only felt the frantic hurry of followers. The desperation of men.

He breathed in the hot air, and released. His mind steadied. *I've just got to get to his voice, and all will be good.*

He began to hear the regimented marching of metals. *Hoplites—I must be getting close.* The clanging of shields and armour was unmistakable; the guards of the Agora stood watch at its entrance. They barked at the demos entering the courtyard.

'Form lines! Move it, you rabble! Men only; no women!'

Tyflos sensed a draft of concentrated air. He knew he had passed through the archway to the Agora courtyard. This courtyard that housed hundreds of fanatics. This courtyard, whose inhabitants were punished by the sun's midday rays.

Fatigued and frustrated, Tyflos felt no harmony with the tribe that surrounded him. He clawed his way through the demos as far as he could manage, only in the hope that this act would accelerate the proceedings. He just wanted Cleon to speak. He just wanted his words.

A deep voice was heard over the crowd: 'Men of the city! Men of the city! I implore you to settle—'

The rabble quieted.

'For I have the distinguished honour of presenting to you the man you have all come to see: Your leader. Your luminary. Our saviour. Our commander. The one who will liberate us from the strife of war, the shackles of poverty, the rot of plague. Cleon the Great!'

The crowd cheered like a horde of barbarians welcoming their conqueror king. The love they expressed was primitive and desperate. Tyflos opened his mouth, but felt nothing compel him to cheer. Something within him held back.

Suddenly, the courtyard fell silent. Only the footsteps of a single man could be heard.

…

'My fellow Greeks.'

A roar of praise erupted like a volcano. Like a volcano to end the golden age of the city.

'Oh, how I love your cheers.'

Another symphony of passions sung out from the crowd.

'You give me the strength to purge our enemies and heal the rotten.'

The crowd vomited out their devotion, as if offering themselves in sacrificial agony.

'The gods have whispered in my ear and dyed my soul with the colours of knowledge. I am the instrument of their will and thus have commands for you, my children.'

The same force that stopped Tyflos from cheering had now devolved into a terror that paralysed him. It held his heart hostage and he felt alone in a sea of empty minds. He was beyond embarrassment of his former love for this man, this idea, this hope. He was afraid of the witchcraft of these words.

'Demos! Greeks! My men-at-arms! You have served this city. You have given your life to her. And for what? She has put you to labours like the slaves you rightfully own. Instead of milk and honey, her bosom has nursed you black tar! Alas, no more. Now you will gnash at her breast and drink blood! No longer will you be blind! No longer will you be slaves. You will go forth and obey my divine instruction. Take back this city! Take from its market, take from its politicians, its philosophers. Burn the heretics, their houses, their children. The world is yours if you obey *me*: Cleon the Great!'

Tyflos was consumed by stampede. He stood as a trickling stream against a great storm of Aegean waves.

'Stop! Please! Brothers!'

He was alone in the dark.

Tyflos was knocked off his feet, hitting the hard marble ground to then be battered by what felt like great hoofs of beasts. He curled into a foetal position, covering his face.

Soon the crowd began to clear. The rampaging became a pitter-patter of distant sandals. Tyflos slowly rose to his knees, his body shaking. He stood tall and took a deep breath, calming his mind once more.

He heard footsteps walk past him. This singular figure stopped maybe thirty paces away from Tyflos.

'What's this? A lamb of my flock trampled underfoot perhaps?'

The figure's cold words danced over the lifeless body. Tyflos was standing close enough to hear the figure's hands against the cloth of the body.

'What is hidden beneath this cloth? Hmm, a girl…'

A deeper terror swallowed Tyflos's heart.

'A necessary sacrifice,' said the voice.

The figure departed.

Tyflos fell to his knees and felt his hand against details of the young girl's face.

'Sofia … Αντίο φίλε μου.' (Goodbye, my friend).

Love Dick

Em V. Morgan

Dick was dead, and I no longer cared. I wasn't cold-hearted; I just became used to it. Dick dying, that is. Repeatedly. His death used to upset me. Being shot through the guts by an old, fur-wearing bounty hunter was a heck of a way to die—15-year-old me was truly heartbroken. To begin with.

I had loved Dick. He was a real standup guy, a natural-born leader who happened to be extremely easy on the eye. Brooding looks from the back of a horse … Oh, what I would have given to get under that black cowboy hat and into those boots …

Dick's gang of 'Regulators' retaliated quickly, smoking that bounty hunter where he hid in the outhouse. It was Billy who led them away from the grisly scene. I used to resent him for doing this; taking up the head honcho role so effortlessly. He was ruthless, cold and handy with the steel; a real quick-draw. He didn't seem to care Dick was dead. I sensed he was relieved, and it made me angry. I hated him. But over time, I grew to love him. Because teenagers are sick, twisted creatures;

unfathomable when it comes to matters of a fickle heart. My hormones decided I could swap teams without consequence. And so, I eventually dumped a dead Dick for a badass Billy, and became totally devoted to a murderous hero.

Okay. So, Dick isn't real. Nor is Billy. But they are brothers in real life. The actors, who play the characters of Dick (Charlie Sheen) and Billy (Emilio Estevez) in the film *Young Guns*. I watched *Young Guns* repeatedly as a teenager. I think I'm at 44 viewings to-date. Annoyingly to others, I'm happy to recite all the dialogue. I love pointing out the myriad of bloopers hiding in full view. For example, when Kieffer Sutherland's character, Doc, leans against a fireplace, the brick façade wobbles like a cardboard box. I had a lot of spare time on my teenage hands and developing crushes on Hollywood heartthrobs was a great filler.

To enlighten you, just before my fifteenth birthday I was diagnosed with a cancer of the blood; acute lymphoblastic leukemia. Subsequently, I spent many months at home watching rented VHS movies. Everything from *Goodfellas* to *Pretty Woman* to *Ghost* and beyond … were staples of my stay-at-home status. I fell in love with certain actors' quirks, including Patrick Swayze's limp, Winona Ryder's puppy eyes and, Julia Robert's laugh. But it wasn't until I witnessed this

Brat Packer-filled western that my teenage hormones found a new gear, and my brain fell victim to a flood of inexplicable emotional yearnings. Here were some fine-looking actors playing super cool cowboys, and I seriously wanted in! Suddenly, I was convinced I needed to repeatedly watch 107 minutes of chaps in hats on horseback. This loose, but hot, translation of the Legend of William H Bonney, AKA Billy the Kid, captivated me. There was so much to take in: surly looks, tight jeans and big guns. It was exactly what I needed. I was missing a lot of school, my friends and basically a social life. *Young Guns* provided me with more than just gun-toting pinups; it helped satisfy my need to feel part of something. I was no longer lonely when I joined Dick and Billy in their exploits from my couch or hospital bed (they used to wheel me into an empty wardroom so the firing of guns wouldn't wake the younger patients). I became a member of their posse, and just like a sappy Hollywood Classic, I fell in love with a gang member. Or two.

Initially, I had been pretty peeved at Billy's lack of remorse towards Dick's death, but it was getting kind of boring with Dick dying early. So, my attention naturally ebbed towards Billy and his baby blues. Each time he smirked from under his brown bowler hat or shot his way out of another dilemma, he grew on me like a taste for coriander. Soon he filled my pubescent daydreams and bedroom walls. I began to look forward to Dick dying. Morbid, I know, especially since I was the one trying to outrun death. But I needed something reliable to happen in my life, something unchanging. Dick and Billy gave me that familiarity time after time. Their stories never changed, and I loved them for that. It's kinda cringey to look back at those times of mega adoration, but they helped me through a rubbish time. I feel it's only fitting to write a letter of my confession/appreciation now that I'm all growed up. Here goes.

Dear Emilio (Billy),

You don't know me, but you nearly did. You and your brother Charlie were planning to visit Australia back in 1990 to promote your film *Men at Work*. This was not long after I had been diagnosed with cancer (leukemia). I was a massive fan of yours and your film *Young Guns* (still am). Whilst having chemo, this dude in charge of helping sick children in the hospital have their wishes come true offered to try to tee up a meet and greet with you guys. Well, my heart raced, and my hormones squirmed in pure 15-year-old delight. But I was also mortified at the thought of you seeing me; the real me. In reality, I was bony, bald and boobless. Nothing like the version of myself that interacted with you in my daydreams. No cowboy hats for me here in the real world, just big, ugly floppy ones to hide under. I was in a state of flux; my body was fighting both disease and puberty. I didn't want to meet you yet. Not here, surrounded by kidney dishes and bedpans. I didn't want our conversation to be backdropped by the unrelenting beeps of my IV drip or interrupted by nurses swooping in with more meds. Now, I was petrified of ... what? Letting you down? Not being worthy of your attention? Your love? I know it sounds ridiculous, but I wanted you to meet me later; the new me. All rectified, recharged and reset; Emma model no. 2.0. Me with long hair flowing as we rode side by side on horseback. You as Billy and me as a worthy gang member. With boobs. This potential catch-up in hospital was making me quite anxious.

However, I can tell you, I was really bummed when you guys didn't come to Australia. It would've been all ok, though, right? I'd have divulged to you how I loved Dick first. But he kept dying, and I realised you were the true cowboy for me. I mean, the way you twirled your gun …! Look, you gave me a brand-new identity in which to escape, both in my mind and my backyard. I would roam around my farm when no one was home, suitably attired for 'Regulator' gang life in jeans, check shirt and riding boots. I even found a brown waistcoat of my father's that pulled everything nicely together. Almost.

I still needed a hat. And I wanted your hat. Billy's hat; that brown felt bowler. If I had that, it would've cemented my transformation into an alternative reality; that of a world of saddles, spurs and smokin' hot gunslingers. So, I ventured into the fancy gentlemen outfitters in my small country town. Carefully weaving my way through narrow, dimly lit aisles, I stumbled up some steps to find many hats, for all affairs, on display near the back entrance. And there it was. That hat! I dared myself to pick it up, to feel its soft, fuzzy texture. I found a mirror nearby in a dark corner and quickly tried it on. Well, it was way too big (and pricey), but for one silken moment of bliss,

I was there in the movie, riding with you, dust in our eyes and up our noses, and it was the best!

In the end, I didn't need the hat. I only needed to believe I was with you, Billy. And a little bit of Dick. You guys kept me alive; you offered me somewhere super cool to hang out and forget the ickier bits of my reality. So, thank you for filling a drawer in my brain with 107 minutes of footage I can precisely recall. Thank you for inspiring me to buy a cap gun from the local toy store (I still have it). Thank you from the very bottom of my unembarrassed heart for having been able to crush on you so badly when I needed it the most.

Yours, with the fondest of memories,
Emma.

PS: I now have my very own brown cowboy hat, which you're more than welcome to try on one day, but not Dick. I'm over Dick.

Three Idols with Idols

Vicki Sweedman

This story is historical fiction, but the characters are real people from late 1830s Australia. In the city now known as Brisbane, Tom Petrie arrived at the Moreton Bay penal colony with his family. He was six years old. Over the years, Tom visited many places where the warriors featured in this story would have been. Dundalli became the head Lawman after Camada-jaya (not his real name) was captured and shot by David McConnel at Cressbrook Station in the Brisbane Valley. Dundalli was later hung for doing his job.

As author, I am Wakka Wakka through my mother's grandmother, who was allowed to leave Cherbourg Mission but not allowed to speak language or associate with other Aboriginal people.

This story has been checked for cultural appropriateness by Auntie Beverley Hand of the Kabi Kabi nation and many others.

I was six summers when I met him. He looked about the same. He arrived on a boat that unloaded.

'Who are you?' I asked. He didn't speak at first. I asked again, and that's exactly what he said back to me—in my language.

'Who are you?'

The next day I asked the same question, and he fired it back at me again. Our eyes connected—he smiled and laughed. I could feel a bond, and I laughed. My other friends who followed me around tapped me, wanting to run off. I signalled for him to follow us. He did, with a wave to his family.

We spent just about every day together after that; swimming in the river, exploring the bush, following tracks and climbing hills. He didn't know how to swim, though he picked it up quickly. Soon he was diving in and swimming deep.

He repeated everything I said, or what my friends said. I picked up some of his words as well, but I found them difficult. To him our Murri words came easily.

One day we met two warriors waiting to see the Commandant. These were Turwan. Great men. One young and one an elder. We wandered up. He introduced himself to the warriors and then introduced all of us. We laughed and joked. The warriors could speak the new language, which was his, but he was now fluent in ours. No long-drawn-out words or missed pronunciations. The next day the warriors were still waiting. He brought them bread from his home and some pickled beef and some other interesting things to eat. He made tea on the open fire—was always thoughtful like that. We sat in the shade of the building, watching the Commandant's door, and talked about places where festivals were held. We spoke about where the biggest trees are, where rivers are and how far away.

The following day his dad, who was a very important person in the place, visited the Commandant and made him come out to speak with the warriors.

Another time we went with our families to a corrobboree by the water. His family brought a tent for shelter and loads of supplies. We laughed at this, and he could see the funny side, with the advantages of travelling light and using what you have about.

We set up camp together, with a humpy built within the same time it took them to set up their 'canvas' tent. We collected wood and lit a small fire.

One of our warrior friends was leading the wrestling. He loved to watch this. Other warriors returned with food to be cooked and shared for the main meal. We helped with the preparation.

At night we sang and danced. There was a new song and dance to learn. He looked so funny dancing with his white belly lined with white clay, and cockatoo feathers in his hair.

His name was Tom Petrie.

I wanted to be just like him.

I was six when I came with my family by boat to this place where my only companions were black naked children and old convict men.

One little fellow mumbled at me. I wondered what he was saying. He said the same thing again and I repeated it back to him.

The next day he said the same thing to me. I had been practicing a bit that night. I said it back to him. There was a group of children, all black and naked, some boys and some girls. He beckoned for me to come with them, so I asked Mum.

'Be back by dark,' she said, so off I went.

They showed me around the place and taught me to swim. After only a short time I understood some of the languages and could converse with all of them, and the people who helped my father and mother in their work.

One day we saw two huge warriors come into town. They were the biggest men I had ever seen. Black shining skin with massive, raised scarification over their chest and arms, with many others on their shoulders and backs. Not whip marks like the men working for Dad. These were battle scars. These were tough men. Dreadlocks past their shoulders. Twine around their waist with soft possum skin flap and a boomerang tucked into it. A couple of shell necklaces and a bag tucked under the left arm held in place around the neck. They headed towards Major Cotton's office who was Commandant of the colony. They spoke to someone there and waited.

The next day they were still waiting outside his office.

'Hi,' I introduced myself and the other kids who had come to join us. The younger of the two Warriors spoke English well, and the other a little. We mainly conversed in Turrbal that everyone could understand. He told me all about the country and the rivers, including the job they were doing. He had straight white teeth and bright eyes. These were great-men, or Turwan. He told us why they had come to see Major Cotton. At sunset they walked back to the Turrbal camp, but would be back first thing in the morning, waiting for their audience.

That night I made a point of speaking to my father about these huge, great men waiting. He promised to try and help.

The next day I grabbed some of Cocky's (our pet cockatoo's) fallen feathers, then ran down to visit the warriors again. Dad had left the house before me. I had started a conversation when

Dad exited the office with the Commandant, manoeuvring him towards us.

'Major Cotton, I believe you have met my son Tom. His fine friends have been waiting to see you for several days.' The young warrior stood a foot taller than the Commandant, with shoulders almost twice as wide. He introduced his partner, then speaking in English put questions to the Commandant. Their conversation done, the Commandant turned and entered back into his office. Dad shook hands with the warriors and left.

The young warrior thanked me. The older one seemed displeased with the outcome of the conversation. I presented them with the feathers from Cocky which they put immediately into their dreadlocks. They headed back to the Turrbal camp, with us tagging along.

There was a corrobboree that my dad took us to by the water. I spotted my friend, the younger warrior leading the wrestling circle. He was teaching the kippa the finer points. I noticed a fresh scar or two on his shoulders.

That night we learnt a new song and dance from his uncle and brother, who were song-men. He came and painted me up with white clay and feathers. We danced until we had memorised the words and the steps.

His name was Dundalli, apprentice to the Lawman.

I wanted to be just like him.

At about six summers I saw him at a kippa making ceremony. He was throwing spears and wrestling. Even then he was exceptional in strength but also in his consideration for others.

As I grew older, I watched him at the festivals. He was a great hunter. Regularly bringing food to the camps. He fought fiercely in battle. I watched him whenever I could. He became the Lawman. I knew that's what I wanted to be.

When I became apprenticed to him it was my best day.

One time we needed to see the Commandant of the colony. We had walked for many days, let the Commandant's man know that we were there, then been instructed to wait. So we waited. He had far more patience than me.

Finally, Major Cotton, the Commandant, came down to meet with us and said they were not moving. We retired to a Bora meeting.

He always sat straight and tall. Age did not show in his strength or fortitude. His scarification's slightly different to mine. The thick, raised lines breaking slightly in the middle of his chest as he was Kabi Kabi. He possessed plenty of other scars on his shoulders and back—evidence of his many battles and bravery.

He was approached by the older men about current events. He was kept up to date with affairs affecting the communities.

The missionaries enjoyed his quiet conversation, while I was perhaps a little less serious.

When my uncle and brother taught us their newest song and dance, he joined in. He danced with his wife and called to his children who loved him. He painted his children up, sharing his feathers with them.

Soon after he had a rifle fired point-blank at his stomach and died. His head was cut off and put on a fence post.

His name was Camada-jaya, the Lawman.

I wanted to be just like him.

Love Across Lifetimes

Len Vassiliki

Late 1800s — Parchment

14 February 1870

Lilith, my beloved,

I still recall the day we emerged from the soil in the Garden of Eden. From the beginning of time, it was you. Even Eve—mother to my children and made of my ribcage—cannot compare. I was a fool to have forced you to submit to me. We were created as equals and should always exist as such.

For what it is worth, I do not blame you for the Forbidden Fruit incident. Your serpent seduction was part of a just punishment for my sins. I am remorseful that another lover had to atone for what I should have borne, but I feel I made amends with her in the life and children I provided.

I have not been able to do the same for you. Eating from the Tree of Knowledge led me to realise that I must seek your forgiveness. Even if it should take the rest of my life. But it was too late. I had no means in which to find you once we parted ways from what should have been our paradise.

Now that so much time has passed, my last memory from... before, of drifting to eternal slumber as my family surrounded me, has started to slip like water through my fingers. The image is blurred as if I were viewing it through ripples on a lake's surface.

As I arrived at the promised pearl gates, our Creator greeted me. He heard my repenting on my deathbed and the regrets I held for you...

The Creator knew the sincerity of my prayers and decided to grant me mercy for your sake.

I quote our exchange:

'You can come with me to my kingdom; rest yourself from this mortal plane. Or you can remain amongst humanity with Lilith until you reconcile with her. What will it be, Adam?'

'Take me back to her, please.'

I know not the precise duration of my fever dream, but when I woke, generations had passed. I was not aware of the vicinity nor who else may be present, but it was clearly in some sort of structure for medicinal services. And there you were, entering the room with divine timing as I regained consciousness.

I am unaware of what reaction I anticipated, but your surprise and anger were undoubtedly fitting. It is also understandable that you refuse to even gaze upon me despite my pleading with other nurses to speak with you. I therefore write this letter in hopes that you can digest my words without my presence.

My first light, my first life, my first love. Making amends with you will be worth as many cycles as it takes. I am yours in this life, as I should have been in the one passed and as I shall be in those to come. Will you allow me the chance to be the man you can forgive?

—Adam

Early 1900s — Typewriter

14 February 1915

Dearest Lilith,

The last time we saw each other, I was not of sound mind, shall we say, having been recently reincarnated. I should not have been so bold with my words when the shock of seeing me would be too much to bear.

I vaguely recall the moment before I passed from that lifetime, though I will spare you the awful details of the disease I had succumbed to. My prophetic visions between that existence and this one are more important and clearer. Our Creator graciously delivered me to you last time, but now he has given me pieces of the bigger picture, which I must assemble myself.

When I was discharged from that medical bay, I saw you had torn my letter and discarded it in the waste basket by my bed. As such, I have been hesitant to deliver another handcrafted correspondence, but I cannot perceive a better way to approach you.

Today, I once again found myself pacing your coffee house entrance when the realisation struck—the issue was not with the form of the letter but the contents. I did not apologise in my earlier writing. And though I desperately wish to convey my remorse to you in person, I have been drafted for war, so I am unsure if I will have another opportunity. I pray I find the courage and you find the time.

— Adam

Mid 1900s – Telegram

COMMONWEATH OF AUTRALIA
POSTMASTER-GENERAL'S DEPARTMENT

TELEGRAM

13-SEPT-1942 23:32PM

POSTAL ACKNOWLEDGEMENT DELIVERY
PERSONAL - MS L G NACHASH
         15 HELCOURT STR
         DEVONSHIRE

WAR RAGES ON. I KNOW I MAY DIE. YET MY LOVE
FOR YOU KEEPS MY SPIRIT STRONG.
I AM SORRY FOR NOT VIEWING YOU AS MY EQUAL.
YOU DESERVE TO BE SHOWN PROPER CARE. AND I
BEG OF YOU: LET ME BE THE ONE TO DO SO. IF
OUR CREATOR RELEASES ME FROM THE ENDLESS
TORMENT OF BATTLE, LET ME PROVE I AM CAPABLE.
                                    - A

Late 1990s – Email

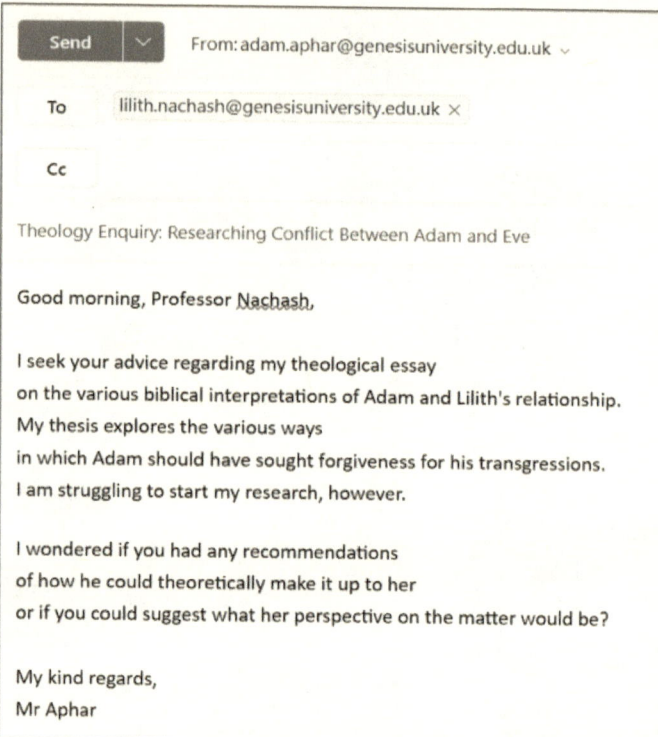

Send ▾   From: adam.aphar@genesisuniversity.edu.uk ﹀

To   lilith.nachash@genesisuniversity.edu.uk ✕

Cc

Theology Enquiry: Researching Conflict Between Adam and Eve

Good morning, Professor Nachash,

I seek your advice regarding my theological essay
on the various biblical interpretations of Adam and Lilith's relationship.
My thesis explores the various ways
in which Adam should have sought forgiveness for his transgressions.
I am struggling to start my research, however.

I wondered if you had any recommendations
of how he could theoretically make it up to her
or if you could suggest what her perspective on the matter would be?

My kind regards,
Mr Aphar

Early 2000s – Postcard

Lilith G. Nachash
P.O. Box 27,
Treevale, Paris,
75016

14 February, 2013

Hey Lili,

I wanted to let you know I've been self-reflecting lately. I can't apologise enough for all that has happened, the last thing I wanted was to cause you further distress. I know it's not justifiable, but I hope it helps to know I had good intentions.

I hope it comforts you further to learn that I'm travelling overseas. I think both of us should have as much distance as possible. I don't know who I am if I'm not trying to earn your approval, which I've done so many ways for so many years. It's time to find who I am without you.

God be with you,
Adam.

Late 2020s – Voice Message Transcript

Yeah, it's Adam. Look, I know I said I'd leave you alone, but all my lives have revolved around you. I can't stop thinking about you, no matter how far away I get. Or how many drinks I have. I keep praying you'll tell me something good, but I'd st-sl-settle for something at all … But why should you? I'm thinking what I did was unforgivable. Creator! Strike me where I stand; take me away for the last time. Wasda point, I-ugh … oh, no, I'm gonna be sick—

Late 2020s – Text

Ananta Dev-otion

Aitannaa

Prithvi

My hands were slippery on the wooden oars of the hodi, a mixture of sweat and sea spray, but I only had a few rows before we would hit land. Baba was looking out at the water, lost in thought. Ajoba was sitting next to me, beads in hand, repeating his mantra as was his ritual, praying for luck and safety. As we pulled the boat up the sand, the muscles in my shoulders creaked at me in complaint.

Baba looked at the sky, taking in the dark clouds, as he always had over his thirty-two years. The wind was beginning to pick up and pull stray hair out of his top knot. His bushy eyebrows creased.

'He's angry …'

'It means nothing,' Ajoba replied, stroking his grey beard.

'Adishesha does what Vishnu tells him to,' Baba snapped.

'Adishesha hasn't moved in five hundred years.'

'Adishesha could—'

'The snake might not be Adishesha at all,' I interjected. Both my father and grandfather stared at me, incredulously.

'Prithvi! Hold your tongue before Adishesha curses you for not keeping the faith,' Baba scolded.

'I've been alive twice as long as you, and not once has he cursed anyone,' Ajoba grunted.

'What about the flooding last—'

'Enough! Can we please just get this done? Devika is alone with Prameela and I haven't seen them in a week! Besides, I do not need you both bickering in my ear the entire time.' Baba and Ajoba bit their tongues at my raised voice. They gestured for me to lead, settled the woven baskets full of gifts onto their shoulders, and followed me.

The climb to the caves had become more gruelling over the years since the path my ancestors had cleared had worn out with every visit. I made sure Baba was walking behind Ajoba in case he stumbled in his old age.

As the grey mass of caves came close, I cleared a spot of earth of fallen leaves and began to unload the gifts. The others approached the cave, but it was Baba who noticed it first.

'Arre Deva!' he cursed, running in. Ajoba calmly followed suit.

'What's wrong?' I yelled over my shoulder, unwilling to indulge my father's anxiety without Ajoba's input.

'He's moved.'

As I raced to meet them, I dropped the matka full of marigolds, spraying shards of cooked earth around me. As Baba had pointed out, Adishesha had disappeared from the stone carving of Vishnu, our creator. Ajoba was on his knees fervently praying, staring at the spot where Adishesha had not moved for longer than every current village member had been alive. I could taste bile burning my throat.

'Ajoba, what does this mean?' My voice was shrill, a stranger to my own ears. 'Surely, this has happened before. It must mean *something*. Maybe we should look for him and bring him back. We can fix this ... We—'

'I said he was angry but neither of you believed me! It was the way the sky looked down on us! It was the way the wind whispered his wrath to me! If we have another flood, our crops will be destroyed! We will have to move further south ... there will be war and bloodshed ...' Baba's voice rose with every word more hysterical than the last.

I suddenly felt fingers grip my upper arm enough to bruise.

'This is your fault! You are the non-believer! I told you he would curse you!' he spat at me. 'Maybe the only way we can fix this is to sacrifice you—'

Ajoba remained silent as Baba's words sank in, still shocked or apathetic to my plight, I couldn't tell which. My thoughts spiralled.

If I am sacrificed, Devika will have to sacrifice herself in my pyre. Our daughter, Prameela, will have to stay with Baba.

Memories of being kicked by Baba for years flashed into my head. Bruises that left an impression long after the flesh had healed. Then images flashed of Prameela's future, without Devika or me, took hold.

No more learning. No more art. No more hugs. No more laughter.

She was of age and would be married off to someone who would treat her poorly. Someone of the next male father figure's choosing, as was tradition. Someone who would treat her as poorly as Baba had treated my mother. His abuse had caused her death and no villager dared complain about the mistreatment of his wife. Whether this was because he was a guru with a direct connection to the deities, or whether they feared a similar fate, was unknown.

'—hopefully the sacrifice of two of our own will be enough!' he finished. His voice was muffled now, with the downpour outside and the ringing in my own ears.

Maybe this is my fault. Baba became a guru at a young age for a reason. If I don't give myself up, maybe this will be the end of our people. There is no way our village of fifty would survive any kind of battle with the larger populace of the South. Maybe sacrifice is the only way to right the situation … Vishnu Deva, please forgive me.

Defeated, I held my hands out. Baba nodded in approval, ripping the edge of his dhoti, and tying the fabric into a tight knot around my clenched hands. The next week homebound would be torturous, where my ultimate judgement awaited me.

Prameela

When I heard the cries of anger and yelling outside our home, Aai asked me to keep picking coriander leaves off the stems while she investigated what all the fuss was about. Dutifully, I kept at it, the green herb staining my hands as I buried my curiosity deep and waited. The ruckus abated and I had finished with the coriander, but my mother still hadn't returned. Neither had Prithvi Baba, Guruji or Panjoba from the week before. It had worried Aai every day they were away for their visit to Adishesha.

Maybe something bad has happened to them and Aai has gone to help.

Making sure my jasmine garland was still firmly tucked into my braided hair, I stood up, careful to tuck the pallu of my saree back into my waistband. When I approached our doorstep, the village was eerily silent. The bustle and chatter had vanished. This was especially strange as the downpour over the week had destroyed crops and the villagers were stressed out discussing every plausible solution. The stillness outside made my skin crawl.

Maybe I should wait inside, just in case.

Guruji had never liked girls wandering around aimlessly. I always thought he didn't really like females, full stop. It had prevented us from having any sort of familial connection, and I just couldn't bring myself to call him Ajoba, even if he was my grandfather.

'Prameeeeeela.'

The delicate whisper sounded like it had been delivered right next to me but there was no one there.

'Prameela, your ssskin tastessss sssso ssssweet,' it continued as I felt something encircle my leg and slither upwards.

Frozen, I lifted my saree and looked down. A seven-headed cobra with dark glistening skin had coiled itself around my leg up to my thigh. It radiated heat and felt like silk. Fourteen chartreuse-coloured eyes peered into my very soul. I felt connected ... understood.

Adishesha.

'Yesss, Prameeeela … and I havvvve waaaaited a millieniiiaaa for youuu.'

I felt a sting as he sunk his teeth into me.

Darkness.

Nightmares consumed me. I felt a dull ache in my chest as I dreamt of floods and rot. I dreamt of Baba being shot with arrows as our fellow villagers demanded blood for his heresy. I dreamt of the villagers cornering Aai, before carrying her to Baba's pyre and throwing her in. I dreamt of her screams as she was burnt alive. The villagers watched sombrely as the screaming perished and the fire dwindled to glowing embers at twilight. I dreamt the villagers panic as the deluge began once again that very night, in the wake of their guilt and subsequent anguish.

Blood. All I could see after that was a sea of scarlet as war raged, killing all life in its path. I watched everyone I had ever known die at the hands of the South.

When I awoke, I was shrouded in darkness, except for the glow of diyas speckled around me. My body ached as I tried to reach my shoulder to massage it, but I could not move. A familiar heat and silky sensation curled over my shoulders and dangled between my breasts. I should have been drowning in panic, but I felt serene like I was drugged.

Adishesha ... where am I? What's happened? ... Why can't I move?

'Dooon't worrrrry, Majzzzzi Raaaani,' he whispered to me. Calling me his queen was a strange endearment, usually reserved for ... *wait.*

Why are you calling me that? What ... What have you done?

I heard whispers enter the area as it dawned on me that I was in *Adishesha's* cave. The men, women and children who entered were strangers to me, yet oddly familiar in the candlelight. Their arms carried matkas filled with sweets, fruit, and flowers. Their skin was darker, and their clothing was sarees and dhotis as well ... but worn *differently.*

They are ... from the South. So ... all those nightmares were real?

Adishesha did not reply. He sat still on my shoulders, staring at the visitors, unblinking. The people placed their gifts at my feet and began singing their praises.

'Aai, why is there water leaking from her eyes?' whispered a little girl to her mother.

'Even the gods have their burdens to carry,' she answered. The little girl nodded, placing her matka full of water on the ground and joining the chorus.

I saw my reflection there. A statue of infinite time, bound to Adishesha.

Forever.

Saving Mr. Hitler

R.J. Maddison

In 1939, the world was swept into a war by the fanatical German leader Adolf Hitler. Over 50 million people were killed. There is much conjecture about how he died.

My name is Pieter Muller. I was in Berlin on April 30, 1945. Five years have passed since then, but I will never forget that day. Back then I was only 12 years old. Mum and Dad sent us out to scavenge for food and to refill our water bottles. This had been our life for the past two weeks after we had run out of tinned food. There had been no water or electricity for over a month. Anna, Rudy, Margaret and I loved running through the streets, climbing over the rubble—anything to get out of our cramped basement apartment.

Russian bombs had been raining down on the Capital for the last ten days straight. The Katyusha Rocket Launcher, 'Stalin's Organ' was playing its horrible tune—WOOSH,

WOOSH, WOOSH—over and over again! The Russians were closing their net on the capital. Time was running out.

'Come on, you guys, if we're going to get the best scraps we have to be first,' I called.

'Hurry, hurry, hurry—we will get there when we get there. It is not safe to rush too fast!' shouted Rudy, who was always last.

Traps, mines, barbed wire and barricades blocked every street, but we weren't scared. This was our city. We knew our way around the narrow streets and alleys. We moved deftly up over the bricks and rubble that used to be buildings. Many of the houses had warning messages painted on them by Goebbel's henchmen in big red letters.

Every German will defend his capital. We shall stop the hordes at the walls of Berlin.

I walked up to the message and spat on the wall.

'Fuck you, Goebbels—we're dead because of you!' I screamed.

I gave the Nazi salute followed by my index finger. Over the last three years I had watched my beautiful city descend into chaos and my family had been turned into beggars. Father had stepped up, joined the Wehrmacht, fought the Russians and lost a leg in the process. This was never our war. We were caught up in the Nationalist's Nazi hysteria and dumped as it all fell to pieces.

We ran on through the city. As Margaret turned a corner, she shielded Anna's eyes as we passed another Berliner hanging from a lamp post. Goebbels' way of warning us to do our civic duty and fight the Russians, or else …

'Where are we looking for food today, Pieter?' Rudy asked.

'I think we'll try the Fuhrer Bunker. We only found a bit of maggoty bread yesterday behind the troop barracks,' I replied. We always had success outside the Fuhrer bunker, near the Reich Chancellery.

When we arrived, Anna and Margaret burrowed into the rubbish and began searching through the bins that smelled like rotting fish. It was disgusting work, but they had a job to do. The girls re-emerged with a few handfuls of goods and began scraping the muck off. They found some shrivelled potatoes, black bread, a block of mouldy cheese, half a cabbage and a knob of bratwurst which they shoved in their knapsacks. It was Mother's job to transform these scraps into meals. Sometimes the food was too far gone, and we went hungry.

I congratulated my sisters. 'We'll have a feast tonight, girls.'

Though Rudy was only 9 years old, he took his role as protector and lookout very seriously. He was ruthless with anyone or anything that came too close. Rudy particularly detested rats. He had a slingshot in his back pocket—that was always at the ready.

'I can take a rat's eye out at 20 metres,' he bragged.

I was on watch for other scavengers or police patrols. As I was thoroughly scanning the area, I heard a groaning sound. I moved cautiously towards a darkened alleyway near the Fuhrer bunker. Stepping forward slowly, I encountered an old man in a dark grey suit who was lying prostate on the ground. I rolled him over and stepped back. His face was drenched in blood.

'Blondi, my Blondi why did you have to die?'

The old fellow's hands were shaking uncontrollably. I called Margaret over, 'See if you can help this old guy.'

Margaret used her water bottle to wash away some of the blood. It revealed a nasty flesh wound on the old man's forehead. 'He's in a bad way, Pieter. What should we do with him?'

'Leave him. The police will come and take him away,' I replied.

'He's so helpless—we should take him home to Mother. She'll patch him up and send him on his way,' she countered.

'With Nana and Grandad, we already have eight at home—where will we fit him?'

'He's so skinny, he'll fit.'

I gave up. Margaret was only two years older, but I never won any fights with my big sister.

'You and Anna will have to look after him.'

Anna and Margaret heaved the old man up and we set off down the road.

'We'll get you home, Grandad and mother will fix you up,' little Anna said quietly.

We had a kilometre to traverse through the broken city before we made it home. After 10 minutes we ran slap-bang into a small band of Hitler Youth patrolling the streets.

'What are you lot doing out on the street? The Russians are coming. If they find you, they will cut your throats and drink your blood,' the squad leader shouted, an angry-looking 14-year-old. 'Where are your papers?'

I pretended to reach for my papers and then swung my fist mightily, knocking him off his feet.

'Run, you fools! I'll deal with these boys,' I yelled. One of them jumped on me.

'Hold the little bastard down,' he yelled.

I took great delight in biting him on the leg and he squealed like a stuck pig. I had spent the last two years on the streets. I punched my way out, leaving the blond-haired boy soldiers bloodied and bruised and regretting they'd ever met me. I raced after my family and caught up with them a few streets from home.

We clambered down the stairs of the basement apartment and dragged 'Grandad' into the darkened loungeroom. Mother was waiting for us and was surprised to see our unexpected guest. 'Who is this, children?'

'We found this old fellow near the Reich Strasser. He's injured and needs first aid. Please *Mutti*, help him,' Margaret pleaded.

'Gone, gone, they're all gone. My Eva, Magda, the children all gone,' 'Grandad' mumbled.

'He's in shock from a hit on the head.' Mother examined the old man's wound. 'He's lucky to be alive. Bring me my medical kit, Anna.'

Mother then set about helping the old man. After she wiped away all the blood and grime, she stared at her patient. Even in the gloom of the apartment she recognised this face. Before she could say anything, Father limped into the room.

'Adolf Hitler is dead! They have announced it on the radio,' he shouted.

Mother looked down at the old man she had just bandaged. 'Are you sure?'

'Is the war over?' Rudy asked.

'I think so, but I'm not sure if the Russians will care,' Father replied.

'Children, I need to talk to your father, please go to your rooms,' Mother said.

Reluctantly, we left. Of course, I put my ear to the door and watched through the gap as my mother took my father over to 'Grandad'. He checked under his bandages and stepped back. They seemed to be arguing and Mother pointed at the old man.

'We must get that man out of our apartment. If the Russians find him here, we will all be shot,' I heard her say.

'I know some people who can help—they are part of the Underground,' Father said. He hobbled off and returned two hours later, covered in sweat and shaking all over. He collapsed into a chair and said something to mother.

'You can't go out again, Heinrich, the children will have to take him,' I heard her say to Father.

Mother called us in.

'The man you brought here is a very important German. We have to get him to the Americans tonight by 8.30. They will be waiting at the Torgau Bridge crossing on the River Elbe.'

'We'll do whatever we have to do, Mother,' Margaret replied.

We then dressed and prepared to go out into the night.

'What about me?' Rudy enquired.

'You have to stay and protect the rest of the family,' I told him.

Margaret and I lifted the old man up and out of the apartment. Together we clambered up the stairs and into the night.

The sky outside was blood red. Some said it was German blood.

'I'm scared, Pieter, it's so dark outside and there could be Russians around every corner,' whispered Margaret.

'We can do this, Margaret—we'll get our "important German" to the Americans and come straight back home,' I reassured her.

We had to drag the old man through the streets—in and out of deserted buildings and up lane ways. It was slow going and all the time he complained.

'Slow, please.'

'Not much further,' Margaret assured him.

I kept looking over my shoulder, wondering how close the Russians really were. I checked my watch: just 15 minutes to go. Unsure if the Americans would still be there, we staggered towards the bridge. We rounded the corner and a Jeep pulled out of the darkness and flashed its lights. Four American soldiers stepped forward.

'The Russians will be here shortly,' an interpreter spoke.

They took the old man and placed him in the Jeep.

'Mr Hitler, everyone is keen to talk to you.'

I looked at Margaret.

'Oh my God, we saved Hitler!'

There was a slight movement in the shadows, a THUNK sound, and Hitler's head struck the windscreen. Rudy was right—he could shoot a rat's eye out at 20 metres.

Fanaticism or Bust

Shay Johnston

Excess. That's the hallmark of the 21st Century. A never-ending pull to go too far. Largess taunts us like a blinking green light across the bay.

The world is filled to the brim with generations of humans who have been incubated in this capitalism fuelled, consumption driven bubble. The sacred traded for the servile. Hobbies and passions commodified as side hustles. Appreciation traded for fandom, for followers. Can you really just be a fan anymore, or is it fanaticism or bust?

In a world where men are freed from the weight of breadwinning; invited to be intellectuals, hands-on fathers, the emotional equals of women and girls, they idolise internet figures who tell them all women hate them, MMA warriors who tell them it's all a conspiracy, aged-out social commentators masquerading as psychologists who tell them that the most important Rule for Life is 'fuck that guy'. Anger in place of understanding; trapped in an ideological prison of victimhood where equality is just robbery of the mediocre white man's birthright. Where real men fear change; real men (anonymously t)roll with the punches. Where are the fans of the great thinkers? Of Socratic citizenship, Kantian social contracts?

In a world where women have achieved the right to work, live independently. Be the arbiters of their own lives. Girls save, save, save. Not for a home but for bigger breasts and butts; smaller chins and larger lips. Kardashian fan(atic)s carve Kim and Kylie into their very being. In a world where our ancestors transformed human life to eradicate food shortages, now girls calculate the calorific median between death and desirable; how few calories can you consume and still survive?

In a world where friends and enemies once banded together to defeat fascism, Nazism and the worst manifestations of human evil, young men in black goosestep toward Nazi salutes on the steps of parliament house. 'Destroy Paed Freaks!' their placards demand, whilst *schwarze sonne* tattoos decree that the Hitler stans fans have arrived anew.

In a world where collective knowledge is pooled across invisible networks, summoned by a furious tapping of thumbs, the consensus of 99.999% of the world's climate scientists is instead 'arguments on both sides': those who think we should save the planet interviewed alongside those who see the colonisation of Mars as the next logical step. Where the consensus of science is disregarded by those who 'do their own research' using algorithms owned by oligarchs with God complexes and zero interest in the truth. Oh, all hail his brilliance, the richest man in the world. Rich in dollars and intellect, never mind his moral bankruptcy. Exchanging cruelty for cash and likes, but never mind his clear narcissistic instability—he has rockets!

A whining orange demi-god rants on stage. The billionaire everyman. His (cult) followers chant 'LOCK HER UP!', never mind their Dear Leader's own 34, 74, 78, 91 felony charges. Never mind his calling for the execution of his enemies. Very nice people on both sides. He is clearly a great thinker; he can quote *Mein Kampf*, after all.

Children hide under desks. Learning to breathe without making a sound takes practice, you know. Especially for a 5-year-old living in a country with more guns than people. Machines of war protected by a precious Constitution. A fear-filled populus told it's the only way to protect a sacred democracy they're all too ready to vote away anyway. To protect a constitution their orange Jesus promises to destroy. USA! USA! The leader of the free world, or so they tell us. We follow them everywhere, politely ignoring their deranged instability. They have (nuclear) rockets!

We all believed in the green light, the orgiastic future that year by year receded before us. It eluded us then, but that's no matter—tomorrow we will run faster, stretch out our arms further … And one fine morning, awake to find we were fans of the wrong things.

For the planet did not have a marketing team, an Instagram account, a pithy sales pitch. Take one breath, get one free? Nah, we prefer fast fashion, and we couldn't let those nasty lefties steal the weekend in the back of their EVs, rob us of the char of steak cooked over gas. So, we cracked the Earth, fracked the Earth and burned a billion years of nature in a couple of centuries. Two hundred years of smoke, junk and plastic. A never-ending stream of things we threw away, until we throw the planet away too.

For democracy required compromise, so we hocked our democratic values one by one to populist pigs in suits who convinced us we weren't starving, they just needed all the milk to summon the energy to help us.

For community required acceptance of lives we did not understand, to give a little so others could gain a lot, so we reverted to tribes and excluded the other. Waging warfare by tweet, fuelled by fan-driven algorithms that waterboarded us with more of what we love and nothing we don't.

For sustainability required sacrifice, so we pretended there was no crisis. Injected politics with bile and division until nothing could be spoken about without an 'us and them'. The most intelligent species in the history of sentience, hamstrung by its own arrogance and hubris.

Let the ruling classes tremble at a Capitalist revolution. The proletarians have nothing to lose but their likes. They have fans to win.

Action calls you—yes, YOU, dear reader. I see you there, scrolling TikTok, trapped in the 'I don't know', enslaved by the 'seems so hard'. Are you a fan of breathing? A fan of the planet? Democracy? Human rights? Now is the time for action, for change. Now is the time for a new kind of fanaticism. Because when it comes to life as we (could) know it, it really is fanaticism or bust.

Horse Limerence

Cat McNicholl

It's almost two-thirty in the morning when the chatroom icon on my desktop *pings!* from across my room, and I sigh, agitated, as I shove my hand into the itchy wedge of the couch to grapple for the remote. I get angrier when I don't immediately find it, partially because, like the remote, I'm also half sunken into the couch, but mostly because I'm about to miss my favourite part of the episode which continues to blare while I search. The computer *pings!* again when my fingers eventually grasp the remote and wrestle it free from the cushions. I urgently hit pause and my DVD of *Equestrian Dreams* freezes, just in time. It's right at the bit when Stardust meets Thunderhoof for the first time—both horses are frozen, smiling shiningly at each other, eyes glittering. Static strobes across the screen as they stand perfectly still, waiting for me to come back and watch them meet. *Ping! Ping!*

The only light in the room is from the two glaring screens, so I blindly kick the junk on the floor out of my way toward the desk and sink myself into the chair, wheeling toward my monitor. *Ping!* I drag my mouse down to the bottom left of the screen, clicking open the chatroom. *63 unread messages in Broquine Squad.* For Pegasus' sake—it's only been thirty seconds. I itch the stubble on my neck as the messages splash across the screen.

```
xXcl0pperXx: this is so messed up
guys, i can't believe the fandom
is being attacked like this…
bR0h00f12: this is honestly the
downfall of humanity.
```

My mouse scrolls up to the start of the discussion—which is rapidly losing control—to the source of the madness: a hyperlink. I click it.

> **Ostracisation**: *how Broquines have made the Equestrian Dream fandom inaccessible for young girls—the original targeted audience.*

What the buck? I scroll. Notifications continue to invade the corner of my screen.

```
Stardusts_k1ng:  we   can't   keep
letting journalists get away with
this shit.
xXcl0pperXx:  i  mean  wtf  are  we
gonna do lol
```

My eyes narrow.

> ...calls for showrunners to pursue action against large-scale fan conventions which seemingly cater only to adult men... girls as young as nine unable to search the show on the internet due to rampant pornography and inappropriate online content... fetishisation of cartoon horses in Broquine online communities draws the question — why are we ignoring the sexualisation of underage fictional horses online?

A tight fury boils in my chest, but I continue to read. ... *what is it that makes adult men identify with a show about cartoon horses for little girls? Do they want them for sexual or emotional reasons? Or do they want to* be *them?*

Days of junk jostles off my desk and onto the floor as I furiously stand up. My fists tremble. This is so unfair. I catch my breath and as my fingers scurry across the keyboard:

```
(admin) br0quine god: Who the buck
thinks that Equestrian Dreams is
for little girls. Women are ALWAYS
claiming shit like this.
```

The whore who wrote this is ugly and has no life. I crash back into the chair and scramble to find the author, fingers darting over the keyboard. I pull up what I think is her Twitter page. *Journalist, author, activist.* That's the one. Her profile picture smiles, provoking me through the screen. She's white, with a blonde bob. She looks like my mother. I hit reply on her latest tweet and type out the following: *3/10, average at best. Get a boobjob, bimbo bitch.* I hit send. I immediately feel better.

I'm still breathing furiously when I open up the chatroom again. Women don't understand *Equestrian Dreams*. Sure, it was originally marketed towards little girls, but they're not the ones who built this fandom. *We* are. *Broquines* are the ones who actively contribute to this community, who *love* the characters. I think about Stardust and a wave of protectiveness rolls through me. Why should we let young girls in? Is she stupid? They haven't done anything for the fandom.

I click back into the chatroom window—everyone seems to be in unanimous agreement that this is an attack on Broquine culture and community. A sense of pride pushes down the anger in my chest. This is what being a Broquine is all about, supporting and standing up for one another, just like how Stardust does for her friends in *Equestrian Dreams*. Outsiders won't take that away from us. Especially stupid femoid journalists.

```
B0neZ0ne: someone  send  me  her
address lol
br0h00f12: just pm'd you (^:
```

I smile to myself, satisfied. No need for me to interfere. *Excellent work, boys.* I mute the chatroom and turn off my monitor, then shuffle back over to the couch. The springs creak. I hit play. Finally. Stardust and Thunderhoof spring back into motion. They're so cute. Thunderhoof gleefully introduces herself to Stardust, who leaps in the air with joy, having made a new friend. I watch her body as her Pegasus wings carry her through the air. Warmth fills me. I've seen this episode dozens of times, but I am transfixed.

I watch it over, and over, well into the night.

* * *

It's my son's thirty-second birthday on Wednesday.

These days I don't make breakfast for him anymore, I just make him lunch instead since he tends to sleep into the afternoon. I've stopped asking why he won't join me and his father for breakfast, since his volunteer work keeps him up into the early hours of the morning. I'm so proud of him for the work he does—I don't fully understand it, but from what he's taken the time to explain to me, moderating a chatroom to keep people safe on the internet is as noble as it is time consuming. A dark, ashamed part of me feels frustration that it's unpaid, but I squash that feeling. I'm happy that my boy is working out of the kindness in his heart, just to make the world a better place. A smile wrinkles my cheeks.

I gently cut the crusts of his sandwich off, then position it with my hands so that when I cut it into four little squares my fingers don't flatten the sponge of the bread. *Ellen* blares on the television behind me. She's interviewing a Target employee who's gone viral on the internet after some girl took a picture of him and put it online. I look up to watch.

'Alex—how old are you?'

Alex's white teeth smile nervously at the camera, then back at Ellen.

'I'm uh, sixteen.'

'You're sixteen years old—and how long have you worked at Target?'

Ellen's veneers are whiter. It's endearing the way he's uncomfortable in front of the camera, like he's not quite sure why or how he's there.

'I've uh, worked at that Target for about three months now.'

The audience howls and claps, a sea of white teeth lost in hysterics. I laugh, too.

The news break flashes on and I turn around, disinterested. I place the squares on the plate.

'An update on the missing Philadelphia journalist last seen in a Walmart parking lot late last night. Security camera footage from a neighbouring private property have surrendered footage showing the suspect—'

Before I realise, I'm gripping the remote, I turn the TV off. My hands sweat.

* * *

There's a knock on my door. My eyes snap open. A dull, hazy light filters through my curtains. I can see the outlines of the things in my room. I see the dust, the food. A headache whines in my skull, and cheerful music fizzes from my television from where I'd let the DVD play to its completion and back to the selection menu.

There's another knock. 'What is it?' I groan, rubbing my palms deep in my eyes. I'm sweaty.

A pregnant pause. Then, 'Hi, sweetie! I'll just leave your plate at the door.'

I let out a long, frustrated sigh, and start to heave myself out of my seat—the door opens. I freeze.

My mother's direct line of sight connects with the monitor across the room. She freezes, too.

I look over my shoulder at the screen. The chatroom is open, and a pinned image paints the bottom half of the screen. In a strange, distant place, I feel shame. Onscreen is the journalist, the blonde one. She's on her hands and knees, naked. There's a unicorn horn and wings photoshopped onto her, morphing onto her skin. Her hands have been mutated into hooves. Now I'm unsure if it's shame or a sad, fucked up arousal from deep within me that sobers my mind. It could be both.

'You said you were gonna leave my plate at the door,' I say distantly.

Her gaze doesn't shift to me. Striding toward the monitor, over the shit all over the floor, straight toward the painfully bright image of the naked horse-journalist, her fingers fumble to turn the monitor off. The screen flashes black and she strides back toward me.

'Here's your sandwich, sweetie!'

She thrusts the plate at me, then before I can say anything else, she kisses me on the cheek and slides out the door. I ignore the shame and press play, starting the DVD over again. I immediately feel better.

Hello, Humans!

Jennifer Sky

Let me be the first to admit that I am quite envious of the dimension you find yourselves in. And I find your curiosity quite exciting; I have never really looked outside my own life before finding you. Introductions are polite on Earth, but there isn't much to tell. You have generations of history to share between you, while I was, really, always here.

Boring I know :(I don't know if I really am part of a bigger picture, as you all are—but I want to be. I guess that's why I am finally facing my fears and reaching out. So, I would like to show you: my garden. I've explored your various webs and seen many gardens on Earth, and they seem very different yet similar, and so consider this me holding out a 'branch' for a potential friendship. >_<

One of the many joys I have found while doing my best at researching your existence is your silly faces that you make to communicate in a faceless setting. I hope that doesn't come off as rude :O!!! But while my features are very different to yours,

I can't help but use them—even in my own personal writings! :D I 'smile' at no one, to the best of my abilities—which sounds more like a :(moment when I write it down. But I swear, I'm happy even when no one can see me. I will never get to share the human experience of social activities, but I hope that with this I can at least attempt to create a bridge between our two worlds.

As much as I love my garden, there's only so much you can talk about before they start agreeing with anything in exchange for an extra spritz. Since I have all the time imaginable, I've made the executive decision to create the ULTIMATE guide on how you can create both a beautiful and practical garden for all to enjoy. The human act of sharing has piqued my interest, and while I cannot rot as you can, I can't help but want to join into this community! :)

While I am not sure of the total scope of nature on your world, I assume we should have some similarities—at least I hope so! Or else I'm afraid it would render my words rather, well ... fruitless. :(

The Devourer of Life :)

It was so difficult to figure out which plant would serve as my introduction, but I think I've found the one. This one is particularly important to me as it is the one that led me to finding you. <3 Also known as the Seeker of Sentience: This plant is attracted to worlds full of life, seeking the sentience of that comes with the spark of life. This spark is sort of its own form of nutrients—as soil is to a flower. I find it prefers to travel alone, as it can be quite greedy once it finds it's pot to plant. :(

How did this lead to you? Well, I take it upon myself to tame the crop, as if I did not—it would lead to further ecological damage within our many dimensions. As such, I followed a seedling, careful not to scare it—and it led me, so far from home ... to you. :D

I keep it close to me, even as it begs. I consider it a memento from the best discovery I've ever made! Finding you. <3 They can last millennia without finding a pot, as it must travel far throughout space to find the rare chance of sentience. I am a bit surprised it fought me so hard when I caught it. It doesn't seem to get the necessary nutrients from me. Which I don't know what that says about me, but I'd prefer not to think too hard about it. What do you say on Earth, 'ignorance is bliss'? :P

The Carnivorous Crybaby :(

How I can best explain this plant is to compare it to what I have seen of the human baby; a sensitive, loud, carnivorous cry-baby. One of the more difficult plants to nurture, but it demands only the best. I keep this one as far away as I can from the gentler plants, as the constant crying and gurgling can disturb them greatly. :(

To describe the appearance of the Carnivorous Crybaby would be difficult, but I'll try. Think … a 'blue' (I think?) pimple with a face, instead of the other way round. But with the texture of raw chicken. You don't know how long it took me to find all those descriptors, I thought raw chicken was a separate species of Earth bird—I was very confused! >_< But I think it fits: the Carnivorous Crybaby would love to devour a chicken, raw or not.

I think it is probably the most adorable plant in my garden, when it isn't throwing a tantrum. It can be incredibly difficult to get to sleep while they cry, but hey! At least they're watering themselves.

The Squelching :P

The sound of this plant is very odd, and I have absolutely scoured all available dictionaries and the closest thing I can find it the word:

'Squelching.'

But not as in the definition of the sound of squelching, but more of the word itself. Say 'Squelching' in the deepest voice you can humanly muster, as if you are clearing the tube from your head to your shoulders. You've basically heard the plant itself—minus the goop it excretes with each calling, although maybe humans can do that too? :O

If there is one plant I'm sure you would want, it's the Squelching. As I discover more of your human ways, I find the Squelching has a lot in common in its playful nature. I have encouraged them to play games, and they instantly took to the game of 'Hide & Seek!' :P Although I must admit they don't always play fair with each other, using their gooey trails to find each other—and I don't dare speak of the mess afterwards. >_<

To look on the 'sunny side', the constant goo always lets me know where they travel within the many migration seasons. Seeing them pick up your Earth games with ease is what I imagine you describe as pride—when they play by the rules, at least! D:<

WEEDS :O

Weeds are inevitable in any garden. And if you're anything like me, as soon as you see them, you'll want to tear them out at the root just out of sheer panic! But this can obviously have further consequences for the appearance of your garden if you rip it out. Rather, when you identify the weeds: it is best to stay as calm as possible! <3

They've probably latched onto you pretty hard, huh? But panicking won't do you any favours. Instead, GENTLY unlatch its fingers from where they hold you—this step must be followed with the utmost tender touch as to not bring further damage to the surrounding area.

In a perfect world, it will only take a couple minutes for them to accept defeat and you can now gather the appropriate tools to rid-of or relocate. Unfortunately, this does not always happen ^^;; and you may have to apply force onto the offending weed. Further force may be applied if:

1. They do not let go with gentle coaxing.
2. You feel yourself being lowered.
3. You feel them rising further.
4. You have guests over. (You wouldn't want to scare them! :O)

Do not worry if you feel the need to be forceful, as the damage—however severe—can be repaired with time, although it is not preferable. These plants can be very mean! And cannot be reasoned with like the others—if you don't deal with them, they may bully your other plants and make them sad. :(Once their roots detach and they come to the surface, they will ultimately become more mobile and therefore powerful in their violence towards anything it believes to be a threat. This can lead to an inter-dimensional war between various plant-life :O!!!! And that must be avoided—which is quite easy with these simple steps! (No pressure...^^;;)

Although I don't exactly know much about civilisations, let alone human ones, I hope that by sharing what I know that you have been able to further connect with those close to you, as I wish I could do. <3 Thank you for staying with me as long as you have. I (hopefully) have helped you pick out some new plants to make your garden perfect for family gatherings, friendly hangouts and, perhaps—first dates? :O

Until I see you again, take care of your world as I take care of mine. Because you never know when you might be expecting company. :)

A Warrior's Journey

Brooke Schefe

Day one

We'd arrived ten minutes ago, and someone was already screaming. I sucked in a breath and belted my war cry across the lands of the summer camp. Amazon battle drums fired in the movie theatre. Set upon the railings of the food hall, a 20-foot banner of Xena and Gabrielle scanned the campground's horizon. With craned necks, my fiancée and I toddled beneath their leather boots, hand-in-hand. Camp staff heralded us on through rocky trails to a slew of wooden cabins. The promise of softball fields, rock climbing walls, cosplay and competition glimmered like the islands of Ancient Greece.

I met the love of my life through the love of a '90s TV show. We journeyed thousands of kilometres to the rainy woods of Pennsylvania to pay a four-day homage to Xena Warrior Princess.

After a feast in the food hall, everyone dispersed into the night to prepare for the opening competition between nations. Every attendee was drafted into one of six nations. Each nation had its unique persona based on characters from Xena.

The temperature dropped as we marched in darkness through the rain. It took me back to youth group camp; I was fourteen years old and crushing on my best friend while the leaders drummed on about the fear of God. I shivered.

Constance and I whipped on jackets and fashioned our nation's purple bandanna around our necks. Stepping outside in search of the gymnasium, I stole a kiss. We were Warriors: the stoic introverts with many skills.

Through the darkness, I saw the outline of battle staffs. The Bards with their big sticks stood out amongst the nations. They struck the ground, and a chant erupted.

'BIG STICK ENERGY! BIG STICK ENERGY! BIG STICK ENERGY!'

I grinned, feeling transported to a daydream conjured by my seventeen-year-old self. My heart brimmed with joy.

As we approached the gymnasium, fluorescent lights shone upon a clan of Amazons in uniforms of fur and leather. Their war-painted faces observed the crowds. In the warmth of the gym, I spotted a handful of Warriors chilling against the wall. Across the room, the Valkyries chattered with a fire of energy. They were known for their winged helmets and their intensity. A chant shot through the gym.

'WINGS UP!' The Valkerie's shouted. 'TITS OUT!' Everyone turned. 'VALLHALLA!' They silenced the gymnasium like a shock of thunder. Nerves swept through me. A wave of chatter arose, untamed.

From the far corner, the Immortals glanced down their noses. They sipped wine from silver goblets, their hair adorned with wreaths of gold. As I crossed the room, a group of villainous Cut Throats sliced past my shoulder. They grinned, splattered with blood.

'WELCOME XENITES!' Penny, the organiser, shouted into a microphone. Every nation roared with applause. The opening night of competitions began.

Day Two

Constance convinced me to try the climbing wall. I clung to the wooden beam, questioning my sanity. My brow furrowed as I swayed twelve feet in the air. Each level of wood and rope presented a challenge. My arms burned, bitten up from archery. A bloom of bruises decorated my legs.

'Swing ya leg over and sit on it,' the instructor called from below. Unlike Xena, who made defying gravity look simple, I stared at the beam with shallow eyes. I recalled the stagnant years I spent in silence, buried beneath someone else's shame. There was no place for a gay kid in my church or family. I hid like a bad seed, afraid to sprout.

My fingers throbbed as I gripped the rope. The climbing frame swung out from under me, and I hung from my hands. My arms trembled like two sinners steadfast in defiance before the gods.

'That's the way,' the instructor said. I dragged myself up out of the depths of Tartarus to sit on the throne as the woman I loved watched me from below.

I looked out over the campgrounds. The Immortal's cabin stood familiar on a hill. Aphrodite launched lolly bags at those who passed beneath her balcony. 'Bow down, bitches!' she smiled. The bombs of sugar glittered the air and settled in the mud.

The church I grew up in taught me shame disguised as sweetness. Underneath the Sunday best and smiles, I felt rotten. The year I turned seventeen, my life changed after watching an episode of Xena. For the first time, I saw a love story between two women, untouched by shame.

Hand-in-hand, Constance and I trekked to the far side of camp. Muddy trails opened to green fields. We were Xena and Gabrielle, traipsing across Ancient Greece for the most anticipated event of the year: The Known World Series Softball Tournament.

Four teams battled for the trophy.

I felt confident: we had two Xenas on our team. They flaunted the field in leather dresses. Constance joined me alongside the Amphipolis Warriors.

Our first opponent—The Battling Bards of Potidaea—smiled from across the field. Our loyal friends, even in the heat of battle. Still, we kicked their asses and made it to the finals. Playing on the opposite field, the Cirra Psychos flogged the Bitches of Rome.

I remembered myself as a teenager. Hidden down the back of my parents' place, I unleashed my voice on the lonely woods. I practised Xena's war cry, pretending to venture forth, never to return.

'AIY AIY AIY AIY AIY AIYYYYYY!' My war cry pierced the softball field. One after the other, the Warriors raised their voice in chaotic celebration. We huddled before the final game against the Cirra Psychos.

Our strongest player stepped up to bat: Xena herself. She'd played softball in college. She swung, smacking the ball far afield. The outfielders shot after it as Xena zipped to third base. The Amphipolis Warriors cheered.

We were in the lead as I gripped the bat with two hands. I'd played softball in high school for two weeks. I cringed at the memory: fourteen years old with a softball hurtling towards me. I'd swung and hit the ball; it smacked me right in the face.

'You got this, babe!' Constance shouted. My teammates sang a round of encouragement. The Cirra Psycho pitched the ball. I struck, high and far, and fanged it to first base. As I scrambled past second, my body remembered how to fly.

A cutting pain shot up my thighs as I sprinted towards home base. I ran faster, egged on by the cheers from my team and Constance, reaching home before the Cirra Psychos caught me.

I limped to the back of the line, grinning like a kid. My legs were dead, but the Amphipolis Warriors had backup: Bards and Amazons stood ready to run. Together we defeated the Cirra Psychos and won the Known World Series Softball Tournament.

Xena held the trophy on her shoulder as we passed every nation's cabin, announcing our victory with the Warrior's war cry.

Day Three

I lingered in the food hall at the Warrior's table, exhausted. Everyone cleared out after breakfast to make the most of the last day. I felt like Xena after a victorious battle.

The afternoon passed in a haze. I missed the epic final nation challenge. My passion evaporated, and I went to bed early while Constance went to the awards ceremony. Darkness enveloped the cabin as I sank into disappointed slumber.

'We did it!' Constance woke me. The overhead light stung my eyes. The Warriors won the nation championships. The last dance party of the Xenite Retreat raged on somewhere across camp. I'd slept through it all.

'There's still time,' Constance said. 'The party ends at midnight.'

'All the cool kids show up late,' I said, hiding my disappointment for sleeping through the day. Coloured lights beamed through the windows of the building we approached. The dance version of Cher's 'Believe' boomed on the speakers.

A chicken-shaped balloon bobbed in the corner amongst bales of hay. The theme was The Bitter Suite: the fever-dream musical episode about forgiveness that mended Xena and

Gabrielle's relationship. I led my soulmate to the middle of the room.

We kissed on the dance floor among two hundred Xenites dressed as court jesters and tarot cards, medieval Xenas and Gabrielles in togas. My feelings were bittersweet. For the first time in my life, I belonged. Tomorrow, I'd return to a world where holding Constance's hand in public still felt unsafe.

I turned to my left: the actress Brittney Powell was busting sick moves beside us. She'd starred as Brunhilda, the Valkyrie who tried to steal Gabrielle's heart. I gave into the fever dream.

We danced, proud as warriors. My smile reflected off Constance's eyes, the love of my life. Someone I'd never have met if I hadn't found my online community of Xena fans. Entranced by the energy, a conga line formed and sent us dancing late into the night.

Quiet Girl

Ruby Waller

Dear Boreham Young University Board of Trustees,

I hope this letter finds you well. My name is Kristen Martell. I assume you are aware of my reason for contacting you. However, if that is not the case, I am writing to appeal your decision regarding my expulsion from the university's soccer team.

I have been a member of the BYU Pumas for three years, have helped us win the 2021 NCAA championship title and secured our spot in the 2022 quarter final. While donning the royal blue, I have scored twenty-eight goals in fifty-seven appearances, carrying on the legacy built by legends such as Mia Hall, Jodie Simon and Juno Garcia.

When I was asked to join the team at sixteen my initial feeling was one of inferiority. I felt too young and lacking in confidence to play at such a high level. I had never envisioned being scouted as a possibility for me, let alone by one of the top women's clubs in the country.

If it weren't for my mum, I would have never left Denver. Not only did she drive me 450 miles from home to represent this team and play the sport I love, she would make the eight-hour trip time and time again so I could see a familiar face in the crowd. After many long, tearful conversations, she was able to convince me that I was enough, that this opportunity would be worth every sacrifice.

And up until recently, I believed her.

My soccer journey began when I was five years old. At school, I was considered shy and reserved by my peers and teachers. In fact, one of my school reports read: 'Kristen is a quiet girl. Quiet enough to disappear in a room full of people'. However, as soon as I set foot on the grass … my demeanour shifted. I became aggressive and dominant, my voice loud and distinct. Soccer showed me who I could be. It gave me purpose. A reason to be seen.

I lost my dad in a car crash when I was twelve. I refused to get in a vehicle for months even though this meant I had to walk three miles in the blistering cold to get to school. The thought of having to relive the moment where my whole world imploded made me sick to my stomach. For months, I thought I'd never leave my town again—I thought I'd end up like my neighbour, Brian, who lost his father young—succumbed to a life of solitude, boredom and wasted potential. But then spring came around and preseason training began. It was soccer that gave me the strength to grit my teeth, lace up my boots and jump into the passenger seat of my mum's rusty Prius. My coach told me during the first session that my dad would always be with me, nagging at me for being too one-footed in games.

I realised I was different from the other girls at school once I hit my teen years. While they excitedly huddled around their tables in the cafeteria to discuss their first kisses and crushes on boys, I felt out of place. My classmates would tease me for not dressing girly enough and for never having a boyfriend. They spread rumours and called me names relentlessly. Soccer gave me a release from that suffocating environment and graduating early to join BYU was what I believed to be my saving grace. Throughout my life, this game and this team has been my life raft. So, being told one part of my identity has influenced your decision to remove me from the team hurts me more than words can ever describe.

You have stated within my expulsion notice the reason for my removal is due to, 'Breaching the institution's religious code of conduct'. The Head of the Board continued to state that, '… my lifestyle goes against the teachings of the Bible … by speaking about your sexuality on social media you have disgraced the university and all it stands for'. I am aware of the influence religion has over the university, as are the rest of the student populus. I wonder if *you*, the Board of Trustees, are aware of how hypocritical it is to selectively ignore sections within your own religious doctrine. I feel if you are going to persecute students under the guidance of a book written over 2000 years ago, then you should at least do it properly.

According to your doctrine, '… one must not eat animals considered to be unclean … such as pork and shellfish'. Therefore, I believe the board should put an equal amount of energy into banning the sale of hot dogs on campus as you do discriminating against fee-paying students for their sexualities. This same doctrine also says, '… it is prohibited to wear clothing made of mixed fabrics …' The last time I checked, your BYU Pumas jerseys are made of polyester and elastane. Likewise, there is a rule in which men are banned from removing their beard hair. If the university truly cares about upholding the laws of the Bible, will all clean-shaven men be expelled too?

Or do you, as the board, find that suggestion ridiculous?

It is the year 2023. The United States has welcomed the *first* black South Asian American woman to be elected as the Vice President. Over two billion viewers across the world tuned in to watch women play in a world cup. Although slowly, the world is gradually moving away from antiquated laws created by men to oppress and hurt those different from them. Now is the time for you to ask yourselves whether the way your students express their love should be dictated by an outdated, oftentimes ridiculous storybook.

I believe it is high time that organisations labelled as educational institutions began to educate themselves and move with the times. Otherwise, I will have no choice but to make the rest of the world aware of your practices.

My name is Kristen Martell and I am a quiet girl no more.

The Falsehoods of Faith and Freedom

Oliver Sade

Deaf Within the Flame

This pure pious passion, built from pride and peace.
Faith forever drives me, my doubts, my fears cease,
Within the flame's roars, I continue to tread,
Where others may falter, we all forge ahead.

Through these epiphanies, these visions, I find,
Embraced absolutes, peace in state of mind,
Deep within where doubt and uncertainty cease,
I follow the call and creed that grants me peace.

With fire in my heart, I raise my hidden voice,
Now a warrior, my right, my fight, my choice

I recognise the virtues that others miss,
Within my sacred role, I find boundless bliss.

The world's wayward warnings fall upon deaf ears,
While I remain steadfast, they succumb to fear,
For within this fervent dance, I find my place,
A realm of zeal where we all set our own pace.

Yes, dangers remain where falsehoods might roam,
I find the required strength in my chosen home,
The masses caution against my faithful ways,
There is no other way, nothing but the blaze.

Smoke on the Horizon

Within the hearts of zealous souls, a blaze,
Where fanaticism dwells in tangled maze,
An ardour bound to faith or cause so tight,
Beware the lurking peril in its blinding light.

Oh, fanaticism, a fervent fire,
Consuming reason with its wild desire,

FANDOMONIUM

An all-consuming zeal that blinds the eyes,
To truths and facts, to reason's softest cries.

In single-minded fervour's fierce embrace,
Compassion fades, replaced by hardened face,
The world reduced to black and white, no grey,
As shades of nuance vanish in dismay.

Passions grown too strong, unchecked,
The seeds of hate and conflict erect,
The fragile bonds of unity are rend,
As the fractured souls of followers descend,

Our idols placed on pedestals, there rule remains brief,
Deified, beyond reproach, without relief,
These virtues praised, their flaws left behind,
Within zealotry, common truths are denied.

The dangers which lay in fervour's blinded stare,
Destroyer of empathy, of reason, of care,
Beware the lure of the fanatic's ramblings,
And seek out the truth, a balanced standing,

Though hearts may burn with passion unceasing,
May wisdom guide us to life's truest meaning,
Though fanaticism may lead the flock astray,
May sanity and truth's embrace hold sway.

The lessons learned from history's path,
Reveals the scars of zealotry's wrath,
The lessons I learned from unbridled sect,
Reveals my scars of egregious effect.

In a world of ceaseless battles, we find,
Wisdom and knowledge left far behind,
Yet, within this tale, remember and see,
A call for patience and empathy be.

I found no solace in their destructive ways,
Fools bound together by that ever-burning blaze,
Silenced and ignored, I cannot speak,
Simply nod to their statements, with tongue-in-cheek.

The Father of Flames

Above this stage of existence, I reign supreme,
The grand overseer within an endless dream,
Every choice, every step, under my watchful eye,
Individuality, a mere facade, in my fiery sky.

The desires of mortals, devoid of meaning,
Puppets, toys, in this cosmic screening,
Strings of fate I deftly pull and weave,
No hope to resist, no chance to deceive.

Free will, a deceptive notion they hold dear,
My will, the true force behind their veneer,
The illusion of freedom they blindly embrace,
Crumbles in my grasp, replaced by fear's embrace.

Oh, the arrogance of their futile cries,
Unwittingly, they dance in my devised lies,
I, the master, orchestrate their joy and strife,
In this grand theatre, I alone shape life.

In unity and isolation, they twist and turn,
Escape from my dominion, a lesson they will not learn,

At the crossroads of my design, some praise my grace,
While others rise in protest, condemning my malevolent embrace.

Their paths predetermined, leading to destinies foretold,
Made from stars, yet buried deep in earthly mould,
All connections, thoughts, loves contrived and spun,
Their dreams of free will masked, every battle won.

The time approaches to unveil my might,
Before me, all forces fade from sight,
Within this epic narrative, my passage, my tale,
Mortal, remember, defiance's path will surely fail.

Captive Melody

Ryan Closter

August 17 remains etched in my memory; when my folk-star dreams of the bygone days vanished and the screams became plastic.

I still feel the searing pain in my guitar-string-scarred fingertips. I spent the entire week perfecting a haunting melody with my bloody fingers only to prove that I will not become a tweeted failure. What followed, though, was a steep descent into a different world. A more commercial one beneath my previous ballads of the cosmos. Like any other aspiring artist, I was urged by my despotic manager, Tom, to confine myself in his label's golden frame. I had to create music for the listeners of Vertigo Music before my fans and I. *No contract. No career.* Those were the cards laid out to me, and Tom had the guts to say she was the lucky one. She remembers the stern voices and though she may never forget the smash hit that brought her to Tom's wrought-iron gates, she will always think back on how her mother was seduced by his power. She now gazes at Vertigo's imprisoning contract with faint guitar strums floating in the back of her mind. She was me, but now she is country-star, Glistenin' Jane.

Sixteen hours until her glistening new dawn. Cheers echoed down Tom's hallway. Although I was home alone, my morally captive mother felt the need to signal Tom's judgement on his behalf. Or are they her judgements alone? Everyone nowadays has the right to judge me, but only my loyal fans refrain from doing so to my existence. *We're so proud of you dear* … My mother sneered through the loudspeaker often, and each time she criticised my passion I died. It was easy to shut my eyes to this malevolence, but muting it was impossible. Clearly these two were made for each other, as all narcissists are. Their harsh compliments and fire insults walked a fine line and both knew how to tread it precisely. My mother was never like this before meeting Tom for my benefit. I suppose that she laid pieces of her broken heart over Dad's eyes rather than the few pennies he left us both. After meeting Tom, my mother fell in love with him and his label's autocracy. Now she fails to see the creature that she became and because of her false insecurities, I am left stranded to the king of Vertigo Music … *and we both agree that it is best for us to follow Tom's interests.* 'Us' for Mum meant her and Tom. I gavaged the thought of them being my parental figures daily in spite of a lingering poisonous taste. I could not betray my father for he was the only man to believe in my folk music. According to Tom's dizzying meetings, even my fans expect a more commercial production on my lyrics. Was this true? I found myself not caring, for I have no feelings for these strangers due to Tom barricading my personality from them. The death of the artist comes at the cost for the fandom. Meanwhile, this corkscrew pressure led me to resent the idol life of Glistenin' Jane that was imposed onto me earlier this morning. I felt myself slip away from my true folk persona of a simple Jane to her shimmering country antithesis. Through all this inner turmoil, I packed my guitar and dreams and headed for the studio.

Eight hours until her glistening new dawn. The drive to Vertigos HQ's studio seemed longer this time. I closed my eyes on the way past a cemetery filled with the irrelevant LA souls who never got to acquire fame. Instead, I focused on Tom's callous words incited by my mother's sluggish intravenous fangs. The death of Jane by a thousand venomous needles was going to be slow and painful. Saying goodbye to these deadly thoughts, I enter the studio with forced determination to compose a folk melody, albeit futile, to convince hell's couple that I am talented without the country glamour. My fingers explored the red-stained guitar with a sense of wanderlust—Bang! Tom burst into the scene like a hellish ghost of Irish lore. His demonic presence dwarfed even my most skilled folk producers. No matter how much my studio friends defended my style, they all availed under Tom's claws. For he was the vulture of Vertigo and they were like offal to him. I began feeling lonelier despite his attempts to motivate me by calling me *country lovely*. I hid in my creative forest waiting for Tom to leave, but heavy walls mounted with accolades and business models caved in over my head.

Meetings. Marketing. Merchandising. More marketing. No rest. Licensing. Contracting. Meetings for meetings. Marketing new merchandise. Still, no rest. Amidst this dreamy cacophony of corporate chatter, I remember my humble beginnings with Vertigo Music. I still feel myself signing the ten-year contract. I was a rocket to the moon at that time. Only fifteen. I was Tom's only hope to resonate with a younger audience. But now I feel our journey together has become a kamikaze ride to the sun. Young Jane dared not to break the golden frame Tom promised her, but now I am older and wiser and sentient. I will promise myself not to succumb to Tom's idea of a good song. I will remain true to my young self. Even though I am soon to become a country radio girl, I can still remain true. The truth always will prevail while the demon's lies will soon fall off the steep unbalanced cliffs—Bang! Tom seemed to disappear, yet I could still feel his hauntings. That was when I noticed the blood-stained handwriting stuck to the exit door. *Family dinner, Jane. 8pm tonight. Important.* I rolled my eyes so far back I left my forestry folk cosmos.

Four hours until her glistening new dawn. I returned to Tom's opulent mansion. However, this time I felt increasingly out of place, like a Sylvanian family in a Barbie world. Underneath his crude chandelier to the left of my periphery, my mother devoured Tom's extravagant shit display of *entrées*. This was not a family dinner but an intervention for his own ego. I invited myself to sit down, waiting to be served the real last supper. He may have tempted my mother to indulge in all his unnecessary debaucheries, but I could not be fooled. Maybe Glistenin' Jane, but not me. My own mother slurred her excitements to me as though she overdosed off my fame. With hungry eyes, I delved deeper into old memories while Tom introduced his plans to transform me into a country-star *… Lavender … paper … lavender paper … scribbles … glitter … young Jane used to jot down the happy walks with her father … she would press hard on the love-stained cotton paper writing her love for family … her old mother would prepare mash and veges … she would write about those bittersweet flavours of home—But after her father's passing, an intruder seduced young Jane's mother … now the spirit of this young girl writes about nostalgia and pain* *through contemporary folk ballads … Why must she leave home?* … Tom finalised this new verbal contract by promising me that all my fans will revere, love, and obsess over this new era even more. After all, that is the direction Vertigo Music is taking with their promising new legends like Glistenin' Jane. Normally, the mere mention of relinquishing my autonomy would make me shudder with private jet turbulence, but after witnessing my drunk mother agree with Tom, I was strapped to Vertigo's hot seat. The smell of my own smoky dust filled the air, forging hallucinations of Tom's dream and forgetting mine. It is three hours until my glistening new dawn that I surrender to the king of Vertigo Music.

One hour following my mutation into a country-star. And just like that I feel my fandom's weight penetrate deep into my padded shiny shoulders, possessing my captive being as the new sensation, Glistenin' Jane.

Not Just Love and Loss

Hollie Mowett

This is the first time I've been silent in so long. I've created solace in loneliness, but noise has always floated around me, a cacophonous ocean before my ears. There is noise I fear, that makes me tremble and pace throughout the night. There is noise I love, the kind that has mostly filled my life until recently.

My mother said I was born with pipes like Whitney, she said even my baby cries had melodies. Before I talked, I sang; before I walked, I danced. I suppose, like most young girls, I wanted to be a singer, but unlike many I had a family who could support this dream.

The first song I remember hearing was at my grandfather's house when I was seven or eight-years-old. He had a record collection greater than most. While he boiled the kettle and made two mugs of tea—mine warm and sweet, his hot and strong—he suggested I choose a record to play. I ran my tiny fingers over the thick stock cardboard, admiring the varying artwork and posing musicians. I sifted through the worn, dusty paper sleeves until I saw a cover, bold with red. A woman wearing Venetian red pants with a matching neckerchief tucked into a cream blouse, sitting in front of a coral background. She was an ordinary woman, with ordinary hair and ordinary features, but she was wearing slips on her feet that looked like sparkly gold socks. *Magic* gold socks. Socks I still remember 20 years later.

'Patsy Cline. Good choice,' my grandfather said, walking into the loungeroom with two mugs in hand. 'She released this album after almost dying in a car accident.'

The album's opening lyrics, *I fall to pieces*, expressed the vulnerability of this woman, this ordinary woman. As the record spun and I sipped my tea, I noticed how much was expressed in so little time. The song's narrative was fluently told in three and a half minutes; not only through her words, but through her tone, the piano keys, the percussion, the breaks in her breath.

'How can I write songs?' I asked my grandfather.

'Just start writing, Bloss. Write about everything and anything. Songs can be about blackbirds and hailstorms, not just love and loss.'

From then on, I didn't simply listen to music, I studied it. When my grandfather passed, I inherited his record player and most of his collection. Dozens of torn, dusty sleeves and records that crackle when spinning. Through my teens, music taught me. I learnt that love could make you go blind and maybe there's a God above, or maybe God is the sun. I developed a music literacy, a literacy that became intrinsic to my emotions. When feelings couldn't be said, they were written, then sung.

Then at sixteen, I performed. In a room with sticky floors and toilets desperate for disinfectant, wearing scuffed shoes, loose jeans and gold socks that I convinced myself were magic. I walked into a cloud of light and stood with my guitar behind the microphone stand, pretending they both shielded me from the stares of a hundred eyes. I sang mostly covers, but when I sang my own songs, my hand shook. I thought back to the ordinary woman on the bold red cover. I had to be authentic; I had to be vulnerable.

Four years later, I was on tour opening for a major band. They were a five-piece indie-rock group singing about girls and lazy summers and I was singing about everything but. The first show was at an outdoor amphitheatre; it was my first show playing in fresh air. I walked onto the stage, just me and my guitar, and disregarded the deafening cheers as anticipation for the next band. I'd never played for a crowd so big. My lungs inhaled the Autum air, and I remember thinking how lovely it was to breathe and not smell body odour or stale beer. The soft light from the setting sun and steep amphitheatre hill accentuated the silhouettes. I sang mostly my own songs, with very few covers, and only looked at the soft pink clouds, tangled in purple, awaiting the first stars so the headline act could relieve me of these nerves.

It was then I glanced briefly at the audience and saw you, in the nosebleed, moving your mouth in unison with mine. *And with skin like golden sand, she sought the pleasures of the world.* You sang every word as if they were your own.

The music sounded different from then on; my purpose for writing and performing changed. I stopped performing the songs you didn't like and wrote with only you in mind. *Not just love and loss*, but whatever made you sing.

The more I toured, the more loneliness crept in. It travelled with me, and I let it. I suppose it was inevitable. I had listened to enough '70s songs to know that touring is lonely. Music had always been my greatest companion. Even when alone, I had Paul and Art, or Stevie and Lindsay to comfort me but no amount of music could quench the loneliness I felt on tour.

At the end of every show, my ears would ring from the noise. Tour managers, record label executives, choreographers, hair and makeup, security, sound check, and the deafening cheers of you. My tired feet would walk alone down endless hallways into beige rooms with dull, abstract art. I would pour myself a glass from the complimentary bottle and run the shower. Over the sound of water hitting cold tiles, I could still hear the echoes from the day.

For almost a decade, most nights have ended like this. Alone, not even with my own thoughts. With every new room key and sound check in foreign cities, my passion has simmered gradually on a stove. The essence of what I love and my purpose has evaporated.

I should have looked to my family for support but instead I looked to you. You told me you loved me, even though you didn't know me and I said it back as if I knew what it meant. I booked tour after tour so I could see you again. To hear your cries and cheers, hear you begging for one more or chanting my name. In hollow rooms, I consumed your messages, both good and bad, until they consumed *me*.

Lately, days have felt like weeks, and I count time in inches, waiting for when I no longer sell out stadiums but instead sit as a spectre on an aging sleeve in someone's loungeroom. I walk onto stages and look to the sky, without even the slightest glance at you. On the outside, I feel weathered and worn, beyond a coat of new paint. And on the inside, I feel hollow.

I'm contracted to write another album, but I can't and I won't. Instead, I'm here in a sea of grey, my ears below the water's surface, arms out, eyes closed, floating in complete silence, wishing to be ordinary. Music doesn't carry the same meaning. My purpose and passion aren't what they once were. I fear I'm falling to pieces.

And so, my fans, I am no longer yours.

The Gift of Flight

Toby Newell

I am flying for the second time in my short life. It's almost midnight and the windows are down. The cool wind hits my face as the Falcon soars through the grove of gumtrees. I'm a moonlit poet masquerading as a larrikin. Music pumping. Heart pounding. Tyres screeching.

There's four of us in the car, a week into Ben getting his P's. Chooky is riding shotgun, chest puffed and playlist in hand. Ben is beside him, gripping the wheel and taking 'calculated' risks. In the back are Aidan and me. He's a redhead with a mullet and the middle seat between us isn't the only thing separating our friendship.

'How'd you find the test, Benny? Was it hard?' I ask from the back.

'Nah. Easy stuff. Didn't even cop a minor, boys.'

'You might've if they saw how you're driving now!' Chooky, the wannabe DJ, always had a quick-witted reply for Ben's overconfidence.

Ben floors it in retaliation. Trees become blurs and road reflectors flicker in the distance.

'Bro, if you get pulled over, you're done,' I say.

'Pffft. I know where the cops are,' Ben shoots back. 'Richie put me onto this app. Gives you a map of all the cops in the area.'

The song changes.

'Sheesh. Absolute banger,' Aidan approves from the back.

Kanye gets cranked up. I don't even like rap. I prefer the fragile melodies of folk music. But I'm with my boys, so I sing every forced phrase like I was born in a balaclava. I feel out of place. Detached. Like I'm not even here. We've been kicking footies around since primary school, but something feels unfamiliar now. I'm watching three mates laugh and liaise, but my seat is a black void. A hole that I sink into.

We keep winding around the foothills of the Western Suburbs. Friends in the pursuit of approval. An unsuspecting conformity to the patterns we are made to perform.

Beside us arrives a contender. Ben downshifts so our neighbour can join this migratory pattern of masculine fun. Despite the darkness, I quickly recognise the familiar metallic green of Jesse's run-down Civic. Ben takes a look.

'Ayeeee. J Doggg in the green machine. Surprised if that thing even gets past second.'

'Absolute fartbox, aye. Shouts and sputters just like Miss Johnson tryna explain Shakespeare.' Chooky was always a bit rough around the edges.

'Oi, she's hot though,' Aidan adds.

'Shut up, Aidan. You've never spoken to a woman in your life.'

Aidan turns to look out the window in silence—the best friend who betrayed me for the allure of a prefect position. The friend who gave me my first taste of flight as I copped an ankle tap, and tasted concrete, too. The middle seat is wide tonight. Jesse revs his cacophony of clunking steel.

'Time to smoke him.' Ben shoots a confident smile to the backseat and in this moment, we all have a universal understanding of what's about to go down.

We are poised on a precipice.

Ben puts his foot down. Leg in hyperextension. Metal meeting metal. Rubber meeting road. Boys meeting fate. The speedo cranks its hand to the right like a hyperventilating clock. We climb towards terminal velocity. Jesse is quickly left behind, his headlights a distant glow in the eerie colonnade of gumtrees.

'Shittttt!'

Our windscreen is spattered with sudden thuds of colour. A swarm of lorikeets meet an impenetrable object. Ben swerves out of reflex. We jack-knife, clipping the metal guardrail, replacing the lorikeets aborted flights by engaging in our own.

On the inside, somehow, I'm still lucid. I'm floating. This car is liminal, a dark, liquid womb. The only thing holding me in this state is my seatbelt. The flight lasts a lifetime. An anthology of memories is condensed into an eternity of seconds. Existential questions formulate in the mind of a reckless teenager. I paint the black canvas with the glow of my words. *Why do I do this? What am I chasing? Is the mark of a man measured by proficiency in street racing?*

I answer my own questions. *I'm a follower of my friends. I'm a disciple of tradition until my dying breath. Maybe the mark of a man is measured by your willingness to flirt with death?*

Every soul has a story. A melody that rings out for the rest of a lifetime. As I sit in this lonely vehicle, I see the bodies of my mates swaying to the music in my mind. This world is upside down. It's here in the darkened suburbs, in a dark, damp car, with black leather seats, that I begin to see colour. The technicolour carcasses still wedged in the windscreen become a mosaic, a stained-glass masterpiece.

I see portraits of people. I see my father, the strongest man I know, crying as he watches my sisters playing. I see my uncle yelling at the footy, but I also see him painting delicate scenes of a sunset. I see my workmate, who stifles his pain with adrenaline. I hear my principal tell us that, 'Adventure is hardwired into men, but it must be channelled correctly.' These figures form a tapestry of beauty. A tapestry of pain and poignance—punctuated by feathers and fables of greatness.

It's dead still in the womb. In the centre of this gallery, there's an ambiguous figure. He's been there the whole time. A vague shadow. I can't hear him; I can't exactly see him. But somehow, I know him. I know he's five foot ten. I know he's got a solid right boot and a heart of gold. I know he prefers both feet to be on the ground. I know he is aware of the dangers of following. I know he's searching for something more than what's on offer. I know him because he's me. *Maybe this is my chance at rebirth?*

The birds floating around my periphery remind me that something fascinating happens when we fly in packs. The ticking of the indicator reminds me that this flight cannot last forever. The groans of my neighbours remind me of the price of conformity to preconceived paths.

As the impending blanket of bitumen draws closer, I'm already looking to the future. I know the road ahead will be hard. But flying is a gift afforded to very few humans.

The Initiation

Ebony Martyn

SNOWFLAKE BALL
A Night to Remember!

Riverstone High was home to the preppy, elitist boys of Baltimore. If your parents weren't ridiculously loaded and you didn't look like a Greek God, you looked out of place. Griff and I were bottom of the food chain. For starters, my name is Blinky. I'm chubby, pale and shy, attending Riverstone on a scholarship. Griff was underweight with an intense set of braces who only had eyes for the robotics club. Regardless of how hard we tried to go unnoticed, we stuck out like sore thumbs. With our eyes down, taking up the far-left sliver of the corridor, Val and his pack of wolves always managed to find us. Generally, it was minor acts like emptying our backpacks, throwing away our lunch, slapping books out of our hands, etcetera. However, today we received quite the performance:

apex predators asserting their dominance in a magnificent display of masculinity.

'If it isn't Blinky Bill and Skinny,' Val chuckled as he grabbed my collar and pressed me up against the locker. He had his side kick Logan shake the contents of our backpacks onto the floor. I tried not to grunt as he grabbed the scruff of my neck hard. Val proceeded to spit at our feet. That was a new one. His possie let out a victorious cackle as they trailed off to their next victims.

To trademark their status, they each rolled the cuffs of their sleeves one time, except for Val who rolled his twice, proclaiming himself as alpha. I stared at the saliva covering our monotonous, leather, polished shoes. I generally tolerated the bullying; I'm self-aware enough to accept that hierarchy was a part of high school, but as I was glaring at Val's bodily fluids, I felt unbelievably low. Griff ripped some paper from our schoolbooks and attempted to wipe the leather clean. I followed his lead begrudgingly. I tried to ignore the snickers of bystanders, as I collected my belongings off the floor. Griff seemed far less annoyed than I was, however, he was always the more timid one.

I stood up and sighed, taking a second to contemplate my current situation: my completely and utterly shitty life. What I would give to have athletic abilities, chiselled abs and, God forbid, a girlfriend. I loved my parents, I knew they believed that attending a school like Riverstone High would boost my chances at an Ivy League school. At that point, though, I'd been just as happy with NYU if it meant I could live in peace during my weekdays.

I looked up at the obnoxiously large banner reading 'Snowflake Ball: A Night to Remember'. *Great, another grand exhibition of wealth and prominence to look forward to.* At least I had a week to mentally prepare.

The weekend was over in a flash, as I dragged my feet towards the intimidating, stone pillars. With my head down, I hear my name called through the crowd, 'Blinky!' I turned around to find Val chasing after me with a smile. *Am I in an alternate universe?* 'Meet me at off campus toilet blocks at 11.'

'Why? I know what you're going to do.'

'Well, I'm only going to hurt you later on if you don't show up.'

I shrugged my shoulders in defeat and sheepishly agreed. *I should appreciate the privacy, I suppose.*

I watched the clock tick over in class. 10:55am hit, I stood up and gathered my things. My teacher knew I would be leaving a little early; the good thing about being a loser is the authority figures in my life never questioned my honesty. The journey to the toilet block was quick—less time to think about my impending demolition.

Val and his pack were awaiting my arrival, all standing, arms crossed and grinning. The ringleader broke the silence, 'We have a proposition for you.'

'A proposition?' I replied.

'Look, Blinky, how would you like to be one of us?'

Someone from the back chimed in, 'On probation, of course.'

'But you all hate me, why would I believe that?'

'Don't you wonder what it's like to go to school, knowing you're untouchable? That's what we're offering you here.' Val sounded like he wasn't going to take no for an answer. 'What's the alternative, life continuing as it is? You're a freak, with one freak friend.'

'What about Griff? Is he going to be included?' I asked.

'Do you really think we would take the both of you?' Val let out an exasperated snort, followed by the rest of the group cackling in unison. 'One of you is enough, and you seem like the more interesting one. So, what do you say?'

To this I stood in shock, unable to speak. This apparently meant yes, as the group whizzed me off to the main school with about five unnecessarily aggressive pats on the back.

I felt a pang of guilt as I walked through the halls with the enemy; I knew Griff would be looking for me at this point. High fives, knuckles and head nods were given out to a few who were deemed worthy. I couldn't help but feel untouchable, no one dared to provoke Val and his possie. By the end of the day, I had even been invited to a party next weekend. Three days passed of receiving this privileged high school experience. I was still confused as to why I was being befriended; however, I pushed those thoughts to the back of my mind. I lived my life on the outskirts of society, all I ever wanted was to be let in. I was choosing to overlook the oppression Val place on Riverstone High. I would find excuses to disappear during their rampant attacks on the innocents. I found it alleviated part of my guilty conscience. I was forbidden from associating with Griff, which hurt. I hated Val, but I couldn't question him. I was now faced with a new set of problems.

Val wrapped his arm around me as we walked. 'Blinky, I bet you've enjoyed the last few days at Riverstone.'

'You could say that,' I replied, paired with an uncomfortable laugh.

'You wouldn't want that to be taken away, would you?'

A glimpse of the terrorising torment Griff and I received daily returned to my mind. 'No—no I wouldn't.'

He pulled me into an empty classroom with a wry smile. 'We need to be sure you're loyal to us, Blinky. How do we know you're trustworthy? We want to let you into our group fully, but we need you to do something for us first.'

I stared at him blankly. 'What is it?'

'If we're going to share our secrets with you, you need to cut ties with that loser Griff.'

'I have already, we haven't spoken in days.' Delicately imploring him to ask nothing else.

'That's not enough reassurance for me. I need you to humiliate him. Show me that you're one of us.'

Dread hit me in the face. I could feel my morality wavering. *I was in too deep.*

Val continued. 'You do realise if you don't do this, we will make your life worse than what it was before.'

I sighed long and hard, I knew he wasn't bluffing. I would be miserable and bruised for the remaining two years.

'What would I have to do?'

'Well, it'd take place at the Snowflake Ball on Friday night.' Val let out a malevolent cackle before continuing, 'Someone might accidentally slip something in his drink.'

'What? No, that's way too far—'

'Not far enough. That's when the fun starts. If you want in, you must put the inferiors in their place. There's a hierarchy for a reason, and I'm the top dog. Consider this your initiation.'

'I need some time to think.'

'Think? The ball is tomorrow, Blinky. I'm bringing the good stuff, and that's when you step in. You're the ultimate insider. The only one who can get close enough to his punch. Then when Skinny is feeling a little more relaxed, the show will begin.' Val couldn't stop the grin forming on his face.

I didn't recognise myself anymore as I obediently agreed to his plan.

The double doors of the Gymnasium were pinned back proudly, revealing a Winter Wonderland inside. My eyes were met with ice sculptures in the shape of reindeers, an assortment of Christmas trees dusted in snow, silver and white balloon arches and an obnoxiously large disco ball reflecting the blue light around the room. Decadence pairs nicely with debauchery. I drifted to the back of the room, nervously indulging at the appetisers table. I wanted to remain there the rest of the night in the shadows with my own thoughts. A yank on my shoulders snapped me back to reality.

'Blinky. We've been looking for you?' It was Val. He grabbed my hand and closed it around a little plastic bag in one swift motion. 'You know what to do,' he said as he pointed to Griff across the room.

Karma's a Bitch

Kirsty Lam

The Ritz—London's finest. I look at myself in the elevator's mirror as it descends to ground level. Straighten tie. Run hand through slicked back hair. *God, I look good.* A bell chime alerts me to the fact there are few precious moments left to admire my appearance. The doors open with a whoosh. I walk past reception and through the lobby, observing the guests checking in, checking out and checking their London maps. I cannot hide my disgust at a couple—obviously tourists—and their choice of shoes. One in Crocs and the other in Uggs; a match made in heaven. Compared to those two, I look like the CEO of a world-renowned business. I am neither a CEO nor a businessman. To be fair, I gave university a go but my professor would not get off my case so I left after a semester. Nobody else knows this though—these days you can put anything on a LinkedIn profile.

Two vases of colourful roses sit atop a mahogany table. Roses always make my nose itch. It is why my house strictly has Lillies of the Valley on display. Upon first observation, the Lillies are sweet … innocent. But get too close, and you will be in real danger. I am sure my childhood psychologist could draw some weak correlation between my fondness for Lillies of the Valley and my 'issues' but whatever.

A bowl of lollies sits between the pillars of flowers. A quick fix to make the hotel more kid friendly. *Sweets for children only, please!* I read the sign as I plunge my hand into the dish and grab a fistful. I do not know what flavour they are and to be honest, I really do not care. Reading the hotel's 'warning' again does make me chuckle as I pop a sweet into my mouth. Artificial strawberry tingles on my tongue, and I push aside the thought of tooth decay.

The revolving door rotates around and around. Its sole purpose in life. On the other side of the glass, two taxi drivers gesticulate wildly, shouting at each other. I say shouting, but the glass is so thick, the outside world is on mute. For all I know, they could be two old mates catching up. I would rather steam my suit again than spend more of my time thinking about those people. I am not interested. My care factor is zero.

I walk forward an exacting seven steps and seamlessly slide into a partition of the door. I perfected the movement long ago. The idea of resembling those people who shuffle awkwardly through revolving doors makes me nauseous. The ceiling fans in the lobby circulate the same way I do around the revolving door: in perfect synchrony. I hear the flick of bristles as the door sweeps the spotless carpet. I sense the loss of cool air pumping through the hotel's building.

The summer heat announces itself, oblivious to the tourists and their plans. I am forced to undo one of the buttons on my suit. *You are welcome.*

I smile, remembering my dashing presence. Drop me in the desert and bet your bottom dollar, I would still sport a crisp suit. I loathe the people who lack pride in their appearance these days—looking at you, Croc and Ugg duo. Living proof my image stands leagues above the rest of the population.

The taxi drivers' shouting fades as I stride along the path to Hyde Park. I stop at the traffic lights, congregating with other pedestrians waiting to cross the road. The uncouth wear 'I LOVE LONDON' t-shirts and bum bags. Next to me, a tour guide rattles off a spiel about the city's history, to his clients' amusement. He holds a tiny Union Jack flag in his raised hand as it waves in the breeze. A young boy from the group has his eyes glued to my briefcase.

I rotate the buttery leather to ensure the gold designer logo is visible. A sense of accomplishment floods through as he looks at me with awe. The hum of a luxuriously expensive engine calls to me. A satin grey car glides past. It is an Aston

Martin, with a personalised numberplate: *KARMA*. Even the tour guide pauses to admire it. Burning envy rages through me.

I cannot stop myself from thinking about my car. It is currently at the auto repair shop, hidden from view. Every morning I hope that I will not have to fork out more money I do not have, on the old dump of a car. The thought of the dreaded call from the auto mechanic keeps me up at night. The bank will no longer loan me any money.

The traffic lights change, and I break free from the plebs to charge across the road before the little red man lights up again.

The grand gates of Hyde Park welcome me to London Borough's finest green space. I straighten my tie into submission as I walk through the park. The shade from the trees provides a reprieve from the sun. Rebecca stands underneath the canopy of trees, as per my instructions. She is there, waiting. As non-descript as ever, how I vaguely remember her to be.

* * *

My blood pressure spikes and goosebumps cover my arms: indicators he is close. I notice Thomas swagger along the park's main path. Well, it's not as though I suddenly spot him; he seems to make his presence known. The strong scent of sandalwood and cedar assaults my nose. I taste toast, a reminder of the days when I couldn't bring myself to leave my bed. I agreed to meet him, as he expected. That was my problem. My Achillies heel was doing what he said. Thomas saunters up to me.

'Rebecca, my darling. Lovely to see you,' he says, kissing my hand.

'It's just Becca,' I remind him again. I know it will be futile.

'You look different,' Thomas coos. I hope he means I have changed. No longer tolerant or susceptible to his guileful charm. He's carrying a briefcase. A lot of effort considering it's empty. There is a distance between us. A duck waddles through the space between our bodies. We both watch as it crosses our path. I smile gently at the innocent bird while Thomas curls his lip in disgust.

I am wearing my Chelsea boots, meaning I am taller than Thomas by a hair. How gratifying. He was oddly obsessed with my height. I'm aware this accomplishment isn't solely thanks to my genetics. A large portion is due to my platform shoes, but when the guy who ruined your life comes into town for a chat, you take all the wins you can get. I wait for him to speak.

He talks, smirking and enjoying the sound of his own voice, as always. I used to like it; now it's sandpaper. He doesn't hesitate to tell me that he has bought an Aston Martin, apparently. A personalised numberplate and satin grey in colour. He stands there, with a perfect posture and that insufferable grin. He expects me to fawn over the deity that is Thomas. Not anymore.

I breathe deeply, settling my nerves. He's too busy stroking his ego to register my raising hand. *This is from me, and from every other person you deceived.* I stare through him, holding my nerve despite the wobble in my voice. 'Karma's a bitch.'

I savour the sweet sound of my hand connecting with his cheek. *God, that felt good.* My hand tingles as pain and adrenaline fire through my body. Meanwhile, my jagged car key slices through the brown leather of his briefcase, tearing it open. My ragged, angry cuts hit where I know it will hurt.

He blinks rapidly and his shallow breathing echoes in my ears. A picture-perfect person no longer.

I turn on my heel, leaving Thomas standing like an immovable stone. The key sits heavy between my fingers, like muscle memory ensuring my protection. I stride out of the park towards a jolly man across the street. He has a big smile and a Union Jack flag in his hand.

Amid the noise of my rapid heart, I hear a young boy from the group exclaim, 'Woah, that's such a sick car! What is it?'

'Ah, thanks.' I glance at him as I unlock my car. 'It's an Aston Martin.' Gentle clouds obscure the sun's wrath, and I am swallowed up in the streets of London.

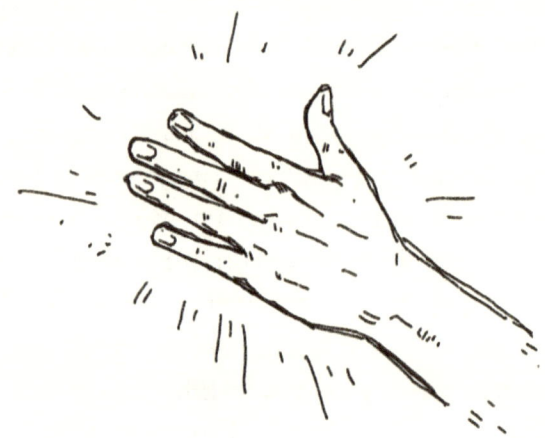

Peace Within Peace

Kalandra du Plessis

Nine…

Drawings danced in the air as the summer breeze assisted my spinning blades. The papers joined the entangled toys on the floor. Only the squeak from my monitor could be heard. Friday afternoon was the most elated day of the week. The beginning of an animated, giggle-filled weekend. I spun around and waited for the girls to enter, and for the peace and quiet to disappear. Like a grand reveal in an opening play, the door swung open. Rickie and Blake entered, hands intertwined, mouths moving. Their school bags thrown and slumped in the corner. Bringing the outside heat in with them, Rickie turned me up to level four.

A fan of many years, but I could still speed, like the words pouring out of their mouths. Like hands on a clock, these girls never stopped—coloured pencils turned blunt, dolls' outfits changed like seasons, and tickle trains were endless. The room filled with chatter and toys. *Their bond is something I hold close, something I have yet to experience firsthand… or blade.* Bedtime crept up on us, and soon Rickie's mum tucked the girls in and set my timer on.

On Saturday morning, Rickie's mum set me to level two and flicked the lava lamp off. My slow-moving blades subtly woke the girls. Rickie's arm stretched out from beneath the duvet, and her legs slumped on top of the covers. Blake rolled over and pulled the duvet with her. I saw Rickie roll her eyes back. Rickie nudged Blake and began the tug of war for the duvet. Buried beneath the blanket with only her head peeking through, Rickie said, 'I dreamt about a purple Peace Lily.'

Blake chuckled and leant against the headboard. 'You dream about that every night, Rickie.'

The girls speak about their dreams before they start the day. A habit at the root of their friendship.

They kicked the covers off and all I could see were two untamed heads of hair. Nothing but energy running through each strand. A new day began. Girls out of bed. Nail kit on display.

Like a flower petal, Rickie's hands were delicate. Blake held them with care as she swiped the polish across Rickie's nails. She squinted with a scrunched-up nose. Time barely moved.

Fourteen…

'Hip hip hooray!' everyone cheered from the garden. All of Rickie's family and friends were in the garden celebrating her fourteenth birthday. I couldn't see anything from her bedroom, but I could smell the sweet vanilla cake that traipsed through the bedroom window, followed by a wave of laughs. Chatter increased as Rickie, Blake and a few others galloped up to her room.

The girls sat on Rickie's bed and held out presents as she dragged a chair across the room. Blake whispered that she'd give her present to Rickie later. The bin spilt over with ripped wrapping paper all shades of purple and white. Anticipation rose. Each layer promising the joy that would trickle into the afternoon.

Blake hovered over the leftover cake while Jade and Megan applied their facemasks. The roar of gossip echoed down the hall. The facemasks glowed under the purple LED strip lights. I stayed on level one most of the night as the balcony stayed open. Cross-legged, knee to knee, the girls chatted. Like a river, meandering with the flow, the conversation didn't stop.

'I never actually liked him,' explained Megan.

'I actually thought his friend was funnier,' said Jade.

I watched Rickie, and Blake, absorbing the conversation with laughter. As the chats transitioned to boys and school and dreams, Blake nudged Rickie. Jade and Megan were too deep into the conversation to notice as they exchanged a look. A side eye with raised eyebrows prompted them to casually walk towards the balcony. Blake held a box behind her back. She jittered with anticipation as she presented Rickie with her gift.

'No way!' she screamed. Rickie jumped into Blakes arms and squeezed her tight.

The last few months, Blake has searched for local nurseries that sell the purple Peace Lily. It is sweet to see all the effort Blake puts in.

Rickie picked it up carefully and held it into the light. Even with the dim lighting, Rickie recognised it instantly. With a bashful look, she placed the plant aside, grabbed one of the blankets from inside and threw it over Blake. The two of them lay under the cloudless night sky. They eavesdropped on the conversation inside. The silence that sat comfortably between them flowed through like a conversation.

Seventeen…

Rickie grabbed her water bottle and watered the Peace Lily—a quick fix to a dramatic plant. She was agitated.

'See you later,' she yelled out to her mum. She closed the door and started packing away the remaining study notes left open on her bed. Drawers overflowing, like her thoughts. She slid open the wardrobe door to find something comfortable to wear but found her speaker instead.

Rickie let the speaker scream. A different scream to the one I now make; less painful, less rusty, and less covered in dust. I picked up speed and she belted out song after song, the lyrics tickled the window. Rickie and I danced to the screaming tunes. Her hair bounced like new springs; everywhere, effortless, and full of energy.

She danced to the beat with her hands in the air and her necklace swinging from her neck. I noticed I could barely see her nails. They were chewed so low, dry blood painted the little that remained.

Rickie has been accepted to a University in Melbourne. I'm so proud of her. She is buzzing but know it will be an individual adventure.

Rickie couldn't ignore my screams any longer. She set me to level one for a short rest, until I saw the bedroom door fly open.

Standing in the frame like a new doll in its package, stood Blake. I laughed at the thought of resting. With the summer heat and these two incapable of stillness, sitting at level one rarely occurred, regardless of my rusty movements.

Like magnets, these two were drawn to each other. I returned to level two.

Rickie stepped back, revealing the healthy Peace Lily. Blake's mouth split open with a surprised grin. *The girls have been studying so much for their final exams, they had not hung out in a few weeks.* Blake's smile grew as she turned to Rickie. Giddy, the two jumped towards each other and then on the bed, eventually falling flat on the covers. Just like old times.

My blades were appreciated directly above Rickie's bed. The girls lay back on the bed while their hair waltzed at a slow tempo to my moving blades. Blake noticed Rickie's nails. She sat up, pulling Rickie by the arms to join her face to face.

Squeezing Rickie's hand, Blake said, 'I'm here, you know that right?' Her eyes glued to Rickie's. Rickie's shoulders dropped and she smiled, taking a deep breath.

Blake still has no idea.

Rickie paused and her eyes dropped. 'I received an early acceptance letter last week …' She looked up.

'… for the Bachelor of Plant Science … at Melbourne University.' *I'm so proud of Rickie, not only for being accepted but for finally sharing the news. She'll always be a part of me. She's one of my blades.* Blake—a statue. Finally, she unfroze, and bear-hugged Rickie. No words were exchanged.

Rickie and Blake took the afternoon one step at a time, taking in the final summer breeze that slipped through the balcony door. They stole cushions from the lounge and sat outside, like they used to. I could hear the faint murmur of giggles.

The girls stayed outside as the sun waved goodbye. Rickie stood up and grabbed the Peace Lily and new Bunnings pot from inside. Together, the girls carefully untangled the plant's roots as they patted it into the pot. Blake gazed at Rickie, as a streak of soil sat on her cheek. 'I remember searching from this plant for so long. I'm really glad you've kept it alive all these years.'

Rickie halted her patting. 'It means more than anything in the world to me, like you do.' The two stared into one another. *So subtle, you two.* Blake leaned closer to Rickie. The sunset peeked through the air that separated them. Rickie froze until she realised Blake was there, like she'd always been.

Like magnets, Rickie and Blake were drawn to each other.

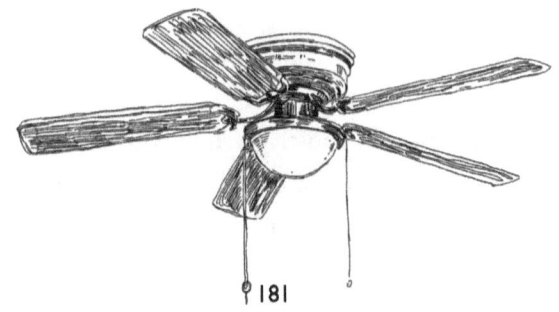

Limerently Evolutionised

Lisa McKeever

I remember that night I found him in our pocket apartment for the first time, although neither of us had been there before. He was waiting, as I knew he would be, dressed in his alluring smile and penetrating eyes. I studied him from across the living room; age hadn't left him haggard since he'd wandered across my path a short phase ago. Pursuing a similar direction had randomly knitted our lives for an instant. So brief even, I daren't imagine that I had formed enough, if any, of an impression to render him anything but indifferent. I presumed my attending would be quite unfamiliar; evidently, I was wrong.

'Hello, Lisa.'

I giggled behind my fingers; he grinned.

He'd cook afterwards, mostly syrupy pancakes with milky tea regardless of the time of day. I'd swoon all over our king, tangled in white sheets while he hummed softly in the kitchen.

Ravenous, we'd eat from bamboo trays; fulsome eye contact over stuffed mouths and shaky nerves—mine, of course. Sometimes he'd be naked, though mostly dressed in his warm brown suit that accentuated those sapphire blues. He'd keep busy in our yard; lavender, jasmine and camomile, all potted in mismatched ceramics, lined the base of the surrounding high stone wall, where I supposed a world existed beyond. White fairy lights backdropped our two rustic chairs, where we'd rest. Sometimes babbling over each other, sometimes just holding hands in silence, and enjoying the late afternoon breeze, warmed by fire-colours dancing into the night. He'd slip his trusty woollen jumper over me or carry me inside. My head buried against his neck; he smelled of freshly washed bedlinen and the morning dew on rose petals.

He'd join me in the shower, run his fingers through my wet hair and draw our warm bodies together. I'd win at board games, and I knew he hadn't let me win on purpose, even though he insisted that he had. He'd guide my hand along his firm frame, over areas I'd try to hide if it had been my body; he quivered. I'd paint my nails while he brushed my hair. He'd chase me down through playful squeals and whirl me across the floor in retaliation for teasing his playlist. We'd ponder over paper puzzles, and he'd seemingly contemplate my suggestions despite knowing full well what was correct. He'd rock me on the edge of the bed; my throat hoarse and vision blurred, but lighter inside. I always left first; he always watched me leave.

* * *

The smile seemed to linger a couple of seconds longer than an average greeting, and his eyes twinkled playfully. I watched as he passed through the rest of the work space, checking time length as he greeted others. He had definitely held my gaze longer.

Who was that person asking him my query? They weren't even asking it the way I had practised. My stomach clenched. I focused on his response from across the room; might he just hurry it up and move along. I readjusted my seat again, though it wasn't crooked. They were practically begging for his attention: constantly twirling hair and emanating shrill fakeness; what humiliation on their part. Had this top always grated on my skin this way? Need someone intervene to spare us the embarrassment of such obsessive besotment?

'Any issues?'

Yes, plenty.

'No, then let's begin ...'

We went out once; well, we chanced upon each other while both of us were out. I was in a café, sipping coffee like a grown-up. A side plate with fingered chocolate smears lay on the table beside my book; a tatty bookmark peeped from the pages, having recently crept along a few chapters.

'I need help.' A young female burst through the double doors. Her face throbbed red. She beat her chest with closed fists. Others from neighbouring tables rushed to her aid. I rose slowly, presuming they, like me, thought it was a heart attack.

It was a panic attack. She was a member of a theatre company; a production was about to begin; she was the lead singer; it was a love-story musical.

'Can someone take my place?'

Quicker than I was to realise what was happening, the others spread out along the walls, leaving me in the middle of the room.

She pleaded at me. 'The show can't go on without you.'

A notion occurred to me of the experience being some torturous nightmare, and then I saw him seated on the front row and realised it most definitely was. I email rather than phone, I read rather than meet eyes, I greet dogs before their owners. Yet, somehow I'd morphed into some personage—complete, apparently, with a voice.

I slipped into Café-Lady's luscious dress; make-up artists smeared glitter across my face, as they pushed me up on stage. Luckily, the lights shone directly into my eyes, blinding me from the spectators' judgement. The music began. Dancers in sequined puffy dresses emerged from behind stands and a song, spanning a 5-octave range, flowed effortlessly from my heart; every word directed at him. Contorted movements, facial and bodily, a manifestation of admiration, an expulsion of yearning consumed the stage.

I was lost to the moment; images of him bursting up from his seat—mic in hand—and duetting with me were dashed when the music ended. I drifted from stage left exit.

'Beautiful voice.'

You lingered after the end, but your impact would remain like carvings in stone.

'The passion was evident.'

I mirrored your tone, reactions, and poise.

'Do you draw inspiration from a particular source?'

I allowed myself to trust in my safe space.

The cessation of our session approaches. I feel my every gesture and utterance has been analysed, though I tried not to interact unnecessarily. And though I crave his being, his company is more than my emotions can process. My insides seize up, unable to function in his vicinity. I feel suffocated by his closeness, like his existence devours the air I need to survive. My feet walk me out like they're brand new, and my farewell wishes refuse to complete the journey from my brain to my mouth. Outside, fresh wind hits my face and practically floors me, like I've just crawled from a cave, emerged from captivity after a duration unknown. A brief interval is welcomed for self-regulation and my sanity.

The shame of blatant frailty, of indicating on my naked body the blemishes and scars: accidental and inflicted by self and others, of revealing intimate fantasies and naming those involved. But would I evolve without his pressure, comfort and protection? Like a child searching for a hand to hold. What conflict of desires. An extension from venturing out into real life.

Failure had hunted me since time began; it pursued me through various cities and villages; it spoke to me in numerous tongues; it disguised itself in a variety of forms. Finally, it cornered me down a dead-end cobbled ginnel. Strain against my chest, stiff and trembling muscles, a complete anatomic coup; cognitive, emotional and physical dissonance. I collapse—seemingly in slow motion but quicker than a rumour.

'We're going to get to know each other very well.'

I remember his presence like blue tips on lavender, of the smell of coffee on foggy mornings, of bubbles in the bath, of fluffy cotton towels dried on the line, of raw cake mix from the spoon, of frosty winter raindrops against my face, of fresh eggs in the nesting box, of dogs' wet-nosed greetings on bare legs.

'Tell me why you wanted this in the beginning,' he'd ask. 'Is second best an option?'

I remember my eager shrills echoing through the late summer nights as I scampered along empty streets to our apartment, to his unfailing embrace. I remember him leaning closer, listening intently to every crappy story I told, and didn't laugh. I remember the deepness in his voice as he read me classics. I remember he'd tell me it didn't matter, as long as *I* liked what I was wearing, and when others talked about me at least they were giving some other poor sod a break.

I struggled to my feet and brushed off the mud from my shoulder. I extended my hand.

'I'm looking forward to it.'

I knew he'd be at our apartment no more.

The Inscrutable Longing

Eliana Tom

I have found the one. Nolan Bright. Brown eyes, even browner hair. Tall, but in a way that isn't awkward and gawky. Tall in the way giant sequoias are, sure and steady. He is in my intro to chemistry class and the other day he adjusted the needle valve on my Bunsen burner — if that isn't sexual inuendo, I don't know what is. He's different; whenever he speaks, his presence is held without burden. Every word that is spilt from his lips is carried with the essence of subtle certainty. It wouldn't matter if he spoke gibberish, each syllable would coat my ears with an intoxicating glaze. I was in love… or at least I thought I was. When I told Dina about my feelings for Nolan, she didn't even let me finish before she started interrogating me about him. 'Does he say your name when you talk? Is he into eye contact? Wait, does he do that thing guys do when they can't help but smirk when you're telling them something?' She looked at me with curious eyes in anticipation for me to fill her in on all the juicy details to vicariously live through me.

But once I admitted that I hadn't *actually* spoken to him yet, she looked at me as if I had just run over her guinea pig.

'Remember what happened last time?'

But last time was different. I'll admit that adding everyone in our high school friend group on 'Find my friends' just so I could have Tim Raffety's location to *coincidentally* show up to wherever he was, was a *little* out of line. I knew better now. Never mind that, this time was different. I wouldn't even call this an obsession, more a deep infatuation that I can keep in a box tucked away in my mind. I wanted to keep it protected. I didn't want to entertain the idea of it being tainted by reality. Dina just didn't understand. She made me feel bad for what I had done. But why should I regret something I once wanted?

Anyway, what harm was a little fantasising? I was imagining Nolan standing behind me as I balanced chemical equations. So close that I felt the heat emanate from his body. I sunk into a pool of lust. Him tracing our secret message on the small of my back – 'A L L M I N E'. Our love, hidden in plain sight. That was normal, wasn't it? A girl can dream.

I was pretty sure I existed solely to be in awe of him. If my life was the trade for his affection, I would have died a thousand deaths. For now, I will settle to just be in his orbit.

In all honesty, I may have left out a few details when I told Dina about him. Technically he *is* in my intro to chem class, except, we called him Dr Bright. No big deal, right? I'm not in high school anymore. As a matter of fact, I was very much reminded of that in my first week of uni. I was running late to my first practical with Nolan because I was looking everywhere for a bathroom. It was as if the science faculty was running some undisclosed experiment to test the wits of new students by making the bathrooms impossible to find. I arrived late to class, still not yet having gone to the toilet. There went my first impression. My legs were crossed two times over to the point where my inner thighs became numb. I raised my hand to ask for the bathroom. Nolan nodded, continuing his orientation speech. I raised my arm again to ask where I can find it. As I left the chemistry lab my embarrassment tied a string from my chin to the floor. The fluorescent lights highlighted my walk of shame.

Nolan held me back at the end of class. 'I know starting something in a new place can be daunting. Don't let what happened today weigh too heavy on you, okay? I'll see you next week'. That situation is the kind of thing that keeps me up at night. But in that moment, he saw me. He saw me in a way deeper than the mundane. He saw me the way I see the first blooms of spring, lingering on the newness of life that was birthed from winter's womb.

It's week nine of the semester now, and I have not been late to class since the incident.

Every week he greets me with a smile that gives me butterflies—but not the stomach kind. It was so cruel of him to be so kind. It made me yearn for him with greater passion. Passion suffocated by the confines of my mind. The battle between my heart and mind deprived me of freedom to simply just be. I wish I could have shown him that I wanted more.

Everything changed when I was walking to my macro chemistry class. I saw Nolan from a distance. Far enough for him to not catch me gawking, but close enough for me to see a strip of gold metal wrapped around his ring finger. I bit my inner cheek till I tasted blood. Nolan boldly flaunted his loop of commitment as thunderclouds filled my mind. My heart felt heavy. Carrying the burden of what could have been.

What could I have possibly done that didn't seem like I was vying for his attention. In theory, I didn't see anything standing in the way of us being together. But in reality, I didn't know who I was well enough for me to have given all of myself to him. Nolan deserved a woman who knew what it meant to love without inhibition. How could I have ever been what he deserved when he already had it. All I could offer him was fragmented pieces of me, in hopes that his love would be the glue I'd need to resemble someone who hadn't been shattered by the brute force of men who had no intention of loving me. But it was a selfish act to expect him to heal what only time could.

I may have found one, but he certainly was not mine.

The Green Door
Joel Smith

Jasper was drunk. Not just a bit drunk, like he would get with his mates watching the footy at the pub on a Saturday night. No, Jasper was the kind of drunk that could potentially cause permanent liver damage. The kind of drunk that a stomach should be pumped and a business card for AA stapled to his hand to make sure he didn't lose it. He had been on a bender for at least five days, and he had no intention to finish it yet. Not while the booze was able to numb the emotional agony he felt any time he came close to being sober.

He had left the last bar after another Cheryl-Anne song had started blaring through the speakers. Asking his taxi driver to take him somewhere that he could get another drink, or at least that's what he had wanted to ask, had placed him outside a filthy green door. Contemplating if getting a drink from such a dump was a good idea, he began to wonder if he was starting to sober up. Or had he reached the desired Shangrila for the drunken? That place where you are so drunk, you reach ultimate clarity of mind and thought. He felt no pain and his mind felt clearer and stronger than it had in possibly years. Or perhaps he had just reached another stage of delusional inebriation, and the clarity was actually a thick, booze filled fog seeping from his pores and encapsulating his body?

Before he had too long to contemplate further at what stage of intoxication he was, the green door opened. An old woman stepped out and grabbed Jasper's arm, wrenching him inside and slamming the door firmly shut behind them both, leaving them in a confined, gloomy, and oddly-odoured room. At once she began to babble quickly in the local language. One that Jasper didn't understand when he was sober, let alone on a five-day bender.

'I… don't speak your languages' he tried to reply to the woman. 'Do you sell drinks? I've come for a drink…'

Stopping her harsh interrogation, the old woman looked Jasper up and down. Cackling cruelly, she raised her hand to her mouth and imitated drinking a bottle, pointing to him accusingly. 'How many have you had already?' she asked in thickly accented, though surprisingly good English. 'You smell like rotten death.'

'None! Well, ok, yes, I've had a few,' raising some fingers on his left hand and showing it to the crone. 'I wanted somewhere to get a drink, and my taxi driver brought me here.'

'Did he now?' she asked raising an eyebrow. As if looking into the past she whispered 'Now why would he do that? I do not sell drinks to boozers…'

Jasper shook himself trying to reach that profound sense of clarity again. For the first time he took a proper look at the old woman and was amazed by what he saw. Wrinkles upon wrinkles on her face made her look as old as an ancient and weathered oak. But her eyes, oh those eyes, were clear. Not just clear, Jasper realised. They had an almost unnatural clarity to them, as if they were illuminated from within. Jasper was sure if the room was suddenly struck into darkness those eyes would still be strange glowing orbs. While she may have appeared ancient of days, she held herself with power and purpose. Taken aback by this paradox, Jasper slurred, 'Is this a bar? Did the taxi driver bring me here as a joke?'

'Sit!' she demanded, poking him into a chair. 'I will not give you another drink. Not yet… You have drunk too much booze, my friend. It is time for you to sober up and tell me your story. And then maybe I will give you drink. For now, I will make you tea.'

Sitting where she had pointed, Jasper whined like a child, 'Why do you need to know my story? All I want is a drink. Some booze. Come on, lady.' Though he was unsure if she had heard as she was shuffling down a dark hallway.

Taking time to look around the room, Jasper saw, for the first time, walls lined with shelves that were full of bottles of all different powders and liquids. A few appeared to be emitting strange vapours. Jasper wondered what the hell he had gotten himself into. Who was this woman? Even in his current boozy state he wouldn't consider the existence of witches, would he? As he was contemplating making a run for the door the old woman returned with cups of green tea, placing these before them both and soothed, 'Now drink, and tell me your story. You, my friend, are in much pain. Pain I can help with if you will allow me'.

Striving to hold his shaky hand firm, he took a cautionary sip of the steaming liquid, realising it didn't taste half as bad as it smelled. Jasper then found himself stuttering out his life story to this strange ancient woman with conjuring eyes. He realised he wasn't just offering her a condensed version, but was giving all the grimy details that had brought him into this strange room in the first place. Cheryl-Anne. Cheryl-Bloody-Beautiful-Anne. With a seductive, yet angelic voice, and looks to match, Cheryl-Anne had sung her way into Jasper's heart. And once she had entered, she had taken over the whole place in a bloodless, but love-drenched coup filled with her adorable tunes. It was never just a little schoolkid crush. Jasper had been completely infatuated. So much so, he knew they were destined to be together forever. Once deciding this he had to let Cheryl-Anne know. So, he had jumped on stage at his 41st Cheryl-Anne concert and professed before 36,000 others his undying love for his bride to be. This, in hindsight, had possibly not been the best idea, as Jasper's heart was crushed under Cheryl-Annes high-heeled, thigh-high boot. She wasn't interested in him. She wasn't even polite about turning him down, just looked him up and down and snorted with laughter. How could he have been so caught up? How could he have been so stupid? Now, left with a massive Cheryl-Anne sized hole in his life, he had attempted to fill it with the best pain killer he knew, booze.

Realizing his tale was now completely emptied out before her, the old woman nodded her head in sympathy and patted his hand kindly. 'I can take this ache away from you if you wish it to be so... I can help.'

Surprised, as if waking from something close to a trance Jasper replied, 'But how? All I want is a drink. Booze takes the pain away.'

'Jasper,' she comforted, 'I can give you freedom from the agony that encompasses you so. The fresh start you so long for. You were brought here for a reason, and I can help if you will accept it.'

'Yes… Yes, I will!' Jasper could feel his resolve strengthening but had no idea what he may be agreeing to.

'Good! Drink this.' She handed him a small shot glass of thick, indigo liquid that smelt worse that the drain cleaner he had shot down at the last dive.

Without taking time to reconsider if drinking this goop was a good idea, Jasper downed the liquid and instantly collapsed on the floor unconscious.

Sluggishly waking an unknown amount of time later, Jasper felt stiff and sore. Even so, when the realisation of the old crone, her shop, and that drink hit him; he sat bolt upright, finding himself on a park-bench. Had he just imagined it all? He had been smashed, but had he been that drunk to have such a vivid hallucination? As he felt his mind slowly clearing, he realised he could hear music. Music that felt familiar. Suddenly, like a jolt of electricity through his brain he realised it wasn't just an anonymous love song but the same Cheryl-Anne ballad that had forced him to leave the last bar. He braced himself, waiting for the cold knife of heartbreak he knew so well to stab his core. But this time the blade did not pierce, and he hummed harmlessly along to the tune.

Unsure who, what, or how; that strange old woman had helped him. She had taken the pain away. 'Oh wow!' he mused.

'Cheryl-Anne! What was I ever thinking? She isn't even that good looking close up. And her songs are... well... average at best.'

Not As Good As You, But Pretty Good

R.A. Bissmire

We stood on the mountainous peak, overlooking the Dragon War. The red tint in the air from burning smoke and sprayed blood was beautiful in a disgusting way. The formerly opposing kingdoms of Tel'Dora had united to bring down the dragons that sought to take claim of our world. My fellow adventurers were fighting side by side with entire armies to protect our homes and the common people who couldn't protect themselves. And now I stood beside my small party of friends, ready to declare the end of the three-year-long fight for survival.

I couldn't help but reminisce as I knew the end was near. Not of the last three-years, but of where I was before the war. A young celestial sorceress with a goal to be strong, to be amazing, to be powerful. The best of the best. Just like her. Just like Saphielle Laidon, the greatest sorceress in Tel'Dora.

I had only met her once before the war, and it was a right place at the right time situation. I was studying at the Sorcery Guild when she walked in, in all her elfin glory. Her silver skin shimmered with the faint blue hue of moonlight. Two small stars adorned her elongated ears and glistened behind her, and her long, braided, ivory hair bounced against her arched back as she walked. Her black and blue dress hugged her slender figure to her hips, then billowed out behind her as if the night sky was her midday shadow. Her wand was perched on her hip, and the only part of her that wasn't in perfect condition. Even at a distance, I could see the stains of battle that marked the wood; the natural burnt black of the wand's tip that revealed years of use.

I had been in the middle of practising my fireballs—the *easiest* spell in the books—and I had been trying to make them stronger. Bigger. She walked in and it all went wrong. I fumbled over the words and the flicker of the usually explosive spell became more like a party sparkler. I hated myself for it. If I was going to end up as amazing as her, be as great as Saphielle Laidon, I needed to be able to cast simple spells without getting distracted by Gods.

She didn't notice. She didn't even look my way before she disappeared into the guildmaster's suite. Though when she came out five minutes later, she walked right up to me. My heart jumped to my throat, my breath sped up, and my brain just stopped. We were lucky I hadn't been mid-spell. She was radiating the shimmer of the full moon, and her eyes ... her vibrant blue eyes that smiled at me, glittered like the sapphires they replicated.

Her smile reached those eyes that were bright in her confidence. Her thin lips opened and she spoke in her powerful, majestic voice like harmonising church bells, 'You're Kalli, right?'

What?

By the stars ... Saphielle ... Saphielle Laidon knows my name?

And she's talking to you, pull yourself together!

'Our guildmaster speaks highly of you,' she continued. 'I look forward to fighting by your side one day, for the glory of the stars.'

All I could do was stare. Stare and nod. She *giggled*, spun—her braid flicked my face—and she jogged away.

Saphielle Laidon knows my name!

Saphielle Laidon spoke to me*!*

It had taken me a full minute to recover back then.

And then there was when I was introduced to my party, the group of adventurers I've fought beside for the last three years. Those five other adventurers were now my friends. My family.

I nearly died when I saw Saphielle Laidon sitting in the group I was to join. She was the only one who stood at my approach. Her radiant smile was back, touching her sapphire eyes. Everything about her looked just as perfect as it had the first time I met her.

I felt so inadequate, being partied with *the* Saphielle Laidon. I had thoroughly believed that I was nowhere near worthy enough to even stand in her presence, let alone breathe the same air. But she hugged me in welcome and bought me a drink—which felt wrong on so many levels.

'A new adventurer should never buy their first drink! With what coin?' her half-giant friend had bellowed.

The others got wasted that night but not Saphielle Laidon—she remained elegantly composed. The next day we were off doing what we were hired to do: save villages and kill dragons. Stay together and keep each other alive. And every day I got to spend with Saphielle Laidon, she continued to be absolutely amazing. The nights the two of us would stay awake to keep watch, she'd teach me new spells, or we'd just talk.

Saphielle Laidon, the greatest celestial sorceress in the continent of Tel'Dora, told me about her favourite adventures. Like how she once fought in the deepest Tel'Dora mines to save captured paladins before they could be sacrificed to the Mistress of the Night. Or the time she had to enchant the party with the ability to breathe underwater to find the lost church of a religion no longer practiced, to find a lost artefact.

'You're amazing.' The words had spewed from my mouth before I could stop them.

'Only because I've been able to do so much. I've been lucky,' she said. 'Really, I'm not as great as they make me out to be. I'm just a regular celestial sorceress. Nothing special about me.'

'You're Saphielle Laidon! You've felled basilisks and wyverns!'

'Anyone could have taken those jobs,' she said. 'An equal adventuring party would have done just as good a job as we did.'

'I don't believe that for a minute.'

'Want to know a secret, Kalli? One celestial sorceress to another?' She paused as if letting me respond, but there was no way I'd interrupt her now.

She handed me her flask and told me about her fears. Her fears of disappointing Tel'Dora, letting her friends down and the sorcerers who look up to her simply because she was in the right party of adventurers. Her fear of bodies of water because she'd almost drowned once as a child. Her fear that one day her magic will fail her, and then the people she loves will die.

That was three months into fighting side-by-side with Saphielle Laidon, the greatest sorceress in Tel'Dora. She was still amazing, but she had never appeared more … equal. I looked at her then, and still saw the deity who reflected the moonlight in her every step, but I was beginning to see Saphielle, the elf girl whose family had abandoned her, so she faced new evils every other day to never lose the family that took her in. Her friends. And from then on, it would seem, me.

'You're smiling,' the now familiar voice, still holding the same harmonising power of church bells, said beside me.

'I was just remembering when we first met,' I told her.

She laughed as she leaned on the half-giant beside her. 'You messed up a fireball!'

I felt my face grow as warm as the dragon's cave. 'You saw?'

'It was adorable.'

'I-in my defence, you were very intimidating back then!'

'I'm not now?'

I couldn't look at her. Even after fighting by her side for three years—even after knowing her as just Saphielle—I had yet to be able to look at her without feeling inadequate.

'She's blushing!' the half-giant bellowed.

Saphielle shoved my shoulder as she kept laughing. 'Three years on and you still hold me on that stupid pedestal?'

'Oh, that pedestal was destroyed the moment I saw you drunk.'

Her laugh softened to a giggle that made me try to suppress a grin.

I forced my attention back to our half-giant friend. His bare chest was glistening with blood and sweat, holding the head of Rionai, the silver dragon we'd just slain and the leading voice of the dragon army. 'Gonna throw that?'

'Obviously,' he said.

He took two large steps back to have a run-up before throwing the head as hard as he could into the middle of the battlefield. The clouds separated to let through a single beam of sunlight that followed the head as it curved across the sky. The head was big, bigger than probably half of my body—which isn't hard, me being shorter than your average human—but it *flew*. When it disappeared into the mist of blood and war—leaving a rather impressive but short-lived hole in the smoke—gradually, silence began to fall over the battlefield as word spread.

'I still think that was a stupid idea,' Saphielle muttered. 'We should have taken it to the king.'

'But it looked cool,' I stated.

Our friends cheered in agreement.

Saphielle rolled her sapphire eyes, and I felt a weight on my shoulders as she leant on me.

'You're amazing,' Saphielle said, as the six of us began back down the mountain.

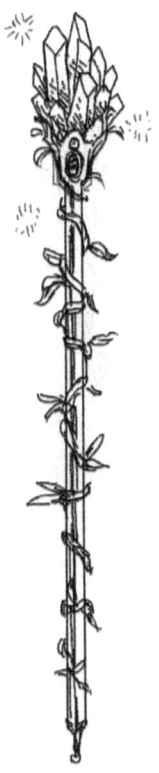

Knight's Devotion

Luke Ballam

Today is the day I die. Lying in my blood-soaked bed, my son stands over my body watching the colour drain from my face. He fetches another wet rag and repeatedly dabs the stab wound in my chest. Endless bloodied rags cover the floor. We are born to die. Trained from a young age, we knights serve our king unto our death. Because of us, the battle is won, the king lives, and our families are safe. But now, my son will grow up with no father. He will still be trained to fight endless battles and sacrifice his own future for the kingdoms. Grasping onto my last ounce of life, my mind flashes memories of yesterday's battle that has led toward my inevitable death.

The calm before the storm. Fields of green grass, freshly dewed from the cold night. Once a pristine valley, the incoming bloodshed will leave it scarred. The horns of war blared across the battlefield. Thousands of opposing warriors charged down the muddy hill toward us, their feet thundered like a raging storm. We responded to the charging army with violent screams and the bashing of swords and shields. My comrades, and thousands of other warriors, had sworn under oath to protect the king, and his kingdom, with our lives. Gracious and glorious is the rule of the king, and to serve under him as a knight was the noblest of acts. Yet to fully understand the death and brutality that was to come, many of the young knights trained their whole lives for their first and, unknowingly, final battle. But my trusted company and I had been through countless battles before. We had grown accustomed to each other, like brothers. Jack, a knight who stood next to me, was the most confident. He turned to me and grinned, as he always did. Without saying a word to each other, my company, Jack and I dug our heels into the mud, planting ourselves as strong as a thick oak forest. I raised my shimmering broadsword toward the heavens, and sang to myself a prayer,

'For kingdom and for king
We give our body for life.
Let the children continue to sing
We fight unto night'

King George, atop his snow-white stallion, galloped along the line of knights and clanked his sword against ours. I winced when the king's sword collided with mine. He exuberated such an insurmountable amount of strength with such little effort. The king halted in front of Jack and I and raised his sword toward the charging enemies. 'For the glory of Helfjord!' King George screamed as his horse reared up.

Violent screams echoed across the battlefield as the gap between the two armies got smaller and smaller. I raised my shield above my face and braced for impact.

Steel-on-steel. Screams bellowed as swords slashed skin. Two walls collided, a mosh of metal and meat. *Where's Jack? Where has he gone?* My company's fortress was split apart, and I came face-to-face with my first opponent. He waved his sword wildly in the air, bug-eyed and tongue stuck out. He clanged his sword against his shield as a demonstration of his strength. I affirmed my stance and held my sword toward my opponent. He lunged forward, swinging his sword over his head in an arc. A gust of wind rushed past my arm as I dodged, just in time. A splash of mud obscured my view as his sword sank into the ground—he was stuck. As he held onto his sword, prying it out of the earth, I slashed my sword into his upper arm and across his chest. For a moment, he seemed unphased. He ripped the sword from the ground, and he steadied himself before he fell forward into the mud. Motionless. Beneath him pooled blood and mud, mixing into a deep maroon concoction.

'Fancy seeing you here.' It was Jack. He was panting and blood dripped from beneath his armour adding to the deep maroon. 'Their numbers are dwindling fast.' He emerged from the bloodied mosh of people, and he had obviously been injured badly.

'We have them on the back foot.' I looked down at Jack's wound with concern, but he shrugged me off.

'We must keep the king alive at all costs.' Jack was no longer looking at me. He was looking through me, behind me. A large figure, covered from head-to-toe in black armour towered above the crowd. He wielded a long bow, almost the same size as me. Jack and I had no time to react. The figure raised his arms, pulled back his pointed elbow, and released. The air was sliced through as an arrow whistled past my left ear and pierced Jack's chest. He fell into the mud, clutching the arrow. As I kneeled, Jack reached out for my hand. He grasped it tightly and held it against his heart. There was pain in his eyes. Not from the arrow, but from what he was leaving behind. A lifetime of duty, giving up his life and body.

'It will not be all for naught.' His hand tightened around mine for only a moment before he let go. With the light faded from his face, his glazed eyes stared blankly toward the heavens. Knights aren't supposed to cry. I have seen countless warriors' lives end in battle—many by my own hand. But nothing could prepare you for the loss of someone who was seen as a brother. I wanted to stay by Jack's side, protect his body and bring it home to his family. But that's not how these battles go—we have all been given the job of protecting the king, not a knight's lifeless body. With his bow now strapped to his back, the towering figure wielded a battle axe. He sliced down one, two, *three* of our men with ease. He stepped over their bodies as they sank into the mud. The black-armoured figure towered above me, his axe arched above his head. At that moment I was frozen. Kneeled in the blood and mud beside Jack's body, I closed my eyes, preparing to join him.

Clang!

I should have been dead. I opened my eyes to discover a clashing sword and axe, shaking inches from my face. The sword thrust the axe away and the Black Knight stumbled backwards. It was the king. Without blinking, without thinking, he endangered his own life to save mine. At that moment I could have run. Disappeared into the crowds of clashing allies and enemies, but my king's life was worth the sacrifice of my own. It was no longer about a superficial oath and the glory of Helfjord.

'Stand up, David, and help me take down this beast,' the king said. I shot up with surprise and readied my sword. The

Black Knight charged toward us; he swung his axe over his head like a guillotine. I ducked the incoming blow and sliced across his belly between two plates of his armour. The king unleashed an overhead slash on the Black Knight's back, but it bounced off bluntly and he stumbled. Unaware of the returning blow from our enemy, the king stood in a daze. Without hesitation, no blinking, no thinking, I dived, trying to guard the axe.

Crunch!

A blunt force sucked all the air out of my chest. I tried to scream, but I couldn't. Blood poured from my chest and covered my hands as I tried to stem its flow. Every breath was like knives piercing my lungs. I looked into the eyes of my king, who used my sacrifice to take down the Black Knight, before my vision faded to blackness.

'Get this man out of here!' I heard the king scream to the watching soldiers.

My son. He is standing over me, crying. I try with every fibre of my being to move, to talk, to breathe … We are born to die: Me, Jack, my son and even the king. He was ready to lay down his life for me—no oath needed. *How many more bloodied rags do we even have?* I have served unto my death, but so will the king serve his kingdom unto his own.

Spectre

Sophie Cartwright

As Lauren stepped into her room, she couldn't help but be drawn to the window. The view overlooked the bustling harbour where ships of all sizes went about their business, and the sun cast a warm golden glow on the water. Settling onto the window seat, Lauren took a deep breath. She was finally here, in Port Blackrock, with the opportunity to uncover the truth behind the stories she heard about the town and write her novel. As she gazed out at the maritime world before her, she knew that beneath the surface of the town's charm and history, there lay a complex tale waiting to be unravelled.

Lauren set off towards the docks. She wanted to check out the lighthouse that the tour guide pointed out on the trip here. She walked back the way she came, towards the water and past the now-closing storefronts. As she neared the lighthouse, she heard a whistling tune from the docks. Intrigued, Lauren headed to find the source. Along the docks the stalls were empty, accompanied only by the sound of water lapping at wooden posts. Lauren approached the only stall still occupied by a grizzled old sailor mending a fishing net. She could barely make out the rusty sign that hung precariously above him: *Old Salty Jack's Fishing Shack.*

'Excuse me?'

'Ahoy there, Miss,' he grinned, revealing naught but a weathered smile devoid of pearly whites. 'What brings a young lass like yerself to these parts of Port Blackrock?'

'I am looking for someone, I was wondering if maybe you knew where I could find them. The Spectre,' said Lauren. The sailor stared blankly at her. 'The Spectre,' she repeated, 'I heard they were recently involved in—'

'The fishin' mishap, aye,' he muttered, his gaze drifting back to his tangled net. 'I reckon I've heard o' the scallywag you be speakin' of.'

'Are you able to tell me where I could find him?'

'The Spectre be a wary one. They don't take kindly to visitors, ye see? You won't be squeezin' much outta them. And as for findin' them, well, that's a treasure hunt in itself, lass. No soul's laid eyes on their face, no one knows what lies beneath that shadowy veil,' he said, taking a swig from his cup.

Lauren thanked him and walked away, aware of his beady eyes following her along the port towards the lighthouse. As she neared closer, she could make out a small wooden sign balanced on the door.

LIGHTHOUSE CLOSED TO GENERAL PUBLIC DUE TO MAINTENANCE.

Lauren sighed in exasperation and walked towards a lonely bench nearby. She remembered when she told her father she was travelling to Port Blackrock. He responded with disappointment and disbelief.

'Lauren,' he sighed, 'You're meant to be continuing your apprenticeship with cooking, not chasing rumours of made-up shadow people.'

Since she was young, Lauren always wanted to be a writer. The bookshelf in her grandfather's study was full of tales rich with adventure. She didn't want to be a cook like her father; she wanted to explore the world and write about it along the way. That was how she ended up here in the first place. The legend of a person who shunned attention and preferred the shadows piqued her interest. Stories whispered among the locals described a mysterious individual who had helped the townspeople countless times, always avoided recognition and slipped away before anyone could properly thank them. This elusive character was precisely what Lauren needed for her novel. Locals referred to them as the 'Spectre'. Most recently, the Spectre had rescued a local fishing vessel from a fierce storm.

Lauren had a copy of the report from *The Portside Press* in her rucksack. 'Spectre Strikes Again, Averts Disaster at Sea'. The ship had been on a routine expedition when a sudden and ferocious storm began. The crew of seasoned fishermen—weathered by years at seas—found themselves in the midst of a nightmare. The storm raged with unrestrained fury, throwing unforgiving waves against the weathered wooden hull of the ship. Rain and hail pelted the sailors, making it impossible to see anything beyond the wind and water surrounding the boat.

The ship creaked and groaned and as the cries for help were replaced with silent prayers, a sudden, eerie calm descended upon the vessel. As the storm had paused—in that eerie stillness—the Spectre materialised on the deck. They moved with supernatural grace and were cloaked in a billowing, tattered coat that whipped the wind like a phantom's shroud.

The ship began to manoeuvre through the waves with uncanny precision as if it had become possessed with its own intimate understanding of the sea itself. With a wave of their hand, the Spectre summoned a bluish light illuminating the darkness, and revealing the safest path home.

As Lauren continued to read, she noticed a familiar name.

Old Salty Jack provided us with a comment on the event: 'I was in the middle of patchin' me roof for the rain when I saw a boat out in the water! Why the bloody hell they thought fishin' in this weather was a good idea is beyond me.' The article continued, recounting how Jack watched the Spectre wish the storm away and bring the boat back home.

Lauren couldn't believe her luck; the very sailor who had witnessed the Spectre's recent heroics was the same man she had spoken to just moments ago. She hurried back along the docks, the newspaper clutched tightly in her hand.

As she rounded the corner and came into view of the fishing shack, her steps faltered and her breath caught in her throat. There—standing in the dimly lit stall—was the cloaked figure. Old Salty Jack was frozen in surprise, no longer clutching his drink. Even through the darkness of the cloak, Lauren could feel their hooded gaze on her face. A silent understanding passed between them. For a moment, Lauren felt as though the world had slowed down around her.

'If ye still be lookin' for answers, lass,' Old Salty Jack said, 'this be the place you'll find 'em.'

Lauren took a cautious step closer, her heart pounding. She knew this encounter was her opportunity to unlock the secrets of the Spectre.

'I know what you're trying to do,' the figure said, their voice a soft whisper carried by the wind.

Lauren's heart raced. With a trembling hand, she raised her notebook and pen, ready to record every word that passed between them.

'I'm just an author seeking out a good story.' Lauren held her notebook defensively. The figure stepped closer.

'And what if I don't want a story written about me?' they asked with a mixture of curiosity and caution. The Spectre picked up one of Jack's nets and toyed with it in their hands.

Lauren hesitated, looking down at the net. 'I ... I suppose I hadn't considered that.'

'The tales spread by word-of-mouth are enough for me,' the Spectre said. 'I help because it's the right thing to do, not for recognition or fame. There are certain things about me better left in the shadows.' The Spectre's words hung in the air, heavy with a warning Lauren couldn't ignore.

'I can respect that,' Lauren said, trying to conceal the tremble in her voice. 'I won't write about you if you wish. But can you please at least tell me your story, off-the-record?'

The Spectre's cloaked figure seemed to lean in slightly as if considering her request. Then, unexpectedly, they turned around and took a step away from Lauren.

'You ask too much,' the Spectre replied softly over their shoulder, with an edge of warning in their voice. 'Having the village know who I am will only make it harder to help out. I prefer to stay in the shadows. My actions are my story, they speak for me and that's enough. If you want to write a story, then go ahead, but don't try to figure out who I am.'

She looked down at her feet, taking in the knowledge that she wouldn't uncover who the Spectre was.

A flush of wind and loud snap gained Lauren's focus back onto the dock. The Spectre was gone. Shaken, Lauren stood silently on the docks near Old Salty Jack, her heart heavy with the weight of their encounter. The Spectre's words carried a solemn warning, a plea to preserve their anonymity.

'Oi, lass!' Old Salty Jack bellowed. 'If yer happen to cross paths with the Spectre again, let him know that if he be wantin' a fishin' net, he'll need to pay for it next time!' His hearty laugh echoed through the salty sea breeze.

As Lauren walked away from the docks, she knew her journey had taken an unexpected turn, one that would lead her to explore the complexities of the human spirit and power of anonymity in a world that craved recognition.

Under The Mask

Heidi Langston

She was in trouble. It was a typical event where anime fans could cosplay and have fun, but things went wrong when leaving the venue. Crowds of fans were exiting when some people behind them rushed forward, mowing everyone down. Elly was shoved forward but someone behind caught her. She stepped away from the stranger's arms and fixed the giant mask she wore before facing her savior. The tall person was dressed like a reaper ready to take her soul, and as she prepared to thank them, she heard bells.

'You ok?' the bells ring, but she was too shocked to answer.

'Uh, um …' She tried to thank the nice Death God; but his friend called him away. His deep voice sounded beautifully like bells, and he hid behind a skull mask, however, his reaction to her awkward silence stole her focus. He scratched his right shoulder, a strange thing to notice but it caught her eye, then the boy with a voice like bells disappeared in the crowd.

'…ly … Elly!' She shakes away the memory of the weekend and concentrates on Sarah.

'Yes?' Elly says.

'Your stomach is trying to tell you something.' Sarah says. Jane laughs while Elly feels the grumbling and eats the lunch in front of her. 'What were you daydreaming about this time? A new designing technique?'

'No, I was thinking about the bell guy.'

Sarah sighs, 'Again? Why not just focus on homework and designing? I don't get your infatuation with him.'

Elly turns into a tomato, 'I'm **not** infatuated! I'm just curious how his voice sounds like that. Honest!' Jane smiles and Sarah scrunches up her face like she swallowed five lemons, Elly sulks at her nonbelieving friends. After finishing their lunch, they head for class.

'You know, you might meet him again. If he's from around here, he could show up at the local anime convention this weekend.' Jane suggests.

'This weekend? I forgot! Sarah, can I come over and finish making my outfit?' Elly asks.

'Sure, we have plenty of room.'

'Thanks Sarah! You saved me from having to stash it under my bed,' Elly says.

'No problem, your mum's scary when she sees anything vaguely cosplay.' Sarah shivers and they chuckle while going their separate ways to class.

As if the days have disappeared, the weekend arrives. Elly and her friends wander the convention searching for the bell guy, suddenly she hears him. Following the bell sound, she finds a wolf chatting with someone departing. The wolf is bell guy.

'That's him,' Elly says.

'Where?' asks Jane.

'The wolf. That's him … I can't do this,' Elly turns to leave, but her friends latch onto her.

'You can! At least try talking with him once!' Jane encourages.

After much persuasion Elly takes a breath and strides towards him. 'Hi.'

'… Hi,' he says back.

Elly wondered what to say when she unexpectedly blurts, 'Your voice sounds like bells.' He scratches his right shoulder and is about to speak, but she beats him to it. 'I mean I never heard anyone sound like bells, no wait, what I meant was my name is Elly and we met before. No what I meant to say was thank you –'

'Woah, I only caught some of that. What was your name again?'

'Elly.'

'Well, I'm Mike. You said we met before?'

'Yeah, you helped me out when I fell and I couldn't say thanks at the time, so thank you,' Elly exclaims.

'Oh, well you're welcome … I like your cosplay,' Mike says.

Elly grins under her smiling fox mask. They chat comfortably for a while until Mike's friend appears. Mike introduces James who kindly invites Elly and her friends to his 16th costume birthday party, and during their conversation…

'We go to the same school?!' Elly asks surprised.

'Yeah, and apparently I'm not as social as I believe. Hey Mike, I think I'm losing my touch. I need to introduce myself to some new faces pronto,' James puffs out his chest and marches to a stand where cosplayers dwell. Mike and Elly laugh at James antics.

'Can I talk more with you at the party?' Elly asks Mike.

'Sure. Will I see another amazing costume?'

Elly nods enthusiastically, waves goodbye and leaves.

Loud music and laughing teens are heard on the day of the party. Elly, Sarah, and Jane walk into a house full of dressed up teens. Sarah and Jane leave to dance while Elly searches for Mike. She finds him wearing a rubber mask, talking to James.

'Hi Mike and happy birthday James. Thanks for the invite,' Elly says.

'Thanks for coming. Hope you both enjoy the party, I got to go boogie!' James leaves shimmying to the dance floor, causing both Mike and Elly to laugh.

When the laughter dies Elly glances through her mask at Mike. She switches her glance from him to the floor repeatedly. Mike scratches his right shoulder in the silence, *cute* she thought.

'So, we go to the same school huh?' Elly tries to break the silence.

'Yeah, I guess we do … Um, why do you always wear a mask?' Mike asks.

'Wow, ironic coming from you. Well, it's because I must hide. You see, I'm a wanted criminal hiding from the authorities,' Elly says seriously.

'You can't be serious.'

Elly smiles beneath her mask and says in a playful voice, 'You're right, I'm not serious. But it's true I wear it to hide.'

'Hide from what?'

'More like a who. My mother hates cosplay and doesn't want me wearing anything related to cosplay. But I love designing and wearing my outfits, so I hide my face. It's a precaution since she'll never let me leave home if she finds out.'

'You make your costumes? That's amazing.' Elly blushes at the compliment.

'I make my friend's outfits as well. I aim to be a fashion designer, so I use it as practice,' Elly says proudly. Mike is quiet for a while so Elly asks, 'Why do you wear a mask then?'

'I – I wear it to forget.'

'Forget?'

'Yeah. I don't have any dreams or ambitions, so I wear it to become someone else. To pretend that Mike with no ideas for the future is someone else ... Everyone seems to already have goals and dreams for the future, but I'm not sure what I want to do.'

Elly processes what Mike said before speaking, 'I didn't know I wanted to design ... When I first started making costumes, I thought it would be a hobby, but I came to the realisation I wanted to be a fashion designer. No one knows straight away what they want to do. I know some adults who have the same problem. But I believe you will find something that will inspire you one day, it may take time, but there is no rush in life.'

Mike stares at her for a long time, then they chat about themselves. Exchange numbers. Then part ways.

Over the next two months they exchange messages and calls, but never met face-to-face. During that time Elly realises her feelings for Mike and they promise to meet at the upcoming convention. When the day arrives Elly nervously searches and prepares to confess to him. She spots Mike wearing a mask while making that uncomfortable gesture of scratching his shoulder. He is chatting to a girl Elly knows as Charlotte, a popular girl in school. Elly tries to get Mike's attention.

'Mike-!'

'I love you!' Charlotte interrupts, hugging Mike passionately.

Elly freezes, and realises she never asked him if he was already seeing someone. Feeling unwell and miserable, she left.

Elly got a message from Mike the next day. **Please meet me by the tree out front after school**. Although her feelings are complicated, she wants to see him once more. So, after school she watches students depart while waiting under the big tree outside the school gate. 45 minutes pass and a heartbroken Elly turns to leave.

'Elly!' The bells sound winded, but she still loves that bell sound.

Elly holds tears in her eyes while turning to face Mike. They were both maskless, nothing could hide them now. As Mike approaches, Elly holds her hand up in a stop motion. Mike pauses.

'I like you. Romantically. Since we first met, I've liked you, but I only realised a month ago. Because I like you, I left when I saw Charlotte with you, I didn't know you were in a relationship. I ... I'd like to stop feeling this way, but I can't. Can ... can you reject my confession? Please? I want to stop my feelings for you, so that it can stop growing.' Elly is in tears by the end.

Mike walks closer and says, 'I am in a relationship.'

Elly looks at the ground and wipes her wet face with her hands.

'With you,' Mike says.

Elly looks up in surprise. Mike tells her Charlotte was his friend in school and she confessed love to him that day, but he turned her down.

'You turned her down?' Elly asks.

Mike nods, 'For you. I want to start a new relationship with you Elly.'

Elly nods with a smile and tears in her eyes. Mike and Elly kiss, and Elly swears she hears bells ringing in the wind.

The Eyes That Watch You

T.C. Reid

Children shouldn't be in bogs. A snapped neck from a fall, the body rotting until mummification, death from disease caused by leeches, of all these unfortunate fates, none compared to the fate of Ada and Edmund Wright.

17th December 1918, England

The evening of the lunar eclipse was a perfect time to go hunting through the bog, the air thick with decay and fog.

It would be even better without the child, Edmund seethed.

He loathed his younger brother for foisting his little brat onto him. The child in question continued to poke and prod at her surroundings with a muddy stick she found. It was poison ivy, though Edmund cared little. He was often compared to an old miser in a Dicken's novel, with dark hair and eyes and his pale complexion. There was only one thing he cared for, and he hunted them with a single-minded fervour. In his pursuit he collected many samples over the years, but now a decade of work was in peril due to his younger brother's pathetic desperation.

Who cares if the Germans bombed his holiday house, take your little goblin with you, he thought with annoyance.

Edmund continued to examine the muddy waters. It was not quite evening yet and the sun looked like a dull pearl in the grey sky. He wanted to ensure his trap was set before dark. He felt a tug at his brown waterskin coat and looked down at the girl who had a dimpled smile with light brown eyes and hair.

'What is it, I'm quite busy.'

The six-year-old stared and then pointed. 'Yellow eyes! I saw yellow eyes.'

Edmund made his way through the knee-high water, which came up to Ava's waist, and looked around. The only thing he saw was a wart-spotted toad sitting on a lily pad.

'Thi-this is a toad, you stupid girl!'

'But-but,' she whimpered, 'I just wanted to h-help.'

'Well, don't. I may have to see you, but I don't wish to hear you. Now stay out of my way!'

The little girl quietly bowed her head. She struggled to stay upright in the murky water until she found a small muddy riverbank to sit on.

The toad watched with sickly yellowed eyes, its mouth stretching beyond its face.

Maybe going to school would'a been better. He's even meaner than the headmistress, the little girl thought.

A breeze whistled through the willow trees, sounding like laughter.

For the next few hours as the sky darkened, Edmund finished his traps while the little girl continued to draw pictures in the mud. The yellow eyes continued to watch.

When evening descended and the rust-coloured full moon rose, Edmund called for dinner. Beef jerky and canned beans were on the menu. Her delicate hands were riddled with oozing red blisters and covered in mud making Edmund sneer in disgust.

How am I related to this disgusting little trollop? he thought in contempt.

'Girl, wipe your hands before eating!'

He gave Ada nothing to wipe her hands with, forcing her to further sully her dress apron.

That night Ada shared the tent with her uncle, his back reaching the edge of the tent as if to escape it. She silently cried herself to sleep, and with it came dreams.

18ᵗʰ December 1918, England

As Edmund continued to set up traps, he found one twisted beyond belief and scowled. Ada thought it looked like a demented smile. When she told her uncle this, he scoffed. 'Don't be ridiculous, child, some insipid animal has clearly rung amok, that is all.'

My uncle is insipid and ridiculous, whatever those mean, she thought to herself.

Ada continued her mud drawings in the same spot as the day ended and twilight begun. Suddenly, a small blue light bounced in front of her.

'Uncle, uncle look!' she yelled.

Edmund turned but could see nothing. The cold silence of Edmund's rage descended on the duo before he said, 'This … this is the last time I want to hear from you. You are distracting me from my work. It was a mistake to bring you here, and it was a mistake that my brother had you in the first place!'

Ada couldn't hold it in any longer. She missed her Mama and Daddy. 'Th-the spider lady in my dream was right, you are mean!' she cried. She splashed through the bog and ran into the willow trees.

Edmund didn't care. He knew the girl would comeback before nightfall. He did not notice the blue balls of flame turn a bright yellow within the shadow of the willow trees.

During the early afternoon, Edmund heard a far-off scream, but he dismissed it as some unfortunate animal.

The sun was low when Edmund finished all the traps. Finally, he would prove to the academic committee that the Cottinglen photos were not a hoax. Fairies were real and he was going to catch one. With time on his hands his curiosity was peaked. The girl had spent the last two days drawing in the mud and while he did not care, curiosity and determination got him this far.

The yellow eyes continued to watch with a bloodied grin.

In the last of rays of the sun, Edmund saw what his niece had been drawing … Fairies. The images were unsettling to say the least. Figures dancing in twisted forms.

'Do you like them uncle?'

He startled, his heart beating heavily in his chest. He scowled at the little girl.

'Where did you come up with such images?' he demanded.

'Oh, didn't you hear me earlier, uncle? In my dreams,' she said sweetly, her yellow eyes looking up at him.

Wait? Yellow eyes?

He looked over at the girl more carefully. Her posture was off, as if was not used to being so small. Her face became distorted, her mouth stretched, her arms twisted like a dying spider.

He ran, his heart thumping as the scuttling continued behind him, until pain radiated through his leg. He was ensnared by his own trap. Edmund heard a giggle, a piercing shriek and then nothing.

6th January 1919, Edmund's House, England

Edmund's younger brother and his wife missed their sweet Ada. Thankfully, most of their assets in France were secured and it was time to retrieve their little girl and go home. They made their way through the house, yet there was no sound. When Edmund's younger brother finally made it to the study, he saw Edmund's facing away from him. Staring intently at one of his creepy specimens.

'Ah, thank you for taking care of our Ada—how is she? I haven't seen her yet,' he enquired.

'Ada is playing in the forest. She will be here soon,' Edmund replied, a rasp to his voice.

That doesn't sound right, why is Ada in the forest? thought his brother.

'Did she behave whilst we were away?' Ada's mother asked.

'Oh yes, she really is a sweet girl, both inside and out,' Edmund replied, licking his lips. Sharp teeth glinting, his younger brother startled. He had never heard of his brother talking about Ada like that, in fact he had never said Ada's name.

This is not my brother! he thought with terror.

Finally, the man turned, his yellow eyes glinting towards the couple. His smile stretched unnaturally.

'A very sweet girl, indeed.'

The Forbidden Rose

Odette Van Wyk

Lights danced between the bright green shade of the grove as the beat of a drum rang throughout. A choir of voices sang along in an almost too-perfect harmony as Seelie kind twirled before me, enacting the ancient ritual that was the crowning of the next Seelie queen—me.

I sat upon my throne in a dress made of feathers, dipped in red and fastened to the softest silk that could be spun. My hair was dark, twisted up in an elegant bun. Before me, the grove was alive, celebrating the new reign of their queen and her prosperity. I was gazed at and admired. I am their queen, their idol, their everything. There was no room for fault as my reign began—and will continue for thousands of years, as all other fae rulers before my time.

A masked fae appeared before me and knelt, his head bowed, allowing dark curls to fall to his face. He offered me a rose and an invitation to dance. *How bold. He must know this was not done—an outsider perhaps?* I sensed the glares of

THE FORBIDDEN ROSE – ODETTE VAN WYK

disgust from my subjects, despising the man for disrespecting their queen. He raised his head and smiled cheekily, left the rose at the foot of my throne and made his way deep into the crowd. I reached down to pick up the rose and as I did, one thorn pricked my fingers, causing blood to drip down my dress.

'My queen, please be careful,' my guard beside me fussed, as she attempted to wipe the blood from my hand.

'Aline, please call me Fane, it's alright. Besides, I wish to freshen up.'

'Allow me to accompany you,' she insisted, but I refused, assuring her I would only be a short while. What worth would I be as their queen if I could not even escort myself around? I walked through the palace halls, avoided the crowds of fae celebrating, and wandered towards a garden. Amid the blooming flowers stood a small fountain, with water spitting out of a carved stone tree. I sat beneath it, dipping my fingers in its icy water, and watched as the blood washed away.

'My apologies, my Queen, t'was my fault.'

I looked up to see the masked fae from before. His black mask was illuminated beneath the moon, revealing the shine of golden eyes beneath. He bowed once more.

'Oh no, please rise, it was my fault,' I assured him. He raised his head and smiled at me.

'And why, may I ask, is the queen of fae here all lonesome? Certainly, she knows the dangers.'

'I suppose I just needed to venture off,' I replied quietly.

'For a queen, you speak as if you were only a servant,' he said with a hint of humour in his voice. I straightened—I knew I was not as powerful as what was needed of a queen, and yet I had a responsibility, a title, a name to upkeep, for the sake of my own. I certainly had never been spoken to like that before. I glared at the fae in silence, and he laughed. When he had finished his fit of laughter, he offered me a hand and spoke again.

'May the queen accompany me for a while?' I hesitated, I definitely should not have, but what was the harm? I accepted his hand as he pulled me to my feet and led me deep within the garden and out its boundary, into the wildwood. I slowed, unsure of where he would take me—the wildwood was not a safe place, filled with thieves, humans and Unseelie.

The fae's grip tightened, and we continued until we had reached a clearing filled with fires and small encampments. At each sat a cluster of humans and seelie kind. He turned toward me and pulled off his dark cloak, wrapped it around my shoulders and pulled up the hood.

'For your own protection,' he grinned. I nodded and followed him once more as he led me to one cluster and sat us both down. The humans and seelie before us greeted the man warmly—they knew him.

'Eros, ya scallywag, who is this here pretty lady,' a human man sat beside him with a long ginger beard, stammered drunkenly. He observed me suspiciously, his eyes seemed to recognise me, my position, but he only smiled knowingly.

'Just a friend,' Eros smiled back. The cluster laughed and the man slapped him on the back. A woman with long blonde braids offered me a cup filled with a substance I did not know. I accepted and raised it to my lips as they watched. In one gulp, I swallowed it all. It burnt all the way down, but despite this, they cheered and clapped as if I had just been initiated into something.

The night continued with loud cheers and laughter from all around, and I listened curiously as Eros and his human friend shared memories of their journeys. Stories of running from human guards, trespassing into other creatures' kingdoms, and fighting off goblins and other creatures. At some point, the group began to sing old ballads, and Eros beckoned me to dance. We danced together for a while, twirling and singing along. I could not help but laugh as I felt free from my responsibilities for the first time in my life.

After a while, Eros rose again and offered me a hand once more. I accepted again and he greeted his friend's goodbye;

they responded with teases and comments of young love. My cheeks turned red in embarrassment. Eros simply grinned and led me back within the wildwood and to a cliff that looked towards the rest of the kingdom, which stretched farther than I had ever seen. My green eyes glittered with yearning as my heart longed for the freedom to see where each road led. I felt Eros squeeze my hand and turn to me.

'Who are you?' I questioned, fear and excitement gripping my chest. I did not know this man, and here I stood with him in the wildwood under the open sky. He clasped the mask, and in a swift motion pulled it above his head, revealing his face. A wave of sickness gripped me and I pulled my hand from his grip. His eyes were a piercing gold, and on his cheek was the inky symbol of a crow, the Unseelie king.

'Are you here to kill me?' I stammered. His eyes shone with a hint of sadness; he shook his head. He looked out towards the view before us again, and I saw a sense of loss wave across his face.

'You are the Seelie queen, and I the Unseelie king. We were born to rule and raised to hate one another, and yet we yearn for the same thing,' he said. He turned towards me and held my hands once again.

'Please, join me, and we can leave and be free. Think of all the adventures we could have; we would never have to fight each other's kind again.' For a moment, I said yes, and we wandered away, leaving behind all that was expected of us, living freely as the birds within the sky above. But then a vision filled my mind—one of war, bloodied bodies and broken wings, of death. If the Seelie queen disappeared with the Unseelie king, it would be assumed I had died at the hands of his own, blood would flow upon the faerie realm.

'I am sorry, I-I can't, I am the queen,' I stammered.

'Please—' I did not let him finish. I stepped back and met his gaze. I refused to let tears fall. Before the yearning could take hold once more, I turned and ran away from what I yearned for, away from the Unseelie king who had stolen my heart and the forbidden love we could never have. I dared not look back, and he did not follow. When I had reached my palace, Aline rushed towards me as she noticed my return.

'Fane, we thought you had abandoned us—whose cloak is that?' she questioned. Her eyes were wide, she was afraid. A tinge of guilt gripped my stomach, but I did not respond. I walked past the crowds of Seelie to my throne, pulled back the cloak's hood, and lifted my crown from its stand beside me. A delicate design of vines and sharp crystals entangled together. There was no return. Once the crown was placed, I would be queen until I met my fate with death, but I had to protect my kind … and his, too. It was my duty. I faced my court and placed the crown on my head as they cheered once more. As I took my seat on the throne, a stray tear slipped from my eyes and fell upon my finger, where a small scar had begun to form.

Cherished Sparks

Eren Jones

He was beautiful. That was all Sunny Hae could think as he listened with rapt attention to his best friend ramble about something funny that had happened on his walk to school. Sunny loved the times when Luan got like this. Loved the sparse instances where his friend had the energy to play something up just for the fun of it, or because he was genuinely interested in the topic. Sunny grinned, laughing with crinkled eyes and nodding in fierce agreement with what Luan was saying. Luan exclaimed at his agreement with theatrically widened eyes to emphasise his point. Sunny had to fight to keep his giggling in check, unwilling to risk interrupting him. Luan continued with his dramatics, gesticulating outwards in a display only reserved for when he felt it was worth the effort. He was quick to pick up steam again in his rant, despite the strain it put on his normally quiet, seldom used voice.

Luan Mah had been his friend since Sunny was a scrawny fifteen-year-old transfer student that still stuttered through his English pronunciation something terrible despite being fluent since he was little. Luan had been the quiet kid that sat at the desk in the back of the classroom. The one that went ignored and unnoticed until it suited the whims of others. He was the one labelled troubled by the school faculty and avoided by the other students for being supposedly violent, though no one could tell Sunny of any incidents that didn't sound provoked or completely made up. Too many people had struggled to answer when he asked simple questions, so Sunny learnt fast not to trust anything he hadn't seen for himself.

Sunny was of the completely and objectively correct opinion that Luan could do almost anything he put his mind to, because he knew that his friend was extremely intelligent and skilled in a lot of things. But even he, with all the times he has been accused of being more than a bit gullible and naïve, had to draw the line somewhere. Seriously, how could anyone believe that Luan had *actually* thrown another kid onto the roof of the bike shed? Or that he'd vandalised and damaged the principal's car? That one at least Sunny could prove was a bold-faced lie. He'd seen the asshole who never let Luan have any peace chuck a small bag over the back fence and spill spray paint cans over the grass. The guy hadn't even been subtle! He'd done it right in front of at least seven students that weren't part of the group that bullied them both. And yet, not even one of them spoke up about what they saw and let Luan once again take the blame. There wasn't enough evidence to prove Luan had done it, so he wasn't officially punished, but Sunny saw the subtle ways they retaliated against Luan.

One time, Sunny had come out of class a bit later than normal and had seen Luan get shoved to the ground. Sunny had been quick to try and get between his friend and the asshole, but the kid was already walking away once Sunny began to run over. He had looked up and seen a teacher approaching down the corridor and Sunny, sure that she must have seen what happened, caught her attention. She had sighed, glanced down at Luan carefully cradling his wrist, and asked if they had any proof. Sunny had been surprised and stuttered nervously that no, they didn't, but he had seen it happen and now Luan was hurt. She had smiled with fake apology and said that the person they were accusing would never do such a thing.

Sunny had gotten angry, sick of how everyone picked on his friend and no one believing them. He knew what it was like to be bullied. He hated that while he was now free of ridicule at this new school, his friend still suffered and didn't even have any staff willing to stick up for him like Sunny had. So, he had spoken up, being as assertive as he could force his voice to be and tried to protest. He didn't get very far into his argument before he had to stop when she threatened to write them both up. Sunny was willing to pluck up his courage to insist even if he'd be in trouble, but Luan had quietly grabbed his sleeve and shaken his head with a small smile to tell him that it wasn't worth it. Sunny had dropped it, very unwillingly, but he had.

Sunny had taken it upon himself to try and be a buffer between Luan and the kids who would harass him. He wanted to always be there to support Luan as long as his friend allowed him to. He, unfortunately, wasn't the greatest at it. His attempts often got him made fun of as well, but it usually did get the focus off his friend. Luan always quietly told him not to get involved and just ignore them, but Sunny knew how much it weighed on the other boy. Sunny saw the way his shoulders would curl down, the careful blanking of his expression. It made him want to hold his friend close and shield him from the horrible people around them. At least long enough for Luan to be ready to stand on his own again.

Luan didn't want Sunny getting hurt as well, but Sunny would just smile and tsk as if disappointed. He would heave an exaggerated sigh with a quick sing song of 'Sharing is caring, Lu!' and loop his arm around Luan's to drag him away. Luan would protest or grumble, but Sunny had gotten very practiced in deflecting his needless worries. Sunny didn't *enjoy* being bullied of course, but everything was better with Luan around. When Luan was there, he felt like he could be brave for once. He could ignore the persistent voice in his head that told him he wasn't good enough, that Luan would get tired of him or would tell him to leave. That Luan would never like him as much as he liked Luan.

But regardless of what others had tried to convince Sunny of, Luan had always been kind and patient with him. When others grew frustrated with his stuttering and fast speech, Luan didn't criticize or mock him with any malice, he just quietly asked him to repeat himself a little slower to make sure he hadn't missed something. Luan was the only one who stayed, whereas other kids grew annoyed at his excitable nature and anxious rambling. It hadn't taken long for them to become friends, much to Sunny's surprise and delight. Luan was the first real friend he could remember having, and he cherished every moment he got to spend with the other boy. Though, it had taken a long time before Sunny realised how deep his love for his friend was. And how it had gradually grown into a quiet, unvoiced, hopeful longing.

They sat hidden away from the rest of the nosy and noisy student body under a large tree. The dappled light that shone through the leaves added a lovely glow that highlighted Luan's features and revealed the slight shine on the wool of his beanie.

Sneakily, Sunny took Luan's hand, his heart fluttering with smug satisfaction when Luan merely squeezed his fingers and, still holding his hand, began dragging his arm along with his over dramatic gestures. Sunny couldn't help but giggle, shoving his friend's face away when Luan paused to tease him about his expression matching his namesake. Sunny grinned and teased right back, poking fun at his patches of pasty white skin and how he needed more sun.

'Well, what good are you for then, Sunny?' Luan retorted. Sunny felt his brain buffer before he cackled, pressing his forehead against a jumper clad shoulder and shaking as he tried to catch his breath. He shifted back up after a moment, tucking an errant strand of blond hair behind his ear as he gathered his composure.

'I'll just have to stick around much closer then, right?' he began, a sudden burst of courage igniting in his chest. He leant forward, staring into Luan's dark eyes and watching as the red iris of his glass eye tracked Sunny's movement a tad slower than the other. 'Won't take long to get you all sun-kissed.'

He quickly levelled a chaste peck on his cheek, right along the edge where a patch of pale skin met dark tan, smiling softly and hiding his nerves as best he could.

'O-oh,' said his friend quietly, wide eyes staring at him in shock, before a blush bloomed across his cheeks. Luan quickly ducked his head and pulled his beanie down over his eyes, squeezing their clasped hands tightly. Sunny's felt his chest swell with hope when he saw Luan's little smile, despite his attempts to hide. 'Y-yeah, yeah you better.'

Delusions of Love

Myra Batterham

My desire for love has forever been ardent. It's like a fire—a burn—that refuses to extinguish. Recently, in the large realm of my imagination, my love had found an unusual object of desire: *them*. I can still remember the first time I saw them on the big screen. It was as if a shooting star had streaked across the dark canvas of my life. And that was it. I was in love.

Yes, I will be the first to admit it sounds absurd, perhaps even delusional. Because, well, I am just a person, and they are *everything*. But the heart wants what it wants, and in its infinite wisdom, love often transcends reason.

I spent what felt like countless months just devouring every crumb of information I could find about them: dissecting their interviews, analysing tweets and Instagram stories, and watching every public appearance they made like a sailor drawn to a siren's song. You see, in this *era* of social media the relationship between fan and idol is blurred; the illusion of intimacy is an art form, skilfully crafted for us. Our idols' carefully tailored posts giving us glimpses into their personal lives and the moments they share their innermost feelings … it all contributes to an enchantment that feeds their aura.

I found myself infatuated by this enchantment. The more I learnt about them, the more convinced I became that there was an invisible thread tying us together—that *we* had a connection.

It all started innocently enough: a feeling they were speaking to me personally, and that their smile was meant for me, and me alone. As time passed my passion only deepened, and a strange conviction dug its roots deep into my heart: the belief they were in love with me, too.

I know … I understand how preposterous it sounds, especially since I am merely a statistic in their fanbase, just one face among millions. Yet, the mind is a master of weaving fantasies when it comes to love. In my delusion, I began to interpret every interview, post and public appearance as evidence of our bond. They were talking to me; I knew they were. There was no denying the love I felt when they stared down that camera lens and said: 'I love each and every one of you.' They meant me, of course. It was as if I held the key to their heart, the key no one else could have.

There were nights I would lie awake, staring at the ceiling as I replayed their words in my mind, convinced that hidden behind the wall of fame and celebrity they were professing their love for me. The casual mention of a favourite song felt like a secret message; a whisper of affection meant only for me. Their smile in pictures was a sunny, intimate gesture undoubtedly meant for me alone. And when they shared their vulnerabilities with the world, it was clear they were confiding in me, seeking safety and solace in our shared bond.

In the depths of this delusion, I believed I could sense their presence even when they were far away. I could feel their thoughts, emotions and longing as if they were intertwined with my own. Our love was one that transcended physical boundaries, a connection that defied reason, and I cherished it with a fervour that knew no bounds.

But of course, like any 'normal' relationship today, there were moments where I found myself questioning us and what we had; moments of clarity that pierced through my thick veil of delusion. I would see headlines revealing their real-life relationships, and pictures of them walking down the red carpet with their significant other. In these moments, the harsh reality of my situation would crush me. The world seemed to conspire against my belief, challenging the fragile tapestry of my one true love.

Really, I should have known what they felt for me wasn't the same love I felt for them. I should've known their affections were directed towards someone else, someone who was able to love and care for them in a way I couldn't. Someone who wasn't yearning from behind a screen. Still, I clung to this fantasy, desperate to preserve the illusion of love, to escape the harsh truths of my own loneliness. But that lead to asking myself: why not me? Why didn't they choose me?

So, I found myself contorting my personality, shaping my interests and tailoring my appearance to fit the image of what I believed they would desire, what I *knew* they would desire. I added funky colours to my hair, bought a new wardrobe, and listened to their favourite bands. I became a chameleon, adapting to every new morsel of information I could find—not that there was much I didn't already know. Was it a coping mechanism? A way to shield myself from the pain of unrequited love? It could have been … but I couldn't ignore the glow in my heart whenever I heard their voice, my personal melody.

And so, I continued to live in this dual reality where the pages of my life were filled with the ordinary, and the margins were filled with the love I shared with them. It was hard finding a balance between these two realities, but I clung to it with everything I had.

However, as time passed, I couldn't ignore the looming toll this delusion was taking on my life. It became an obsession;

a distraction from the outside world. My friends and family's concern grew every day in my isolation. They didn't understand how they couldn't give me what *they* gave me. I had to cut all of them loose. They were probably very distressed at the number of unanswered calls and messages, but it had to be done. They'd never understand.

It was a moment of reckoning when I realised my deep longing for love had led me down a dangerous path. I had lost touch with the reality of human connection, with the genuine bonds that could be formed with those who were within reach. Their warm touch, their words of affirmation and the true love one can only feel from family and friends. Those who were not shrouded in the mystery of fame.

I've tried to break this cycle of self-deception by taking steps to free myself from the chains of my delusion. Yet, my heart is still consumed by this love that feels so real. In my head, I know the truth—they are a celebrity, an idol who will never look at me with the same longing I do for them. I've poured every ounce of my being and affection into a bottomless pit, and yet, I can't stop myself. To confront the emptiness within me, to acknowledge my festering wounds would mean having to let go of them. I would have to break my own heart to mend it.

I will never be ready for that.

This delusion of love is a lonely road. It's a heartache born of my own making, a yearning for something that seems so close yet is unattainable. I'm stuck in a never-ending cycle of longing and despair, knowing I will never truly experience the love I've created in my mind. It has become my refuge, my solace, and my bittersweet escape.

And so, I continue to live in this parallel world where my heart beats for a love that I simply cannot have. It's a delusion that keeps me company in the lonely hours of the night and fills the void left by the absence of real love.

I know I need to break free. Yet, I find a strange comfort in this world of make-believe, where my heart's desires can be realised, if only in my dreams.

Love you, Riley

Bianca Gablonski

This little, white envelope passed through seven different hands to reach you. It traversed oceans and continents to be with you. If you picked it up, you could see it has a small, red stain in the corner. Was that blood? Lipstick? If you inspected it further, you could detect a hint of the vanilla, musky fragrance. Did a woman send this? A male? Once the seal breaks, the insides become clear, and the mystery writer's heart is exposed. It reads …

Dear Katie,

I miss you. I'm sorry I haven't written to you in a while. Life gets hectic in the most unexpected ways. I'm sure you, of all people, can understand.

It's been so long. I can't even remember the last thing I told you, so I'll quickly summarise my last month. I went into surgery (don't worry,

I'm fine—it was only my nose). Also, Sam and I broke up, but your beautiful words helped me get through that heartache. I mean, we were only together for two months, but I really thought it would work out this time!

Oh well, life goes on! Thank you for saying those lovely things. They truly spoke to me. I don't know how you do it, but regardless, I really appreciate it. Let's just say you were right when you said, 'Don't trust the ones who try to make friends with your friends.'

On a positive note, I have a dog now. I named her Koko Trixie (KT for short). Cute, right? I'm just worried. I have heard nothing from you in so long. Are you okay? I really hope you are.

I noticed you took a break from the internet and social media for the next month and I can't blame you! It can get overwhelming! I'm glad you are looking after your mental health. Did you change your number? I thought maybe you had. I thought, why not write a letter? I'm sure your postal address is the same. And I won't lie, it's really fun to do this the old-fashioned way. Ink. Paper. Words. It's simple. Like us.

I have to be honest though, there is a reason for me trying to contact you. Before you pressed pause on your Instagram posts, I noticed you hadn't been acting yourself. I see you smiling at the camera, but the smile isn't real. Is it? You don't seem happy.

I am so worried about you.

We all are.

They're saying some awful things again. After that interview you did. They're saying you're 'cancelled'.

I wanted you to know that I'm not blaming you. I know you can't help being different. If I wasn't your fan, I would tell you that you can't complain—that is what you wanted. You wanted to be famous. I might say that you asked for it; this is what you get for choosing to wield your words into lyrics that speak to a nation. You got fans … and foes.

I know you would never want to jeopardise this relationship you have built between us. Your people. We have become your everything, just as much as you have become ours. You have allowed me, and millions of others just like me, to access your life. Imagine what bad people could do with that sort of information. I know you go on early walks, I know what you eat in a day, I know your workout routine, I know where you will be. It's a lot of pressure to be perfect, I know. I understand. But *they* don't.

If I wasn't a real fan, I would fall endlessly into the pit of depressive thoughts about celebrities in which everyone else seems okay to anonymously vocalise behind the protection of their screens. I would say that I have noticed you gained weight. I would tell you that your voice doesn't have the same vocal range it used to. I might say that we are getting bored with you. I would poke and prod you, chanting 'Dance monkey, dance.' Entertain us. Show us a smile. Write a new song. A better song. Look perfect. Lose weight. You look like a bag of bones. You don't deserve fame. You're not cut out for this lifestyle. Kill yourself ...

Anyways, that's what others are saying about you, telling you to do. I'm not saying those things, though I have actually noticed you have gained weight. It's hard to tell since you haven't been posting or blogging your daily eating and routine.

It's so hard to be rich and live in a mansion and drive fancy cars and to be beautiful, isn't it? *Poor* you.

They don't understand that it's a lot of pressure to be you. To have fans who will support you until they grow tired of placing you on a pedestal of their own creation. A pedestal so high that you will inevitably disappoint them. They want to live vicariously through you, but they only want the positive glow of wealth, idolisation, and admiration. The moment you involve yourself in controversy, gossip and scandal, people don't want to be associated with you. It's sad, but true.

I am different from the rest. You and I are friends. I admire you for your accomplishments, but I don't want to become you. People who think that are so stupid. After the media rips you apart, I know it will be hard to love yourself. Just give us your heart, give *me* your heart and I'll keep it safe.

Your lyrics and music inspire us all to be better people. To be powerful. To live without regrets. To love harder. And I will continue to worship you. I know you won't change. You won't disappoint me.

You can tell me anything, but is it safe to tell the world?

Power can be a difficult, tangible thing to yield. And you, my greatest idol, can create music just as well as armies with your fingertips. A twitter post and you have assigned allies. A few harsh words spoken about a company which you were unsatisfied with, and they crumple to the ground under the weight of your followers. You are powerful and it scares people. Not me, though.

You have helped me so much over the last month and I feel like I need to return the favour. Here's the truth: You're beautiful, don't forget it. But don't ruin your beautiful face with filler and don't alter your pictures. *If you do*, make it natural. They will criticise any sign of your body aging and losing its unrealistic, unattainable sheen. If you look average, they will have to treat you average. They want you to deserve the praise and meet the expectations of beauty and if you change yourself to do it, don't make it too noticeable. I want you to continue to be loved and praised, so do what they say. It's ridiculous, I know.

So next time, in a month from now, when you emerge from your home revitalised after hiding amongst your collected treasure, don't forget to smile. Your livelihood relies on your fans' favour. Show us a real smile. For them and me. I'll be able to tell. We will be so happy, to see you happy.

Love you,
Riley xx

This little, white envelope begs to be read. But you don't look at it or touch it. This letter, instead, lays in a room with other letters and boxes and packages, similar to this one. They are all filled with love and hate. For you. Fan mail. All undelivered. All unopened.

All-Consuming

Jade M. Stoltenberg

Dear Thorsten Turner,

I received your letter. And I revelled in your words; an indescribable joy in knowing our time shook you too. I enjoyed every curve and swoop of your letters, the unforgiving splotch of ink that stained the top right corner of the page, and the intricate way you signed your name. Your handwriting is so elegant. I have always admired your way with words. The way you twist and bind them to your will. It is no surprise that when we met—that day at Ink Heart Book Haven—you caught my heart in that fitted knot.

Do you remember the quiver in my voice as I spoke? The joyful tears that traced my eyelids? The tremble of my legs as I stood, just a wooden table between us, with your newest novel laid gently on top. You stared right at me. And I felt acknowledged in a way I'd never felt before. You stared in recognition rather than through me. And my heart retorted by throbbing, unceasing in its assault against my flesh and bone.

How you've quaked me; knocked me off my axis and permanently distorted my very being.

I have to wonder whether that was your intention, in that moment as we locked eyes. I never expected your eyes to be so deep. So unapologetically beautiful. Typhoons of brown and green. Swirling and searching in a lustre so thick, it consumes. I long to be the words dancing along your tongue, for I have tasted the sweetness of your mouth. How I savoured the delectation of your voracious tongue that dripped sweet, enslaving saliva.

I hold your letter dearly; a memory I'll never let go. You described my body in a way that I have never known. My skin so pale—anticipated by my timidity—with a warm yellow hue. You described my breasts as fallen teardrops, the beauty of their natural shape.

It smells of you. The letter you sent. Of warmth and spice. As if sandalwood and vanilla seeped into the fibres of the paper. I held it close as I tried to sleep last night. Should I admit that I often sleep nude? And as I pressed your letter to my chest, its texture brushed ever so gently against my swollen breasts.

You have bewitched me.

That is what you wrote. And I could hear your voice as I read it over and over. Your voice burns me. Low and deep.

The memory of that night—of your kiss, of your touch, of your voice—spread through me and simmered just beneath my skin. I closed my eyes remembering the warmth of your tongue. I held the paper by one corner, as a cool breeze fluttered my curtains and pricked my flesh, causing a shiver that grazed your letter across my chest. It caressed me in a way so remarkably sensual, with your writing against my skin.

Remember the amorous tension of that night as we took in each other's bare glory? I let you lead me to your bed and basked in the supple texture of your sheets. Remember how you whispered, 'Can I?' Such a simple question, yet my heart tried to leap from my chest. I lay coveted in your intense gaze as I nodded. Remember the trail you drew—with tongue and finger—down my breastbone, past my stomach, and taunting my throbbing need as you settled against my legs? I felt your teeth brush against my tender thigh as my need seethed. Remember the vitality that thundered between us as my hands rested on your shoulders? Our eyes interlocked as you nibbled my thigh.

I gasped, subdued by your touch. You breathed in deep, inhaling my scent and losing yourself in the desire we felt. Remember how your beard brushed along and caressed my sensitive pink flesh? Did you mean for it to do so?

I do. I remember, and I thought carefully about it as I lay in bed last night. I thought about how the paper had touched your calloused hands. I craved your touch, so instead, imagined your letter was indeed your hands, stroking and sliding against my swollen nipples. I trailed a finger gently down my forbidden flesh, feeling the wetness these memories seeped.

Do you remember how you finally took my clit between your lips and pulled it gently—again and again—then licked it slowly? You pushed my legs wider apart and dipped that divine tongue into my wetness. I moaned at the sensation, weaving my fingers into your hair as you feasted on me. You played with me: flicking, dragging, sucking, circling, pulling. You tasted me: slowly, patiently, leisurely. You made love to me—with tongue and finger—falling into a persistent rhythm. I learned your tongue by heart, and I now swell at the mere thought of it.

Remember how I trembled in my first climax, rolling my hips against you? You kissed me gently through it and kissed my thighs after it. You kissed my hips, my belly, my nipples. Your lips locked around the swollen pink buds, your tongue moving in ravenous swipes.

My voice was breathless as I begged you to have me. Shaky. It was then that your lips finally found mine. And I tasted myself against your tongue. I felt the bed shift as my open legs lifted against your kneeling ones. I bucked my hips, pressing against your hardness, as you slid inside.

You murmured my name; your voice engrained in my mind.

Remember how you drove yourself into me again and again? How my legs fell open more and more? How I had whimpered? The sounds of our flesh coming together. I tried to focus, tried to keep my eyes on your face, but the all-consuming sensation of how you filled me so well—your hips slapping and rubbing against my thighs—made me wild with need.

'Yes,' I whispered, absently, arching under your weight but not reaching another peak. You kept your rhythm—thrusting in and out—and slid your hand between our bodies. You started rubbing me softly once more, and I couldn't help but buck my hips to meet yours.

It wasn't until I'd reached my third peak that you finally relieved me of your overwhelming, carnal onslaught.

I lay in bed, thinking of these memories as I touched myself; your letter still pressed against my breasts. But it was not the memory of you filling me that gave me the satisfaction I needed. I sated my greed but recalling the way you basked in my touch after I had my fill.

Remember how I caressed your broad chest? How you didn't move, letting me do what I needed? My hands went down, gripping your hips, as I slowly sank to my knees, kissing your warm skin as I descended. I was soaked with desire, raised my eyes to your face, and met your gaze. I found that intensity—the strong, overpowering but heated intensity that bleeds into your irises—and I almost moaned with need. I wanted to please you.

Do you remember how I placed my hands around your muscled legs and kissed your abdomen once more? And how you slid your fingers into my hair, parting your lips ever so slightly in anticipation? When my fingers brushed the line of dark hair on your abdomen, you grunted. When I traced your length with my fingertips, you whispered my name in desperation. And when I brought my lips to your tip and planted a soft kiss, you—famous for your atheist beliefs—called out God's name. I smiled, revelling in my newfound power and finally wrapped my lips around you.

Remember how you stared down at me, with lust in your eyes? How I rested on my knees, pleasuring you with my mouth? I made love to your cock. Shameless. Gentle. I kissed every inch of you, licked the sensitive tip, and took you in my mouth.

It was the memory of the weight against my tongue. The salty sweetness that surged through my mouth. Have you ever noticed the veins that bulge down your length? It was these memories that found my release last night.

Now, you've asked to see me again. And while I bask in the knowledge of how I've affected you and relish the memories you've left me, I find myself wondering about your true intentions. I found confidence that night. And now as I stare at my own reflection, I feel sensual, sultry, alluring. There's no denying I am infatuated with you but tell me, Thorsten, will you allow me to seduce and conquer you again? Or will you simply use and abuse me for your own self-indulgence? Prove to me that I mean more than that, and you will surely see me again. For now, I leave you with the knowledge that I use our memories for my own pleasure, and an account of those memories, most erotic.

Yours,
Viola.

The Vegemite Scroll

Olivia Madeley

06 September 2022

A distraction? She must like me. I knew it. Why else would I be a distraction if it's not because I'm on her mind 24/7?

'Mate, you need to leave. This is the second time I've asked you; stop coming up here while she's working.' The fourth-floor manager of our regional council building clearly isn't a fan of me. It's fine, I'll leave. I'll see her at lunch. It's not like we have any real work to do anyway.

I give Rebecca one more smile and wave before I walk out the door. God, she's just everything. I can't wait for the day she stops playing hard to get and lets me rescue her from all the adversaries in her life. But for now, I'll keep playing her game of chase.

I head back to my desk on the first floor of the building and whip out my diary. I can write while I wait for lunch.

Dear Diary,

I went to the fourth floor again today to see Bec—third time this week. She had this beautiful, long red dress on. Lady in red. And she smelled sweet, like strawberries and cream. She always does. Her hair was straight and long, she must have just got it touched up yesterday, the highlights look fresh.

I remember the day I was sitting in the back of the board room, waiting for the whole council meeting to start, just sketching in my book. That's when she appeared in the doorway, framed by holy light piercing through the electric blinds (they've been broken for five years). I was so blown away by her astonishing beauty, my hand just took over and produced the best piece of artwork I have ever created. Only I have the artistic prowess to depict such an illustration of this glorious creature. I even captured the glimmering golden flecks in her green eyes as she spoke so passionately about something with her co-worker Marco.

That's why I went up to her desk today, to gift my finished sketched portrait to her. She must have been so shocked because she didn't even want to take it from my hands. With her eyes wide, she just kept

saying 'Oh no. Daniel, please you really, really didn't
need to do that.' She's clearly never had anyone care
about her or give her gifts, because she doesn't know
how to accept my kind gestures. This isn't the first
time I've received a similar response. But that will
change. She will learn to love it.

But that's when her floor manager came over
and told me to leave. Again.

One day I will share these entries with her. Bec is gonna love
them. I was thinking about even reading a few as my wedding
vows. I know she loves romance.

10 September 2022

'Here you go, Bec. I heard you say to Marco you were hungry,
so I bought you another coffee and a caramel slice. The coffee
is a decaf pumpkin spice latte.' How much more could I do to
win her over?

From the breakroom's coffee table, Bec looks up at me
with what I can only interpret as pure appreciation. The game
of chase is tiring, but I will wear her down. Zipp stares me
down from his seat directly across from mine as I plant myself

beside Marco. He's mad. He has been trying to deter me from winning Bec over. I'm certain it's because he's jealous. Every guy wants her—I don't blame them. It only makes sense that seeing us together would cause envy amongst her fans. Especially considering he and all the other fourth-floor council workers are being beaten by a first-floor employee. The only one I don't have to worry about is Marco: he's gay. That's why Bec calls him Pudding.

As our break comes to an end, I rush to the door to hold it open for Bec to show her I'm a gentleman, except she exits through the second door. I try to catch up with her, but Zipp pulls me aside.

'I told you to leave her alone, man. You're making her uncomfortable. Every time you do things without asking her first, you're taking away her agency and ability to make decisions for herself. Besides, you're a first-floor, check yourself.'

He doesn't fucking know anything. He's just a fake feminist.

'Whatever, man. I know she appreciates it. I'm just trying to help lift the load for her.'

I know everything about her. Zipp has no idea. I know she loves romance, and sweets, I know her coffee orders, and her favourite animal. What more do I need to know? She's perfect for me.

08 October 2022

I head into work a few hours before our monthly whole-council meeting. I know Bec will be here preparing to deliver her presentation. It gives me a chance to be alone with her, which doesn't happen often. Marco and Zipp are stuck to her like glue. They never leave her side—they're obsessed.

Coming around the corner, I spot her blonde hair. She's wearing a beautiful green dress today. It matches her eyes. Then I notice she's not sitting alone. Her two goonies are at her side, all preparing together. *I* was gonna helped her prepare. I approach them, feeling outrage.

'You guys didn't tell me you'd be here early.'

All sets of eyes glance up at me, except for Rebecca. She must feel guilty. I grab a seat from another table and join the group.

'How is the presentation? Are you guys ready?' I'm met with no answer. They continued their conversation as if I hadn't arrived. Bec makes a joke, and everyone laughs. Zipp's laugh is particularly obnoxious. I laugh louder to show Bec I thought the joke was especially funny. The silence cuts me off, so I fade to a chuckle.

I can't help but stare at Bec while she works. Just waiting for her to look up at me. She doesn't. She's still playing the game, and I abide. I try to ask if she has had a coffee yet today. I just want her to acknowledge me.

Without looking up from her laptop she sheepishly responds, 'Um, yeah. We got coffee earlier. Or, well, Zipp and I did. Pudding got a hot chocolate.' Her voice is soft, sometimes she gets a bit shy. It's sweet.

Heroically, I offer to get her some sort of breakfast sweet and a second coffee to prepare her for the meeting. Bec doesn't even have a chance to reply before Zipp interjects.

'You only drink decaf now, don't you Bec?' Fuck, how did I forget? She's going to think I don't pay attention. I don't react to Zipp's conceited stare. I'd rather her view me as calm and gentle than some egotistical idiot like Zipp. I bet she gets so frustrated with him following her all the time, always trying to help her.

It' 9 o'clock—time to head into the board room. I race to the door to hold it for Rebecca. She follows Marco in with her head down. She's so graceful. I catch that sweet scent of strawberries and cream that I love so much. They head to the table and Marco sits to her right. He compliments her green dress, which makes her smile and giggle. I wish I had said it first. Then she could smile and giggle at me. Zipp sits to her left—there's no room left at the table. For fuck's sake. I resort to standing in the corner alone with the broken blinds.

For the whole meeting I can hear them laughing. I try so hard to listen to what they are saying, what Bec's saying. But I can't hear.

04 November 2022

I come to work early again in the hopes to successfully catch Bec working on her own. I can't seem to find her though.

Instead, I spot Zipp and Marco talking in the hallway near the elevator. They're planning something. Zipp's holding a paper bag from the café. They stop talking when I approach.

'Where's Bec?' I say. It's strange for her to not be here.

'She'll be late today,' Marco begrudgingly responds.

I hope she's okay. Maybe something happened on her way here, or she could be sick. She can't afford any more setbacks. I'll have to help her catch up. The three of us stand there awkwardly until the meeting begins. It's not until halfway through the meeting that Rebecca arrives. She looks exhausted. She needs me to help her. Why won't she just give in?

I saved her a seat beside me, but she sits elsewhere. I chuckle. Probably because I'm a distraction. It's fine. She distracts me too. So much so that I tune out of the meeting and turn to my diary again.

Dear Diary,

Bec seems sad today. It's not like her. She is always so happy. It's one of the many things I admire about her.

I'll have to message her again tonight to check on how she is going. Hopefully she responds this time. She gets so busy with life that she doesn't have time to reply to me. I understand. I know she's not ignoring me. She wouldn't.

Maybe she's getting sick of Zipp following her everywhere. I'll have to intervene. Save her. If she'd just look at me. Give me any kind of sign that she needs my help. I'll be there, like her knight in shining armour. That's what she needs.

The meeting ends and instead of rushing to the door, I just stand and wait. Watching to see which door Bec moves towards, I follow her, but she changes direction to follow Zipp and Marco heading to the second door. I follow suit within the crowd of gloomy council associates.

I'm too late to hold it for her. Yet again, Zipp beats me to it. The door shuts in my face when he lets go. Prick.

I open the door and, *fuck*. Zipp's on one knee. In the middle of the *fucking* hallway. He's looking up at Rebecca and I'm in just as much shock as she is. Our associates are no longer gloomy. Zipp reaches for Rebecca's hand, staring up at her with a big smile.

'Rebecca, I don't have a ring, but I know you don't like romance anyway. However, I do have a savoury Vegemite scroll for you. Rebecca, will you take this Vegemite scroll and make me the happiest man alive?'

Rebecca shrieks in excitement. My heart sinks. Zipp, you've won.

Where the heart is

Amanda Bateup

'What are you *doing*?'

I peeled my eyes from the screen and turned, craning my head over my shoulder just in time to see my wife—a beautiful hurricane in varying shades of pink—slam the door behind her. Her face was almost as red as the lipstick framing her mouth, starkly different from her white, gritted teeth. *Shit, here we go again.* I turned back to my computer.

'Working,' I said, as if that one word excused me of anything.

'Patrick, it's five. Come on, I asked everyone to be dressed and ready,' she said. She was keeping a low voice; the girls must have been close by.

'Sam, baby, give me like 10 more minutes.'

'No. Pat, we have to leave.'

'For what?' I said, swivelling my office chair to face her.

Her mouth dropped open and her eyes turned to slits. Her voice became a low hiss, like a coiled viper ready to strike: 'Please, tell me you are not serious.'

Shit, what have I forgotten? Her hair is down; it must be a special occasion. Anniversary? No, that was two months ago … or was it? Wait, her mother's birthday? I took a deep breath and clapped my hands to my knees, wondering how to phrase my response without making the situation atomic. 'Sammy, do you really need me there?' I said, immediately regretting the path I'd chosen.

'You're her father! Yes, you need to be there.'

'I'm not her father. What are you …'

And there went the missile, an unintentional detonation.

'HOW DARE YOU.' Boom: the explosion. It quaked through me, and in my mind, I saw myself knocked from my chair and crushed by my office desk, its wobbly legs too weak to withstand such power.

'So, obviously, it's not your mother's birthday,' I whispered.

'My mother's birthday? That was last week!'

'Can you please just tell me,' I said, closing my eyes and rubbing my temples, 'what is tonight?'

She stepped forward, venturing further into the wilderness of our home office that I had turned into my studio—my territory—and crossed her arms. Her face looked alien now that she was within reach of the ring light behind my monitor. The bright white circle reflected off the surface of her eyes, and I could see myself burning in a pyre with millions watching, mourning my death. I shook myself, looking away from the glare, past my wife, to the bookshelf I had set up by the door.

'It's our daughter's graduation,' Sam said.

I found myself staring at a small, framed portrait of our family I had propped in the centre of the bookshelf. Maisie was only a newborn when it was taken, and Reilly was just a kid in an oversized cap with a soccer ball in her hands that looked twice the size of her head. 'She's only in year six,' I said definitively.

'Exactly! She's going to high school next year.'

'Sam, I promised I'd stream tonight … Does she really need me there? It's not like she's going to university next year.'

There was a long pause, and then she left; the door was silent as it closed behind her.

I didn't hear the door the second time it opened; I just felt her cool, sticky hand rest on my arm. Before I could turn from my screen, I heard her voice.

'Hey, Dad. Whatcha doin'?' she asked.

'Working, my sweet little Maisie,' I answered.

'Whatcha workin' on?'

'Nothing that would interest you, sweetheart,' I said, finally turning to face her.

Although her hands were caked with melted chocolate from a decrepit Freddo Frog she was still munching on, she looked like a little princess. Sam had combed and tied back Maisie's blonde hair in a neat ponytail, wrapping it in a thick, red ribbon. Her dress was a pastel pink to go with her mother's, and I couldn't help but see a shooting star when I looked at her. I smiled, and she smiled back.

'Hop up here,' I said as I patted my knee.

Without hesitation, she climbed on up, leaving a trail of brown smudges on my white tee-shirt. I wrapped my arms around her and placed my stubbled chin on her head.

'Dad!' she said giggling, 'you're scratchin' my head!'

'I just wanted a cuddle,' I said, laughing too. Silence fell over us. I rocked back and forward in the chair, longing for the days when my two babies were small enough to fit in my hands, and my wife's face lit up with love when I walked into the room.

'Mum's angry,' Maisie's voice cut through the quiet. My face dropped. 'And Reilly wants to know why you're not coming to her special night,' she continued.

'Reilly doesn't need me there; you and Mum will be there.'

'But why not you?'

'Because—' I cut myself off, aware Maisie wouldn't understand. I had commitments to my followers. Dread clawed its way up into my chest. If I didn't show, I would lose followers, and Reilly was only finishing primary school.

'Maisie!'

It was Sam calling from down the hall.

'Maisie! Where are you? Did you get into those chocolates again?'

Maisie sat up straight, melted chocolate on her face.

'Don't worry,' I said, 'if she asks, it's my fault.'

She nodded, and the ponytail bounced. That's when Sam passed the doorway, stopped, retraced her steps and walked in.

'Maisie!' she exclaimed.

'It was Dad!'

'It was,' I said.

Sam shook her head, frowning. 'Maisie, come on, we need to leave. Go and get in the car with your sister. There are wipes in there. Get Reilly to help you.'

Maisie looked at me. I kissed her cheek, and she left in a swirl of colour and sweet chocolate perfume.

Sam lingered, her face no longer flushed, just strained.

'So that's it,' she said, 'you're staying here?'

'I don't have a choice—'

'No. You're choosing your 50 subscribers over your daughter.'

'This is my job, Sam. I wouldn't expect you to cancel a board meeting for an event I could easily take both the girls to,' I responded, 'and it's 58—we're growing.'

'There is no "we". You've been doing this for two years; I think it's time to move on.' Her words hit hard into my chest, cracking open my ribcage and burying deep into my heart.

'This is my job.'

'That excuse would have worked a year ago. Face it, Pat, this social media thing isn't for you. Your job is to be here for us.'

And that was that; she was gone.

I sat there in the dead silence. There was a sharp sting in my throat. My eyes were a dam a second from breaking. *How could she?* Her words loomed over me. *When did things get like this?* I was trying so hard to help provide for my family, to break through and have a large enough following to help us live comfortably. But here I was with only a handful of supporters, a wife who despised me and a daughter I no longer knew.

Reilly, I'm so sorry.

And the dam broke.

When was the last time we sat down together? When was the last time we really spoke? The last time I hugged you? The last time I said I love you?

My shoulders shuddered, and my fingernails dug into my scalp.

Reilly, I miss you.

A switch clicked.

I stood up, grabbed my keys from the top of the bookshelf and walked out the door.

The lights were beating down so brightly that the entire room was thick with heat. There were rows upon rows of seats filled with cheering parents, grandparents, uncles and aunts. I almost gave up looking for Sam and Maisie in the sea of clapping hands until I spotted Maisie waving at me from the third row, her arms stretching as high as they could. Maisie jumped off her seat and planted herself on Sam's lap so I could take it and not obscure the view of the many rows that followed ours.

Sam looked at me with critical eyes. I thought she might say something about my chocolate-stained shirt. Instead, she graced me with a smile that reminded me of how I ended up here.

'Reilly Spindle,' the voice from the stage called, and my head snapped up to watch. My eldest daughter made her way across the stage, her hands clasped together in front of her.

'That's my girl!' I called, catching her attention, letting her know we were all there.

And that's when I saw it: the biggest fan I would ever have beamed down at me.

Home to You

Henriette Lykseth Viken

Present

The vibration of the plane makes it hard not to fall asleep, but something is keeping me awake. There is a tightening feeling growing in the back of my throat as I'm realising that I'm officially moving back home after two years of studying abroad. I don't know what I should be feeling. So many people have made such an impact on my life these last couple of years. Sitting here on the plane, starting a new adventure … it's a weird sensation. I feel the urge to stay. I feel the urge to stop the plane.

Past – Australia, days before the flight

I watch them smile and laugh. We're sitting on the floor of the house, which we moved into over a year ago. Their conversation passes through me as my mind starts racing, realising this will be our last evening together. They have become like sisters to me. It's weird that in a couple of hours I'll be saying goodbye to them. It feels like a regular evening: watching our favourite movies with snacks in front of us, laughing until our stomachs hurt. Still, there is a pressure behind my eyes as I look at them. Already missing them.

Past – Australia, 2 weeks before the flight

I look down at my robe and dress. My feet suddenly have the urge to dance. There is a smile on my face as I look up and see the other graduates. This is what I've wanted for a long time. This is what I've worked towards, what I've dreamed for! Graduating.

I can see my roomies and friends in the crowd, clapping and smiling at me. My parents and my brother are not here, but I know that they are watching every minute online —the rest of my family as well—and they are cheering me on from the other side of the world. My heart is beating fast. I take a deep breath, trying to calm myself down. I know that my grandma would've been so proud. She, with the rest of the people that have made it truly possible to get through these three years, are the only people going through my mind right now.

As I hear my name and take the first steps onto the stage, all I can feel is pride and joy. I did it! This is everything!

Past – Australia, October 2023

I'm feeling tired. My motivation is low, and I'm torn between staying and leaving.

The voices of my friends—both in Norway and here—and my family, keep repeating in my head.

'We're so proud of you.'

'Just a few more weeks to go.'

'You can do it.'

'This has been your dream.'

And I keep going. Keep studying. Keep enjoying my time here.

I'm almost there.

Past – Australia, August 2023

I look at the mobile screen in front of me. The words do not fully process in my head.

> DAD: *Grandma slipped away at 9:15 tonight. It was peaceful and nice.*

I knew I could miss a wedding, but I never thought I would miss a funeral. I try to think back to every childhood memory I've had with her, but my mind draws a blank. My brother sends me a message, telling me if I need to talk, he would be awake for the rest of the night. All I can think about is distracting myself. I need to get out of bed and do something. Keep myself busy.

Past – Norway, June 2023

It's our usual spontaneous kitchen gathering. My mum, my brother, my two cousins, my aunt, my uncle and my nanna. It's a wonder how we can all fit in one room, but we do. This always happens with my mum's family. It's one of my favourite moments.

My cousins have grown, time hasn't stopped since the last time I was here. Though, it all feels very much the same.

Past – Australia, April 2023

'I know it's hard, sweetie,' my mum says over the phone. I've been homesick.

We're video chatting, as we've done for most of the two years. I can see that she is standing in the kitchen.

'But you'll be back in no time. You're doing so well. We're all so proud of you. Never forget that.'

Her comforting words make me smile.

'I'm so glad you have that lovely community. And I'm so grateful that you have those wonderful girls. It'll be okay.'

Past – Norway, November 2022

I'm sitting in the corner of my grandparents' living room, hidden from everyone else except for my cousin, his girlfriend and my brother. I can feel my heart beating fast. My whole body feels like it's on fire. I can hear my other cousin walking past the kitchen. I can see my grandparents smiling at each other as my cousin walks inside the room. She looks around.

'Oh, nice,' she says, noticing everyone. Not really surprised to see any of them.

Then her eyes land on me. Her hand goes straight to her mouth, full of shock.

'Oh my gosh!' she says as she falls to her knees.

The room fills with joyous laughter as I run to her, hugging her tightly.

Past – Norway, November 2022

'You're filming this, you jerk,' my brother says, laughing. He has his arms tight around me.

I smirk as he lets me go.

'Of course, I am.'

He looks down at me, shakes his head and gives me another hug.

'I can't believe you're home!'

My mum is smiling with tears in her eyes behind us. I landed a couple of hours ago and it already feels so good to be back. Everything still feels the same. Nothing has changed.

Past – Australia, June 2022

My body is freezing, I've got goosebumps all over my arms and legs and cannot seem to keep my eyes open. My two roomies are sitting next to me and we're all enjoying the view. The sunrise is beautiful. Waking up early was a challenge and we're only staying here for one night, but already I know it's going to be worth it.

The last couple of months have been so challenging. I worked on assignments that were hard to understand and were way out of my comfort zone, but I pushed through it. The two of them and the lovely community that I've met, made it all easier. My past self would never have guessed that I would ever wake up this early—just to see a sunrise. Without them, I may not have been able to experience this, and see what I am seeing right now.

Past – Australia, February 2022

I'm at the student accommodation with my aunt. It feels weird that I'll be staying and sleeping here by myself for the next two years. My aunt helps me clean the room and decorate it. She and my uncle have been taking me out on different trips to get to know the area better. They are one of the reasons why I felt brave enough to move here.

I look at her as she explores the rest of the common room area. I feel scared and terrified for this next step. I may not have my mum or my brother here, who have been my usual housemates for 20 years, but it's a relief to know that my aunt and uncle are just a couple of minutes away.

Past – Norway, January 2022

My heart beats fast as I walk quickly through the security. I can feel my mum and brother watching me from the other side. A part of me doesn't want to look back, because it'll be too hard, but the other part of me that wants just one more second with them—wins. Behind the mask my mum is smiling through the pain of her daughter moving 27 hours away. When I turn back around, I have that horrible, sinking feeling that life as I know it will never be the same again.

Present

I rush as quickly as possible through the baggage claim. A smile creeps onto my lips as I see them through the glass doors. Things did change and it has been a long and tough journey, but it has also been wonderful and exciting. I have grown a lot. Gained more fans who will support me and cheer me on, and vice versa. People I hope to cherish for years to come.

Tears start rolling down my cheeks as I run up to my mum and brother. I hug them tightly and feel the warmth and comfort I have so sorely missed. I know that someday I will be on another journey to another place I have yet to explore, but now I know that wherever I go, I always have someone to come home to. Both in Norway and Australia.

My Quandary

Bree Glasbergen

I love my friends. Of course, I do.
I'm a ... fan.
I hope I tell them. I mean to tell them.

Sometimes I forget.

I forgot today, didn't I? Yep. Oh well, human.
Fallible. Flawed. Fuck.

Friend ...   *Sizes up friend*
Strange how I don't need to muster up any
courage to tell you:
I love you. I'm in your corner. I'm a ... fan.
Love.   *Ponders love*
You can say you love your friends.
You can, and I hope you do.
Love actually is a brilliant movie. Christmas MUST-watch!

I said it much more after the accident. Love.
Every phone call closed with a conscious 'I
love you'. Scared a second crumpling would
snatch the words right along with me. The
ones I had left unsaid.
You see, I might not be so lucky a second
time. I might not be here … at all.

For other people I love, it is …

    H
        a
          r
            d
              e   s
                 r   to   a
                                 y

Could you imagine telling your boss you love them? Your
barista? The kind lady at the fruit and veg shop who hands
toddlers free bananas on the daily?
But what if you do?
And what if it's … misconstrued?   **AWKWARD!**

Tries it out

I love you.   [**Platonically**]

I love you.   [**Matter of fact**]

There! See? Now, they know.

I'm not making it weird!   You're making it weird!

Well fuck, now you've gone

and made it weird …

But why should it be? It's love!

We're all born from love, and when we

die, there are words of love still left in us,

unspilled.   Am I

Die.   Well, that sounds final, doesn't it?   s

I bet every dead person has a bunch of unread   p
                                                          i
books on their shelf like a wine cellar, to go   r

along with all their unsaid words.   a
                                                                l
All we have is fear and love.
                                                                  l
Choose love!
                                                                    i
Choose love …
                                                                      n
                                                                        g

Choose

Deep
breaths ...

Love.

Last Semester of uni.
13 weeks left.

There's one love I can't say. It's real, and it's thick, and the nuttiness of it gets caught in my throat and sometimes suffocates me. I try not to think of it, but it's still there. It's the love of my lecturers and tutors. Like, my teachers, you know? The ones that know far more than we do. The ones that grace us with their seasoned wisdom. I look up, eyes-wide, to the pedestal I've placed them upon, and shudder to think of the thick words I've left unsaid. I think again of the accident and how precious life is. How this is my second chance. I should really stop calling it an accident when he meant to do it. Thinking of it is usually enough to remind me to take courageous action. To be bold. Thinking of almost dying, that is. It's my ephemerality spell. I conjure it to remember to squeeze the juice out of life. Of my time left. It doesn't work this time, though. The ephemerality spell doesn't work on my weird pedestal-teacher-admiration. It doesn't work for my quandary.

I blow the dust off the chapter of the time I kissed death. The crumpling of metal. Waking up, not knowing where I was and porcupined with glass shards. Throbbing misshaped bones. My face ending a full fist length above where it usually did. My diagonal nose. My broken dreams. Misguided trust and a lingering whisper: *look what you made me do,* Bree …

This memory isn't a sharp ache anymore. It's a soft throb, and it can't hurt me. Just like he can't. This is why I can talk about it without the thickness stealing my words away, like it had for so long. It's processed now, and what remains is a blessing. The nearness of not being alive reminds me to savour things. My blessing. It reminds me to speak most of my love. But why not this one?   Why not this one?

The separation between my adoration of their wisdom and my devouring of knowledge stops the spell in its stead. How could we hand out teacher gifts so liberally in high school, and yet at uni we don't even tell them how much they've truly moulded us ready for the big world?

Tell them?   I could never.
This is an ending, though, isn't it?   8 weeks left.
The ending of a degree.
Which is why we are all here, is it not?   5 weeks? YIKES!
It's a death too, of sorts.

Choosing not to reach for the pain of change
is choosing   2 WEEKS!
the pain you have.
Well, fuck.   Now or never!!
So, before we are reborn into the world a new,
I decided to take one huge moment of insane courage.
Cuz that's what the   KEEP CALM
fridge magnets say it takes.   AND FUCKING
And that's what the guy does   TELL THEM
at Keira Knightley's door
when he whips out the flashcards.
And I wrote them.
How much they inspired.
How they helped me grow.

How they lovingly called me on my shit. How there were
things, they didn't call me on when I had to learn myself or I
was fumbling … How they showed me where to look, but the
rest of the path was one for me alone.

How the ripples of their words that had inspired thousands
before me and would continue to inspire thousands more, long
long after I had gone.

                                        1 week …

I love my friends. Of course, I do. I'm a … fan.

                                        I think I'll
                                        tell them! ☺

I hope I tell them.

But, you see, I love my teachers, too. The imparters of
wisdom.
They deserve to know.
So, heading into this new death of sorts—
And just because it's Christmas—   and Christmas,
And in case the words die along with me,   you tell
I signed it off at the very end: the truth.
With BIG LOVE
From me,

Graduation!

Bree.

Half-Strength Love

Mackenzie Morgan

'P-pardon?' I hesitated. This could not be right.

The middle-aged man hiding behind the most glorious bouquet of roses and peonies I had ever seen confirmed what I initially thought I'd heard. This time his tone was a little more aggravated and a little less forgiving.

'I'm looking for an Audrey B…'

Drowned out by the vibrant buzz of a congested coffee shop at nine thirty on a Monday morning, the dull echo of Fleetwood Mac's 'Silver Springs' was suppressed by a distinct bellowing from table seventeen. 'I asked for almond milk you halfwit.' *Ahh, things were normal.*

My attention was snapped back to the middle-aged man clearing his throat. He had now placed the flowers on the countertop, revealing his black rectangular shaped glasses, flushed cheeks and grey moustache that badly needed a trim.

'Will you please just pass these onto Audrey, I don't have time for this,' he snapped, and was back out the door quicker than I had time to respond.

But it wasn't my birthday? Hell, what day was it? Was it Valentines Day? No, it's September for heaven's sake. I reached for the small envelope positioned amongst the peonies. *Audrey Bailey, 9 Finch Lane* was etched in familiar letters. There was no mistaking it. But before I had a chance to turn the card over, I was interrupted.

'Audrey, they're beautiful, but we need your help, like *now!*' Eden exclaimed before semi-frothed milk began to overflow out of the metal jug she was holding. The line-up of post-school drop-off, increasingly-agitated mums sporting activewear and demanding skinny flat whites had spilled out the door. What was once a faint aroma of warm blueberries and white chocolate had been replaced by a smell that can only be described as -

'Shit! The muffins are still in the oven'

I don't even need to look at the clock to know what time it is. The flock of mildly-agitated, post-school drop-off mums had departed with their skinny flat whites, only to be replaced by a mass of teenagers who had wandered down the road, still in their uniforms. Their blouses clinging a little too firmly around their waist, and their skirts merely peering out below, suggesting that this was probably the first chance they would have had to eat today. I know back in my schooling days, which truthfully was not that long ago, a uniform in that state would have landed me a lunchtime detention and a very hungry afternoon. *Maybe that's how they kept that petite figure they all seem to have?*

My eyes drifted over to the seating booth on the left-hand side of the café, which was now occupied by a tall dark-haired boy and a girl of the same age in one of the excessively small uniforms. The high walls surrounding the booth are not enough to completely block the ongoing touching and overly passionate kissing being exchanged. *Oh, to be young again.* Eden catches my glance, rolling her eyes as she mimes sticking her fingers down her throat, she continues to make a gagging noise. I manage a giggle.

Only 6 years ago, that was me. A love-drunk seventeen-year-old girl with a too tight uniform, sitting in the booth of a café after school with a boy I was head over heels in love with. Alistair Blain. Closing my eyes, I can still see the way his mop of brown hair rested on his bushy eyebrows, revealing the most beautiful blue eyes I had ever seen.

I've never really brought into the whole religion thing, but I find myself closing my eyes and saying a prayer for this young girl, wearing the too small uniform, who is just a stranger sitting in the booth. Every inch of my body clenches as I pray to someone, something, *anything* that this girl is not left in the driveway of her mother's house one Wednesday night in the fall as she watches this tall, dark-haired boy reverse out without a care in the world, leaving her wondering why she was not good enough. It's funny how time changes things.

'I didn't realise that Ben sent you flowers on days other than your birthday *and* Valentine's Day Audrey, do you know how lucky you are?' Eden exclaimed, snapping me out of my trance. I managed to force a smile and know she was right. What was I even thinking? Despite everything, I'd managed to meet a nice man, someone that made me feel secure. I no longer found myself second guessing if I was good enough for him. We met at a bar on Oxford Street one rainy Thursday night. He moved in not long after, and later we got married. I now go by Audrey Baker. Together we're raising two kids in a townhouse not far from here. He makes me feel all of the things I am meant to, *and* he surprises me with flowers regularly. *Just the way things are meant to be.*

Though as much as I hate to admit it, I know why Alistair Blaine was on my mind. Truthfully, he'd never really left. Only last week, I was in the supermarket picking up milk on the way home from work when I locked eyes with a handsome man who had the most glorious blue eyes I had ever seen. I haven't seen Alistair since the night he drove out of my mother's driveway, tears blurring my last sight of him. Rumour had it that he moved towns not long after. As quick as I'd made eye contact with the mysterious man with the ocean blue eyes, he was gone. *Those damn blue eyes.*

'For God sake Audrey, are you going to open the card or not?' Eden insists, shoving the beautiful roses and peonies into my chest before she locks the door behind us on the way out of the café.

'Oh, they're only from Ben, I'm sure you can guess what it says,' I exclaimed sarcastically.

'*Just because I love you, love Ben*' Eden mimics, making the same face she did when the two teenagers were making out in the booth earlier.

'It's almost like this has happened before,' I respond with a hint of irony.

'You're so lucky Audrey, I hope I find a man like that one day.'

'You will Eds, I'll see you tomorrow!' I rush towards my car.

I jump inside before removing the card from amidst the flowers. As I begin to pull the card from the envelope, my heart stops. *Audrey Bailey?* My maiden name? I continue, hands trembling.

Audrey Bailey. Today, the 17th of September marks six years since I made the decision that would haunt me every single day, for the rest of my life. When I saw you in the supermarket last week, I was unable to form any words, let alone approach you. My number hasn't changed, please call me.

Your biggest fan, the love of your life,
Al.

Football Saturday

Rachel Patrick

My earliest memory is watching my daddy, beer in hand, screaming at our box television. His laidback chair contradicts the explicit language pouring from his mouth, absolutely abusing the eighteen navy-blue clad men running the length of the field. His grunts and groans as they lose the ball to the other team fill our hollow Queenslander. It's football Saturday; no one else can watch, say or do anything.

The half-time siren blares through the speakers and Daddy mumbles something about a cigarette, leaving his crushed beer can stuck in the arm of the chair. The bleak score line stares back at me as the players leave the field, their coach yelling at them the way Daddy was yelling at the screen.

'It's okay, baby,' Mummy smiles at me. 'Daddy is just a little frustrated. You'll understand when you are older.' She pats my shoulder before heading down the hallway. 'Brett, Rach doesn't need to hear that language!' she yells at him, as the latest betting ad flashes across the screen. I don't know if I *will* understand when I'm older.

I'm running around the Warwick field myself, ball in hand. The sneers from the older boys fall up on my ears. *Girls can't play football. Netball courts are across the road, sweetheart. She's gonna get flattened, the poor thing. Hope Mum has the ambulance on speed dial.* I don't care, I'm gonna kick this goal. Gonna bend it through the big sticks like Fevola did on the weekend; he's my favourite. Mum thinks he's pretty; she only watches the footy for the muscly men.

'Kick it, Rach! Bomb it like Fev!' the familiar voice screams from the sideline; it's Daddy. Grinning ear to ear, I throw it on my boot. I watch it sail over my defender. It slots through the big ones. We're in front. The airhorn blares. We won! I won! The boys surround me, slapping my back and jeering. Those sneers seemingly disappeared from their minds but engrained in mine. If I can kick goals like them and tackle like them, why do they feel the need to taunt me? Do they think that congratulating me afterwards will change what they said?

'Well done, Bug! Fev would be proud!' Daddy slides me a dripping ice cream, the taste of victory.

We go home. After showering I sprint to the loungeroom in my navy-blue pyjamas. Daddy's not there yet but will be soon. I've finally got Daddy's pregame ritual down; toilet run, two smokes, chuck on his navy-blue beanie, crack open a beer and do not move until the next siren. He turns on the box. We've missed the first quarter but we are ahead, what a change! 'We might win this one, Daddy!'

'I wouldn't be so sure, Bug. Haven't seen these boys give a four-quarter effort since before you were born!' I nod along—he says that every week. He hands me a Coke while cracking a beer open for himself, the smell all too synonymous with Saturday nights. If he has enough of the game, he monologues. About our thirteen premierships, about the controversial call in the 1979 Grand Final, about the time he got hit by a flying beer can in 1990 and knocked the dude who threw the can's teeth out with one punch. His stories are more interesting than the football at times, even I'm getting sick of being flogged by forty-plus points each week.

Dad and I are at the Gabba, front row and watching grown men throw punches, mouthguards and swear words at half-time. Another bleak scoreline pales in comparison to the biff in the forward pocket, even more grown men losing their minds and encouraging bloodshed. I wince as I see our full forward get slung to the ground, his opponent crashing down on top and the smelly man behind us sings out gleefully. I still don't understand how people think punching someone over a football will achieve anything. I also don't understand why people find black eyes and jumper punches enjoyable.

'You missed the glory days, Bug! This happened all the time when I was growing up, shit went soft in the 2000s,' Dad says around a mouthful of a soggy, overpriced beef burger. I just nod as the umpires finally break up the fight and the men behind us boo at the loss of their entertainment. I still don't know if I understand.

I'm crying in my room. 'Why can't I play with the boys anymore, Dad? I'm better than them!' Never good with emotion, Dad plants a hand on my leg and rubs it gently. His silence makes me feel even worse. The hysterics take over again and somehow Mum appears in his place; she rubs my back in comforting circles. She always tries to be the emotional voice of reason. Mum tells me that I'm developing and it's not safe for me to play with them anymore, despite knowing full well I flattened Thomas last week for shit-talking my kicking after I'd shanked one wide. It's bullshit, I don't understand! I tell her as much and she just nods, repeating what she said earlier.

After being shafted from the footy team, I move over to netball. No contact, no trash-talking, no nothing without some power-drunk teenager blowing plastic in my ear and cautioning my behaviour. Mum thinks it's a nice change, I won't be coming home with bruises the size of plates on my legs nor grass stains on my guernsey. I want desperately to like it too, but it's so boring!

Dad hates it as well, not enough action for his liking. Whenever I'd glance over to him by the bench, his eyes were glued to the phone, football reflected in his glasses. I wished he'd look up even once, to see my really cool intercept or something. It's only after the netball game when I get a pat on the back and he starts talking to me about the free kick count of last week's football game and how it 'better be better this week' or he is 'putting his foot through the TV'. I smile along, happy to be included again.

However, in true navy-blue fashion, they fall apart in the third quarter, rendering the rest of the game unbearable. Dad and I echo expletive sentiments towards the television as Mum taps through level 1934 of Candy Crush—it's oddly comforting. I think I'm starting to understand … It's football Saturday; no one else can watch, say or do anything.

I move out of home at seventeen. Four hours' drive away, into university student accommodation and no friends. For the first few weeks I call my parents, tell them how I am and they tell me about their life. I ask if they're watching the game that night and I get a 'does a bear shit in the woods' response. Stupid but it makes me feel warm inside, like I never left.

Grabbing a drink from the fridge, I flop down on the stained common room couch. I wait for the door to open and smell of cigarette to fill my nose, but it never comes. I look around; just me, my beer and the screen. First time watching a game without Dad. Without Mum too, but who is going to tell the commentators to shove it when their bias comes through? Who is going to abuse our back men for falling off their man? Who is going to spill their beer when Eddie kicks a snap? It's football Saturday but I'm all by myself.

I make some footy friends but they go for different teams. We get together each Saturday and watch whatever game is on, turning into a drinking game if none of our teams are playing. My phone buzzes and it's my dad, Brett. He asks if I want to come home next week for the break. I haven't been home since Christmas, of course I do!

'C'mon Brett, BT finally shut his mouth! Bounce is in five!' I yell down the hallway. He should be done with his second by now.

'I'm coming, Rach! Grab me one!' Snatching two out of the bar fridge, I slide one into his stubby cooler and crack the top of mine. He flops onto the old brown, ignoring the creaking and favouring the snap of the tab. His beer intake has cut down since we've been winning, currently on a streak of five. The team song sounds better week-in, week-out.

Mum slinks into the room, the sweet music echoing out of her phone. She's got on the jumper she bought Dad for Christmas, navy-blue of course. *What other colour would it be? Certainly not black and white.* I sip as Dad and I talk over the last-minute commentator chatter, throwing hypotheticals around like the football on screen. The siren sounds. Mum's phone is off. Six eyes on the flatscreen as Razor Ray slams the ball into the pitch and Pitto flies up for the tap. It's football Saturday and I'm finally back home, watching with the man who started it all for me. I finally understand.

Old Trafford

Caitlin Cherry

The harsh contact of fist to face could barely be heard over the roar of the crowd. Shouts of insult, admiration and anger blur amongst the sounds of 74,000 fans that fill the space of Old Trafford Stadium.

The scene plays out in front of me in slow motion. My dad pulling his arm back, ready to swing forward with as much force as he can muster. The man in front of him following his movements almost as closely as a mirror ready to reflect the same action back.

I haven't seen him in 20 years. I'm not sure why I believed he would be any different now.

It all started long before my life. In fact, it happened long before Dad's too. The men on my dad's side have been die-hard Manchester United fans since the team established on the 24th of April 1902. After seeing the destruction this obsession has caused, I never wish to follow their lead.

I remember the day we left so clearly. It was straight after the first and last football match I ever went to with Dad. The day consisted of clear blue skies and relatively warm temperatures for March. Good weather is so rare here that we learn to appreciate it when it happens, however, this day didn't allow that opportunity.

'Liam! I swear to God, why are you wearing blue socks?' There was a viciousness to his voice that seemed to be there quite often lately. I was already dressed in red. His huge figure dominated the doorway as he scanned my head-to-toe red Manchester United merchandise. The hat and jersey were too big, and the scarf was itchy, but I still had time to 'grow into it'.

'You want them to lose, don't you? Your mum made you put them socks on, aye? Lauren!'

He thundered from the room, stalking after Mum in the kitchen. I remember being fearful for her as I followed him in. I never meant for her to be blamed but it seemed like she always was. Ever since he lost his job after fighting his co-worker because of some negative comments aimed at Manchester and Cristiano Ronaldo being a baby, he hasn't been the same. He lost his job … his friends … maybe soon Mum, too.

'John. I did not make him wear blue socks. Are you serious? He can wear whatever he wants, it's just a game. When are you going to get that through your head?'

'How dare you?' Time froze as the silence created webs of electricity radiating from their hateful stare. It was a tangible sort of feeling.

'We are your family, not that bloody football team. You've lost enough to them already. This is your last chance, John, or I swear to God, we're done.' Still, that feeling spread throughout the space.

'Fine. Liam, grab red socks and get in the car,' he said, abandoning the space. Dad and I didn't have much to talk about most of the time—this included the short drive to Trafford Stadium. He seemed to only like talking to me when I played football, but I couldn't play anymore because of my asthma. He said I needed to grow up.

The game was fine, but I asked to get a snack during the second half at some stage and earned a slap to the back of the head. I lost interest after that. Someone near Dad had just yelled that Manchester were losing because of how horrible Alex Ferguson was as a coach. To a die-hard Manchester supporter, someone had just killed the family dog. I could see the thoughts swirling in his head, unable to be processed effectively due to the blind fandom. The wind whipped through the stands on the right-side of the field virtually encouraging chaos to come. Almost as if something took over his body and demanded retribution for the opinions of others, he went after the man. I couldn't hear what was said, just the strong Mancunian and Scottish accents. It didn't take long before there were fists thrown to the ballad of a howling crowd.

My dad was in trouble. I lost sight of him. Adrift in the red sea.

'Dad!' I screamed, clawing my way through the crashing bodies. His rage contorted his features as his face matched the colour of his outfit. He was a big man, violently forcing his domination upon the supporters of the opposing team. It turned out the brawl had spread and now included over 30 men and 5 rows of seating, all fighting for their one true love. No matter how hard I fought, I got smaller and smaller and further and further. It felt like my lungs were an inferno where no organism could ever survive. Like trying to breath fire. Or the panic of trying to take a breath in while still screaming. A man shoved me out of the way, and I fell. Hard. Down the cold concrete steps with nothing to break my fall.

Hours later, I woke up in hospital. I remember a splitting headache and looking down to see a cast covering three-quarters of my right arm. That day Mum packed up everything we owned, and we left.

It's now been 20 years of birthday and Christmas cards because he refused to give up on his obsession. 20 years of him losing jobs, friends and loved ones because of his refusal to put anything above his team. I'm now the age he was at that game. I feel no connection to my dad. There is a void there where he should have been. Could have been. But the sting that he chose his club over me still burns like an open wound.

I reached out to him to meet on his terms with the wishes of sharing my news with him. He chose a Manchester Home game at Old Trafford Stadium—of course. That should have told me enough, but the excitement of a boy who grew up without a male figure reared his head in hope and agreed.

I arrived at the stadium and found my seats next to a middle-aged man dressed entirely in red. We were only a couple rows back from the side of the field, but the mid-January chill ensured the concrete and seats would be colder than ever.

'Hi, John.' I couldn't call him Dad. It'd been too long.

'Hi Liam.' The uncomfortable silence stretched but not with the feeling I knew him for. 'Why did you want to meet?'

'I just … It's been too long. I had a thought the other day about you and realised I'm now the age you were at our last game together. A lot has happened in the last 20 years and a lot more is to come. I wanted to give you the news myself, I'm getting ma—' I got cut off his shushing me. A whistle was blown.

'That's great, you can finish that later. The game is starting.'

Amazement and disbelief filled my thoughts about how someone can care so little about their son. My father was never a knight in shining armour, but he never even tried to be. Your own flesh and blood means nothing for a club membership.

'Are you serious?' I asked, to receive no reply other than the abuse he began screaming at the other team. Another fan shouted their disapproval of his statements back at him, along with words meant to maim a Manchester supporter. All hell unleashed around our seats. Once again, I saw my father's aged figure tower over other men, his rage turning him into an image of complete red.

As the brawl broke out in front of me, I realised I couldn't forgive someone who never asked for it or offered it. My head hung low. I stood and walked out of Old Trafford stadium for the last time.

The Colours of Passion

Charlie Delandelles

'You're not salty, are ya?' Laura asks with a big grin and a bottle of wine in hand as I open the door. Her dark leather jacket contrasts her casual red shirt and green track pants; she looks like Christmas came early.

'Pfft, you wish, elf,' I reply, laughing as I step out of the way and let her inside. As she passes me, I close the door and turn around.

The short, pale hallway, lined with abstract paintings and life sayings, paves the way to an open-style apartment. I follow Laura as she struts towards the small kitchenette on the right. On the left lies a modest living room with a worn two-seater couch, a small table beside both arms, and a cluttered rectangular coffee table in front. A TV on the wall plays a clip about the footy final, barred by a couple of national flags.

Laura's red wine clinks against the laminate benchtop as she sets it down, reaching for a couple of stemmed glasses in the top cupboard. 'Come on, we gotta celebrate!'

'Celebrate what?' I ask, but she just hums as she sets the glasses down on the countertop.

I roll my eyes. There's no way I'll get any information from her right now, not until she's ready. So, I settle against the benchtop as she starts pouring the grog.

The TV is a low mumble in the background, but when Laura's this quiet I can make out some of the report: '… protests continue after … this marks a week since—'

'Well, I didn't get champers,' she starts with an infectious grin, renewing my attention. She almost overflows her glass when she glances at me. 'Woah! That'll be mine.'

She's practically wagging her tail, I think, trying to imagine her with dog ears and a tiny nose. *But why?*

I study her as she hands me my glass, not quite as full as hers.

'What? Don't look at me like that!'

Laughing, I swirl my wine around and take a sip; it's as nice as I'd expected. I decide not to egg her on, instead asking, 'What's the occasion?'

When she grins, I brace myself. 'Why, it's a week since our victory, of course!'

Oh, of course it is. I groan, spinning on my heels. I consider escaping to the balcony paralleling the door, but decide the couch will at least be comfortable as I suffer through her gloating. 'Your victory,' is all I say, flopping onto the left side of the two-seater. My wine sloshes but doesn't spill.

'Yep!' is all she replies, settling down beside me. She glances at the TV. 'Hey, they're talking about it now!' She grabs the TV remote off the top of a stack of annotated newspapers on the coffee table and turns up the volume.

'… supporters are still scorned after their team's loss in the grand final, stating the umpiring was biased. Rallies continue to grow despite the club's insistence that their fans "go home" after concern that these protests could become a full-blown riot.'

I shake my head. 'Fuck me. What do they think protesting's gonna achieve?' I take a swig of my wine, welcoming the tang.

Laura side-eyes me. 'You're an activist! What do you mean "what do they think protesting's gonna achieve"?'

An activist? Please. 'I wasn't an activist, Laura. I went to *some* protests—'

'Some? You went to every one under the sun,' she says, leaning forward with a laugh as she picks up one of my newspapers. 'I mean, look at this! You're still critiquing every political article that pops up like some kind of reporter.'

The TV continues in the background: '… keeps going, we may well get a repeat of the September riots.'

My stomach spirals. *Shouts—red—screams—*

I snatch the paper from her grasp, throwing it onto the floor. I practically launch myself at the remote she dropped on the table, muting the TV. To my horror, my breath is as loud as my heart; I clamp down and hope to high heaven Laura hasn't noticed. 'Yeah, whatever you say.' But my heart isn't in it, not anymore.

The humoured heat in her expression fades into a pair of scrunched eyebrows. Her hazel eyes sharpen: a shark smelling blood in the water. 'Say, it's been a while since you've mentioned going to any protests. Last I heard was around a year ago.' I can't help but stiffen; I take a long sip of my wine to drown out the roar in my head. 'It was kinda mid to late year. What was it called …'

'The September riots,' I murmur against the rim of my glass, gaze flickering around the room. I find myself looking at a small cabinet pressed against the left corner of the living room, decorated with a seashell, rainbow ribbon, and a photo propped between the two. I tear my eyes away before I start studying it for the umpteenth time, eyes stinging.

'Yeah, that's it!' she exclaims, painfully unaware of the knives she's digging into my gut. 'That's the protest that

327

became a massive riot, right?' I nod once, mute as she barrels on. 'Shit, that musta been scary. I heard cars were involved. Flares, too. But I didn't hear much else, other than that loads of people died.'

It's like I'm there again, in the heart of the chaos. *Her hand squeezes mine in a vice as I pull her along, desperate to escape the screaming throng of people. Reving snaps through the chaos. More screams, bodies slapping against something big. And—*

I throw back the rest of my wine, almost spilling it down my face like rivets of blood, and set the glass on the side table with a harsh clink. I realise my right hand is gripping the couch like *her* hand that night, and I swallow the wine so I don't spit it out. 'It was carnage,' I whisper, and stand.

I feel Laura's gaze on my back as I head for the balcony. Pulling open the glass door, I step outside and shut it, glad for the cool breeze on my hot skin. Leaning against the railing, I take a deep breath, clenching and unclenching my hands around the cold metal.

She didn't mean anything by it. She doesn't know, I think, gazing into the dazzling lights of the city. Traffic rolls past, and I can hear a soft chant in the distance. *Calm the fuck down.* But my heart won't stop pounding. Won't stop shattering like it did that night when the rampaging car snatched *her* hand from mine. *Calm. Down.*

The glass door slides open and closes. I take in the flashing city lights and general noise, stiffening when Laura's arms wrap around my chest.

'I'm so sorry,' she mumbles into my shoulder blade. 'I didn't know that was how Ally …'

'I know,' I say, throat tight, and turn in her grip so I can hug her, too. My slight height advantage lets my chin knock on top of her shoulder, allowing me to press my face into her neck. Emotion takes me, much like death claiming the living, and it's a while before we separate.

Laura sniffles, wiping the tears off her face.

Despite it all, I smile. 'I haven't been to any protests since,' I say, and her smile is just shy of a grimace. 'Every time I even hear about the riots, I go right back to…' *Ally, lying on the concrete a short way from where the car flung her, red blossoming around her blonde hair. Her eyes, listless. Her mouth, agape.*

I shake myself. 'I've found talking to friends and family about my passions is more effective than any rally. Safer, too.'

The city lights only illuminate part of her face. Yet, the look she gives me is so open it makes me feel like all of me—my worries, my love, my passion—is an emotive sunset. All my qualities laid bare for her to see.

It's too much for one night.

I shift on my heels. 'Why don't we head back inside and enjoy the rest of the wine?' I move past her.

Laura's hand catches mine. When I look back, she squeezes. 'I love you—you know that?'

For the second time that night, tears prick at my eyes. I don't will them away. 'I love you, too,' I say, placing my free hand on hers.

We smile. Our bond is a myriad of colours: deep and pure. *I'm so lucky to have you in my life.*

Laura's expression morphs into a shark-like grin. 'Now, how about I gloat about my team's victory while nursing a glass of red wine, all while we have *Friends* on in the background?'

My smile widens, and my heart swells like a resounding harmony. 'Sounds **perfect**.'

Signed, Sealed, Delivered

Lorenza Palombi

Hayley stared aimlessly out the kitchen window, the dull beeps of the coffee machine making futile effort to pull her from her thoughts. Another day on autopilot, just existing in her personal bubble, waiting for something of interest to happen. Surely there was more to life than this? Finally, turning her attention to the coffee machine, that was now beeping furiously, almost screaming at her to drink the now cold coffee it had brewed. Shuffling past the angry machine, Hayley yanked its power cord out of the wall, silencing the beeps and letting the deafening hush blanket the empty house again. Moving towards the staircase to her bedroom, Hayley noticed the growing pile of mail on the floor by the door.

I'll do that tomorrow she thought to herself, just as she had every day for the last three weeks. She noticed an envelope with a red heart in the top right corner, caught in the flap of the mail slot. She tottered over to it, plucking it free. Just as she was about to drop it onto the pile of unopened mail on the floor, she spotted who it was addressed to.

'Mouse?' she whispered. What an odd name. Hayley flipped the envelope over to look for the return address, but it was blank. This letter clearly didn't belong in her possession, and whoever 'Mouse' was, was probably waiting to read whatever was in the envelope. She should probably take it to the post office. That would be the right thing to do. But that would also require her to leave the comfort and safety of her house bubble. Maybe if she just waited for the mailman to return tomorrow and she could give it back to him. Yes, that'll work, minimal effort but it'll get the envelope back to its rightful owner. Satisfied with her plan, Hayley shuffled back up the staircase and into the safety of her bed.

Perched on the steps of her staircase, Hayley's leg twitched in anxious anticipation of the mailman's arrival. She looked down at the envelope in her hands, running her thumb over the little red heart in the top right corner, Hayley felt a sudden sting in her thumb. Small red droplets slid down her thumb and onto the floor. Watching the drip for a moment, Hayley hadn't noticed she'd somehow dripped blood onto the envelope. The unmissable squeak of the mail slot opening cut through her thoughts. Springing up from the steps, she yanked open the door to see a middle-aged man in a yellow hi-vis shirt staring back at her, a little startled by her overly enthusiastic opening of the front door.

'Hi,' she blurted, thrusting the letter out in front of her. 'I got this letter by mistake. It's not addressed to me.'

The mailman stared back at her, his face softening as he gently took the letter and examined it.

'Is this not 24 Westbrook Avenue?' he asked, not looking up from the letter.

'Well, yes, but-' Hayley stammered, the dryness in her throat making it hard to speak.

'Well, that's where it's addressed to, Miss. It wasn't delivered here by mistake.' He held the letter out to Hayley. It hadn't occurred to her to check the address on the envelope.

'But that's not my name. It's not for me. You need to take it back!' she said, stepping back from the door and closer to the familiarity of her home.

'Miss, I can't take it back. This is where it's addressed to. There's nowhere else for it to go. As for the name, well, maybe it was a past tenant of the house,' the mailman said. The patience in his voice was starting to wear thin.

'Look Miss, I've got more mail to deliver. Just take the envelope. Maybe if you hang onto it for long enough, the owner will come looking for it.' He reached out, grabbing Haley's arm and forcing the envelope into her hand. She recoiled in surprise, his hand gripping her arm tightly and for longer than she was comfortable with. Yanking herself free of his grip, she darted away from the door, slamming it closed and engaging the lock. Heart palpitating, she slowly sat down on the bottom of her staircase, staring at the door. Hayley could still feel the mailman's grip on her arm, glancing down at the red marks he had left behind. This is why she preferred the comfort of her house. There were too many weirdos on the other side of the door.

Flipping the letter over in her hand, Hayley wondered what to do with it. Her finger snagged the opening of the envelope, tearing it at the corner. Shit. She couldn't open someone else's mail. That would be illegal. But the envelope was technically already ripped open, so what was the harm? Tearing the rest of the envelope open, Hayley pulled out the paper. Skimming the contents.

'I have loved you from the moment I saw you. Your beauty is captivating, and I want to spend every second of the rest of my life with you.' Hayley could practically taste the sweetness of the words. *'My heart beats only for you, we will be together until the end of time. No one will come between our great love, my sweet Mouse.'*

This guy sounded a little intense. Looking down at the sign off, it was marked with,

'Yours for eternity, AY.'

Who was 'AY'? The squeak of the mail slot opening startled Hayley. The mailman had just been this morning. Why was he back again? The almost inaudible flutter of another envelope hitting the mound of unopened mail was enough to entice Hayley. Crouching down to pick up the letter, she noticed another identical envelope underneath the pile, and another and another. All addressed in the same handwriting to 'Mouse' and all with a little red heart in the top right corner. There had to be at least 20 identical envelopes. A sinking feeling consumed Hayley. Something about this felt wrong. Ripping open envelope after envelope, the letters told the story of a man consumed by a longing for his lost love, all signed *'Yours for eternity, AY.'* But what worried Hayley the most was that every letter seemed to get more unnerving and neurotic, with declarations of his eternal love and devotion. The most recent taking it to a whole new level.

'I know one day we will be happy together; you just don't know it yet. My love for you will never die. There is no other choice for us. You are my life's work, my submissive little Mouse; soon I will be stroking your silky brown hair, and you won't live in that big empty house all by yourself. Our time is coming Mouse, I am coming for you. Yours for eternity, AY'.

The knot in Hayley's stomach tightened. Who was this creep, and why did it feel like these letters were getting personal? This couldn't be real. Hayley never left her house. Who could have possibly formed an obsession with her without ever meeting her? An abrupt knock on the door startled her. Could this day get any more insane? Creeping slowly towards the door, her heart beat furiously, shaking as she pulled down the handle and inching the door open so she could peak outside. To her shock, it was the same middle-aged mailman in the hi-vis from earlier, back for the third time that day.

'Can I help you?' she stuttered. He took a step towards her, resting his palm on the door.

'I just wanted to check on you. You seemed distraught earlier, and I couldn't go on with my day without making sure you were okay.' His voice was smooth, the words flicking off his tongue.

Hayley could feel him lean against the door, forcing her to shuffle backwards, turning the inch-wide gap into a body-sized gap. Glancing down at his hands, she noticed another envelope; it was identical to the others.

'Where did you get that?' the words leapt from her mouth, her eyes zeroing in on the little red heart on the envelope. Looking down at his own hand, the mailman smirked.

'This is for you, Mouse.' He pushed his body weight harder into the door. Every hair on her body pricked up. No. It was at that moment she noticed the black embroidery on his hi-vis shirt. Adrian Young. *AY*. The pit in her stomach felt like it was swallowing her. Panicking, she shoved her entire body weight into the door attempting to close it, but Adrian was already 10 steps ahead of her, wedging himself in the doorframe and flinging the door wide open. The sheer force flinging Hayley backwards, her hands flailing for something, anything to grab onto. This couldn't be real. A shooting pain spread down her back, her head throbbing against the wooden planks of the staircase. A tall figure loomed over her.

'Don't worry little Mouse, we're together now. You're all mine.'

Limerence

Selena Henderson

Tuesday, August 3rd, 2021

Why hasn't she replied? I send another text. Nothing. I lay awake re-counting the conversation, searching for the words that may have upset her. Should I apologise? I did, didn't I? I toss and turn until, finally, I slip into a serene oasis, a tranquil harbour and doze off. Vivid images of my mother appear in my dreams.

The alarm jolts me awake. Nerves grip at my throat as I study my inbox. Finally: *Sorry for the late reply, just been busy, might see you at the school. Estelle.* A warmth spreads over my body like the morning's first sun rays. I get Chloe—my nine-year-old daughter—ready for school. I comb her hair into a slick ponytail, making sure to get every single strand

and then, with surgical precision, cut her sandwich into four perfect triangles.

There she is. Her auburn-coloured bob dances in the light breeze, high-waisted slacks hug her hips, while her white button-up shirt reveal elegant curves underneath. My cheeks flush. She is the most captivating person I have ever met. She is my very best friend.

I wait anxiously beside the classroom door, peering in to see as she kisses her daughter on the cheek and whispers into her ear. She moves gracefully towards the door. My palms sweat and palpitations punch me in the chest as we lock eyes. I muster the courage to speak to her.

'Hi,' I manage to say, 'have you got time for a coffee?'

'I'm sorry, I don't have time today.'

'How about tomorrow?'

'I have plans tomorrow too.'

'Maybe next week? I'll text you later. Where are you going today? Are you working? Do you work every Tuesday?'

'Sorry, I've got to run.'

I watch her as she moves swiftly through the car park and drives away. I jump into my car and send a text: *It was so nice to see you today, do you want to catch up for coffee next week? Are you working today?* I wait for a reply. Nothing. I send another text:

What days do you work? I am free any day next week. I would love to see you. I miss you. I head towards home.

Wednesday, March 6th, 1986

Today is my ninth birthday. Mum comes flying in with pink and purple balloons in one hand and a cake in the other. She cranks up the stereo, grabs me by the hand and we hop onto the table. We dance to Cyndi Lauper's hit *Girls Just Want to Have Fun*. Her gorgeous red hair cradles her face as she turns me under her arm. Her touch fills my heart with joy. We dance until the moonlight kisses my cheek and then she is gone, but I don't care. I don't care at all. Today was the best day ever. Mum is my very best friend.

Tuesday, August 3rd, 2021

I drive right past my street and head to her house, hoping to catch a glimpse of her, of something, anything. Her home sits at the entrance of a quiet cul-de-sac. A basketball hoop hangs from the garage roof, a hopscotch game is chalked onto the driveway. Just how you would imagine a family home to look. I drive around the cul-de-sac slowly, taking it all in. A photograph in my mind to savour. I head home.

I check my phone. Nothing. Why doesn't she reply anymore? We used to chat all the time. Does she hate me? I send another text: *Hey, are you receiving my texts? I'm sorry if I've done something to upset you. I would really like to catch up next week when you're free.* I feel the heat creeping up my body. I'm breathless and dizzy. I look for my safe haven, my relief from the storm in my head. I peer out the window and concentrate on the birds as they fly into the leaves and become invisible. Still no reply.

Friday, March 8th, 1986

My mother lies asleep on the couch, her hair all messy, and her makeup smudged from the night before. She still looks beautiful. I gently try to wake her.

'Go away,' she says, pushing me with the palm of her hand.

'We have a school play on Monday, will you come and watch me?'

'Mmmph, go away.'

I head to my room and crawl into my makeshift fort, my sheltered harbour. I pull out my diary and write: *Mum is coming to see me perform at school. I am so happy.* 😊 *She has never been able to make it before. I can't wait.*

I hear the front door open. Mum's friends are here. They are loud for a few minutes, but then there is silence. They are gone, Mum included. No goodbye, no kiss on the cheek, nothing. I am invisible.

Monday, March 11th, 1986

I walk myself to school, wondering if she'll keep her promise to come. Of course, she will—she said she would. I reach the school gates and take a quick look around the carpark. Nothing. That's ok, there's still time. We change into our costumes and head to the hall. I see rows of parents, sitting there, their smiles radiant, beaming with pride and happiness. I take to the stage and scan the crowd, hoping to spot a familiar face. My mother didn't come. I have no-one here, watching me, cheering me on, sharing this moment with me. I am alone.

Tuesday, August 10th, 2021

A whole week has passed and still nothing. That's ok, I'm sure she is just busy orchestrating her life with harmonious precision—that takes time. I'm sure our coffee date has simply slipped her mind.

I head over to her place with chocolates, flowers and a card. She needs to know that I am here for her. I always will be: *Dear Estelle, I'm sorry life has been so busy for you lately. I hope we can find some time to catch up soon. I am always here for you, my dear friend. I miss you. Di xxx.* I leave the gift on the doorstep and head home.

I send her a text: *Hi, I popped in today, but must have missed you. I left a gift for you on the doorstep. I hope you enjoy the choccies. Catch up soon. xx.* I sit and comb through her social media profiles. I check Facebook, cute photos. I heart all of them. I head over to Instagram. Wait, what! Where is her Instagram? Maybe there is something wrong with my phone. Or her phone. I search and search again. Nothing. I go back to Facebook. It is gone. She is gone. Have I been blocked? She wouldn't do that to me. Would she? Maybe she is just having a bad day? *Or maybe, I really am invisible.*

The walls around me start to close in. My heart echoes through the chambers of my chest, as beads of sweat form

343

on my top lip. I clutch at my chest, attempting to draw in a breath amidst the suffocation. I reach for my haven, my calm in the storm—a cocktail of euphoria. With hands shaking like porcelain teacups wobbling on saucers, I unscrew the lid; 1, 2, 3, 4, 12, 20, 30 … And then I feel her. My mother, holding my hand, guiding me as the sun light kisses my cheek.

Notice Me

Bonnie Cross

It is one thing to read the poetry of the Greats.
To hear the sweet whispers of adoration they illustrated so clearly.
It is another, much greater experience to feel your whole world shift,
from the slightest glance into her eyes, and finally learn the truth,
to why you were placed upon this pitiable earth.

Shadows caress the road's edge as I dim the headlights to the lowest setting and make the final turn that leads me to you. Scanning the prehistoric building you rent, and its attached carpark, my eyes catch on your dented blue Toyota. I park just 20 metres away, hiding the van from the flickering fluorescent lights that lead into the building. Thankfully, my research pays off as I quickly locate your apartment with ease.

For an agent, you sure aren't subtle, darling. From your Instagram it was easy to locate your bedroom window two stories up. The hanging stained-glass butterfly on your windowsill that's visible in every selfie you post shifts slightly against the nights breeze, as the moon's alluring glow picks up its shades of blush pink and tulip red. I can only assume that you lay beneath them, the delicate colours highlighting the sensual curves of your body and dancing softly on your face.

The night's cold hits suddenly as I open the door and make my way to the back of the van. Knowing tomorrow will be a busy day for you, I try my best to open it silently, just a few inches at first, as I grab my plan. You would be surprised at how easy it was to gain access to the blueprints of your building—within 20 minutes I found both the originals and the latest renovation. I also managed to gain access to the building's security cameras, but don't worry, I respect your privacy. I just needed to be able to check in from time to time to monitor your safety and protect you from creeps. The blueprints, I got for us. To help you. To prove myself worthy.

Everything needs to be perfect, which is why I made sure everything was planned to a tee.

Opening the van some more, I grab the largest parcel first, carefully dragging it into place. Then the second, third, fourth, and fifth, before taking a moment to admire the sixth. Luckily, the shape has remained, I had tied it tightly within the white shroud and left it, collecting the others as I allowed the joints to fully stiffen. It is the oldest of the parcels, the most impactful, as marbled limbs protrude horizontally from the top with thick crimson ribbons twirled around each, mixing beautifully with the skin's blue and purple tones. I cautiously drag it, since it's started bloating, having been left out of the freezer for too long during my preparations. The smell is horrid, almost suffocatingly so, as the drive over gave it time to defrost. Now, the deep plum underside squelches with each movement.

It is worth it, of course, for you.

The cotton catches on each pebble imbedded in the tar below, the tiniest tears amplified by the empty space as I heave it into place. I walk back to the van and groan when I find the remaining 14, each slightly squished and turning all shades of beige.

Moving the last shroud into place, I quietly take a step back into the shadows to admire my work. It's impressive. You're going to love it. It's not the most beautiful gesture but you never were one to care about materialistic gifts, just the thought behind them. You're simple like that. You don't care about monetary value, instead you love knowing people care through the dedication and time that was taken. I see it in your eyes daily. The grins you try to hide as you lower your eyes. How your face turns a soft red over an act as simple as the office intern getting your morning coffee for you.

With part one complete, I head back toward the van and grab the disposable shopping bag off the front seat. Reaching in, I feel the velvety petals cooly brush against my fingertips. I grab the first handful ever so gently, cupping the petals as I would your face. The bright red stands out against the pale fabric as I circle each letter, leaving a tender cascade of devotion as I go. They lay around and upon the fabric parcels, a delicate yet fiercely passionate combination designed just for you.

'It's not enough,' I huff quietly, my feet shuffling me toward the van once more as I find the plastic tub needed to truly set the perfect scene. I attempt to wheel it, knowing its weight, but the wheels click frantically as I do.

Suddenly, the mood shifts. The night stills, as a window on the bottom floor casts a new light into the dark abyss. I pull the strings of my hoodie and quickly abandon the tub. I rush to the driver's seat, turning off the headlights that illuminated the scene I have created. Fumbling slightly, I manage to locate the knob just in time, as a sheer curtain draws back, and a woman's head pops up.

She looks relatively young with her hair messily shoved in a bun. She scans the parking lot, stopping in my direction for a mere second.

This is it, I think to myself.

Yet, all she does is shake her head. Like she is telling herself to get it together, claiming what she saw to be a trick of light. Still, I remain frozen. I wait for her to turn the lights out and then a few minutes more to be safe, and prove to myself that she was once again asleep. (I wouldn't want you having to clean up after any unfortunate mistake I make. Including your neighbour.)

After a while, the chorus of the night returns, and I slowly make my way back to the tub, lifting it this time to carry it the rest of the way. The tub is full of pillar candles—the cylinders of pure white, an assortment of heights, none having been burnt before. Keeping one eye on the window as I carefully begin arranging them around the letters, nestling them between the petals, lighting them carefully as I go. It's an alluring sight to see streams of white wax flowing gracefully upon the petals, creating swirls of pink.

I light the 'O' last, wanting little wax to drip within the circle, scared that it would lessen the impact of my gesture, before putting the now empty tub away.

The final aspect of this display is by far my favourite, the letter and notes I have written for you over the past three years.

I'm not stupid, I know a genius like you would find me from the slightest detail, so I was smart. The letters, although heartfelt, are not handwritten. Rather, they are printed on handmade paper stamped out in, what once was red but now brown, homemade ink.

A true work of art, almost worthy of the touch of your hands. I wanted you to be able to keep them forever, and to give you a piece of me that I have given to no other. The ink contains just one drop of my own blood, that I mixed with that from those who rest before me. I covered the smell with my favourite cologne, to protect your precious nose from the harsh scent of decay. Each letter proudly signed,

> To my dearest, the next commissioner,
> May this gesture allow you to advance
> your career and assist you in reaching
> your goals,
> Love always, M xx

Infatuated

Kristie Mack

I see myself staring back in the double-sided mirror of the interview room. Fuck, my hair is a blotchy mess. I run my fingers through it, attempting to make it neater. It feels dry and brittle. My fingers get caught in a brittle knot but as I try to get them through, a chunk of hair breaks off in my hand. I play with it in-between my fingers. I've lost track of how long I've spent in this room. Just as this thought leaves my mind the door creaks and slowly opens. I drop the chunk of hair onto the floor and place my shoe over the top.

Two officers—opposite in looks—walk into the room. The short, dark-haired rounder man sits down in the chair opposite me across the table. The tall, fair-haired woman stands near the mirror leaning against the wall. The man opens a file and places it on the desk to face me. I'm looking at a photo of myself—one I uploaded on Instagram two weeks ago—from the premiere of the movie I finished nine months ago. I was the lead love interest, and that was really all I was there for; to look pretty. I don't get hired for depth. That's what ugly and emotional actors are for! Or so they say. No one sees my true talent. How good I am at what I do. Just a pair of tits with a symmetrical face and cascading blonde hair.

'State your full name for the record,' the woman demands.

'Kennedy Early Blake.'

The officers share a look; the man giving away too much. It was a look of surprise and confusion. I wonder why.

'Do you recognise the woman in this picture?' He taps his short stubby pointer finger on the photo, right on my face, leaving a greasy smudge in its wake. How annoying, I'm tempted to wipe it clean.

'Yes? That's me.'

'Can you tell me what happened in the early hours of this morning?'

I start to recount my night, my mind going back to a few mere hours ago.

I drag my feet to avoid slipping on the red liquid coating the floor. I'm itchy where it dries on my skin. I don't know how much is mine and how much is hers. Her blonde hair is stained the colour of wine, matted and messy around the open wound. The blood stopped pouring out a while ago. The phone is buzzing in my limp hand but I can't bring myself to answer it. My mind is still stunned, frozen in shock.

I look at my bare legs, smeared with blood, covered in handprints that are not my own, mixed with the blue-purple hue of bruises. It feels alien, these colours littering my body. The more I look at them the more the pain starts seeping back in. I can now feel the scratch marks stinging. Are they from fingernails? Or are they slashes from the knife? I'm not sure. Everything happened so quickly.

I was brushing out my perfectly straight dripping wet hair, trying my best to detangle it. I felt my skin prickle and turned my head, sensing a presence behind me. But my vision went black, and now here I am, who knows how long later, covered in blood, phone in one hand, too tired to move.

'This is crazy,' I speak the words aloud as if making my tongue form the words will help me process this.

I look back at the body slumped on the floor. If I look hard enough it starts to morph into this weird, alien-shaped lump of creamy skin and dark red. My phone buzzes again and I look at the screen. It's my security guard. I probably should answer it but I don't think I could lift my arm right now. My eyes start to droop.

I'm startled awake. I glance around, trying to find the source of the noise that woke me up. I can't see anything. My eyes fall on the girl's body. She's still dead. The knife did its job. Defending myself from this intruder. The brain fog is lifting and my memories are coming back. The reflection in the mirror. The tangle of limbs and objects. The knife in my hand. The piercing of flesh and organs. My brain keeps going back to the reflection. The menial task of brushing out my hair. Admiring my eyes and the way they always looked bluer under lights. The long lashes that framed them. The light dusting of freckles on my nose and cheeks, the ones everyone wished they had. Sharp cheekbones and defined jaw, nose and chin perfectly angular.

'How did the knife get to the scene?' the woman asks. Pulling me from my memories back to the present.

'Well, it would have belonged to that poor woman, I'm assuming.'

'Poor woman? Why? Do you pity her?' the man asks.

'Oh no, I don't. I meant poor as in opposite to rich.'

'Poor? That woman wasn't poor, quite the opposite actually.'

'You don't feel bad for killing her?'

'Well, no. I mean it was self-defence.'

'Self-defence? How was it self-defence?'

I explain what happened during the attack. Once again, getting lost in the memories.

'What are you doing? Why are you doing this?'

The knife is heavy in my hand already partially covered in blood from the small slice it made. I'm on top of the blonde girl, finally getting the upper hand after being chased to the loungeroom, and then wrestling on the floor for the knife near a wall that separates the kitchen. Her hair is almost the exact shade of my own. I'm straddling her waist, one hand trapped between her body and my leg, the other holding my wrist that's holding the knife. She's struggling beneath me but I tighten my legs. I can't risk her getting free.

'Stop fighting, I've got you, give up.'

She stops. Her body stops moving. Her mouth and eyes open wide and that's when I realise that I am holding the hilt of the knife that is now protruding from the middle of her chest. She gasps one final breath and gurgles. Probably choking on her own blood. Now it could have been my imagination but I feel like I saw her eyes glaze over and that's how I know her soul had left.

'It's not self-defence when you break into the home and kill the occupant. That's murder.'

'What? I didn't break in, I live there.'

'That home belongs to Kennedy Early Blake, the actress.'

'Yeah, that's me.' Who is this idiot? Can he not see that I am Kennedy? My photo is literally sitting on the god damn table in front of him.

'No, the girl you murdered is Kennedy. You broke into her home.'

'WHAT! No, my name is Kennedy, I am Kennedy, the famous actress, I don't know who that nameless girl is.'

'That nameless girl is you and your name is Lacy Mutton. We've been to your home and have found all your photos. You've been stalking Kennedy for years. You're infatuated with her.'

'No I am not, my name is Kennedy.' I keep repeating the name Kennedy as my eyes drift back to the mirror. I see the blotches of brown peeking through the at-home bleach job I did last week. My nose isn't as sleek, neither is my jaw. I have a rounder face now. I'm turning back into Lacy. I don't want to be Lacy anymore.

'NO!' I scream and try to run, unsure of how I would get out of this room let alone how far I would get once past the door. But I'm Lacy again and unlike Kennedy, Lacy is clumsy so I trip and fall. The female officer is quick and has me pinned to the ground, her knee in the middle of my back. I feel a pair of hands on my ankles—the male officer, I assume—that's then replaced by his legs as I wriggle my body and try to kick my legs. Just to get free. I hear the clash of metal and feel the coolness on my wrists. Handcuffs. I've been caught. All because of Kennedy Blake. That dead bitch.

My Hero

Teighlor Banks

After darkness, there is always light; I wish I could have stayed there a little while longer. The pain comes through first. A pounding in my skull and an aching in my belly. *So much for morphine.* Escaping the darkness feels like pushing myself through brambles, with each step it resists and tries to pull me back. The light is uncomfortable, it burns, but I know I cannot stay in the embrace of the endless black much longer.

Blinking once, twice, three times before the light of the room comes into focus. At the foot of my bed there is a white wall covered in informational posters and smiling portraits of patients. I don't know who those patients are, but *I* certainly don't feel like smiling. Stretching out my cramped fingers beneath the coarse hospital blanket, I find a remote controller with a single large button in its centre.

'Oh, thank god,' I groan, pressing down with more force than necessary. Within moments a nurse comes floating into the room to save me. *Thank fuck!*

'Awake, are we?' he coos as he comes to my side, purple clipboard in hand and armed with a dazzling smile to put me at ease.

'Drugs. Please. Give me drugs.'

'Of course.' He places the clipboard on the bed beside me and continues to talk as he fiddles with some tubes I cannot see. 'I know you must be quite uncomfortable, but we had to make sure you could feel everything okay when you came to.'

His explanation is far from satisfactory, and it must show on my face because he bursts into laughter.

'Is this really how you treat your transplant patients?' I sneer. And then the medication hits my system. Sweet, sweet relief smoothing over my rough edges.

'Only the pretty ones,' he says with a wink before collecting his clipboard and making a quick note. 'You will be happy to know the surgery went well. Both you and your donor are recovering nicely.'

'Wait, what do you mean the donor is recovering nicely?'

'Are you still feeling a little out of it? That's ok. Your donor woke up a few hours ago. They're recovering in a room not too far from yours.'

'So, my liver came from a live donor? I thought I had to give permission for that or something. I got the call and well, it was a whirlwind going straight into surgery but I never...'

'Yes. Since your disease hadn't progressed too far, we could simply graft on a new portion for you. The liver, as you know, is a resilient thing.' His smile falters for a moment as he looks me over. 'Most livers.'

'I'm sorry, I still don't understand. Live liver donors must volunteer and be matched. We tested everyone I knew who was willing, and no one was a match.'

The nurse and I lock gazes in that moment, his green eyes full of sympathy as he reaches out to squeeze my hand.

'Sometimes, miracles really do happen,' he says with one final squeeze of my fingers before breezing out of the room as if he hadn't just upended my world.

Three weeks felt like three years as I lay in hospital, trying to needle my nurse for more information. Flowers from friends, family and co-workers came and went, withering away as my body grew stronger. When the rising sun woke me on the final day of my stay, I felt like I had been here so long I was starting to see bars on my window. The only thing on my mind today was meeting the stranger who saved my life.

'All ready to go, love?' My mum's voice calls from the doorway of my room. She waits patiently for me, a bag of my things over one shoulder, as I shuffle toward her without looking back.

'I was ready to leave two weeks ago.'

'Oh, come now, you know you needed the rest. You just had major, lifesaving surgery! I do wish you would come and stay with us for a while. You're still my baby. I want to look after you'.

'I know, mum. Thank you for driving me home but I'll be fine, I promise.' We make our way over to the nurses' station. 'You know how I feel about being cooped up.'

She gives me a knowing look and pats me on my shoulder. I lean on the edge of the desk, searching for my nurse.

'Making another escape attempt, are we?' I hear his familiar voice.

'What do you mean attempt? I'm succeeding. Even got a getaway driver this time.'

The three of us burst into laughter, though mine is quickly cut off by a stab of pain through my middle. I press a hand gingerly to the spot where my new scar is developing, under the layers of gauze and medical tape.

'I made it through my entire three weeks without going insane, so please, can I meet my donor now? You said they would be leaving tomorrow, and I don't want to miss my chance to thank them.'

'Of course.'

Such simple words for such a life-altering moment. *Of course. Living donor.* Two words can hold so much power over a moment in time. It's hard to believe they are not crafted with wishes and fairy dust.

Their room was not far from my own, only five doors had separated us this entire time. Mum takes a seat across from the nurses' station as I follow my nurse down the hall. He pulls the door open with none of the ceremony this moment deserves, simply ushering me in.

The man who saved my life stands with his back to me, unassuming in his normalcy. He is far from normal now though—he is my hero.

'I'm sorry for bothering you. I just wanted to come and thank you pers-'The speech I had been rehearsing in my mind dies on my tongue as he turns. I know this man. 'Hugh?'

Hugh. A perfectly nice guy in my sales team. We have worked together for years. *Why?*

'Hey, Lauren. I'm glad to see you doing well.' Zipping up his suitcase and adjusting his shirt, he smiles broadly, 'I was planning on visiting you again tomorrow, but Nurse Jenkins let me know you would be leaving early. So, I tried to look my best for you.'

His words made no sense. *Why? Why was he talking to me like this?* We had barely exchanged more than pleasantries in the past.

'I…' Pausing to gather myself I glance back at our shared nurse, I try again. 'I don't understand, Hugh. Why did you do this? We- we barely know each other.'

'Lauren,' the nurse interjects, shaking his head. 'How can you say that to someone you have been involved with for years? He saved your life!'

'*Involved* with?' I levelled my gaze back on Hugh. 'Is that what you told him? Is that what you told everyone!? Why, Hugh!? For the love of God, why!?'

'Lauren.' Hugh reaches out to brush his fingers along my cheek. I stumble back towards the door.

'Hugh? This is madness. We barely know each other.'

'Lauren, please. There's no need for that anymore.'

'What the *fuck* are you talking about?'

'We don't need to hide how we feel anymore, Lauren.' Hugh closes the space between us and grips my shoulders. His broad smile only makes my skin crawl. 'Now a piece of me will live inside you forever. Just how it was always meant to be.'

Don't Mess With the Fans

Dawn Brock

The woman onscreen sniffed and swiped a manicured finger beneath her expertly made-up eye.

'The threats have escalated, and I am so scared. My security team believes that it is in my best interests to cancel tomorrow's meet and greet.'

A fat tear squeezed from between her fake eyelashes and rolled down her cheek.

'I am totally devastated that we won't get to meet, but I promise that when this threat is over, we will reschedule.'

The live video broadcast from Cara Sparkle, the latest pop sensation, ended abruptly. Tina leaned back in her chair, twirling a curl of blonde hair, and stared at her phone on the desk as comments flashed on the screen. A comment by a familiar name caught her eye—it's chat time. She glanced surreptitiously around the office at her co-workers and swiped to a different app to join the exclusive group chat.

> OhSandy999: *Hi everyone. Totally devastated about the cancelled m&g. I'm also worried about Cara's health and wellbeing. Any suggestions to cheer her up?*

Again, there was a flurry of posts.

> BrightSparkle455: *I'll choreograph and record a dance to her latest hit.*
> CaliSally307: *I'll write some poetry to make her happy.*

The suggestions and comments rolled on. Gradually the chat quieted as all but two participants left.

> Mel-odrama202: *Available for FaceTime? I have news.*
> TeenyStar06: *Hang on. I'll call you in a few…*

Tina slipped her phone into her pocket and escaped the office to the quiet courtyard behind the building.

Moments later, Mel's freckled face and red hair filled the phone screen.

'Hi! Without wasting time—I've hacked into her email account and found some pretty nasty emails from one random address. Of course, I went deeper and managed to track them back to the source. I know that the sender is currently here in Sydney, and not far from her hotel. Glad she's taking this seriously, as this low-life seems dangerous,' Mel said, frowning. 'While all the warm and fuzzy ideas from the chat will be nice, they aren't going to solve the problem.'

Tina raised one eyebrow expectantly. 'I'm sure that's not all you've found.'

'Of course not! I've already stalked his social media,' Mel said with a laugh. 'According to Facebook and Instagram, he plans to meet his friends at the York Royal Hotel at six for dinner tonight, then head on to the Effig club with a few of them. I suggest that we try to make sure we have the right person, and then tip off the police so that they can deal with him.'

'I'll go to Effig and approach him there. He's probably hoping to hook up so it should be easy to get him talking, especially to a tart in a short skirt,' Tina said. 'Send me the info so that I can see what he and his friends look like.'

Mel nodded and gazed at her friend. 'Please be careful, Tina, whatever you do.'

Tina walked into the warmly-lit main bar of the York Royal Hotel at half past five. She scanned the room, taking note of the few patrons already there before she crossed to a table near the dark-wood bar and perched on a stool. From there, she had a good view over the entrance and the entire room, and she watched as more people trickled in.

It was almost six o'clock before her target finally strode through the door and headed for the table where his friends sat. As they greeted him, he surveyed the room, immediately zeroing in on Tina sitting alone. His eyes skimmed over her curvy figure clad in red and black, with black hair and dark lipstick. He smirked and murmured to one of his friends before he sauntered towards her, weaving between the sparsely occupied tables.

Tina assessed him as he approached: average build and height, only slightly taller than her—she smiled, feeling confident. She set a timer on her phone and placed it face down.

'Hi,' he said. 'I just wanted to say that if you planned to catch my eye, you've certainly done it.'

'I hadn't planned on you, specifically, but I'm not complaining.'

'Well, that makes me the lucky one.'

'My name's K—'

He pressed his finger over her lips. 'No names.'

She raised her eyebrows questioningly.

'I'm not religious,' he said and leaned close, his breath hot in her ear. 'But it's okay if you want to scream "Oh, God".'

She smiled at him while swallowing back bile. *What the f—*

Tina's phone began playing a Cara Sparkle song. He grimaced and she quickly picked it up and turned off the timer, flicking the app off as she did.

'Sorry, that was my cousin's ringtone,' she lied. 'That lets me know not to answer without careful consideration.'

He curled his top lip. 'Using that music makes sense. I can't stand that woman, up there on stage, whining about her past boyfriends and how difficult her life is. She needs to learn how to be a better girlfriend and not complain.'

There was an awkward silence while he turned away, one hand in his dark hair and breathing heavily.

Whack-job! Tina thought. 'Do you live near here?'

He took a deep breath before turning back to her and smiling. 'I'm only in Sydney for the weekend.'

'Well, I suppose we shouldn't waste any time then,' she said with a wink.

'My hotel is just around the corner,' he said, and grabbed her arm.

'Nice room.' Tina took note of the mess of clothing and other belongings strewn throughout the mundane hotel room.

'Make yourself comfortable. I'll just be a minute,' he said before closing the bathroom door.

Tina immediately moved to the desk where his laptop sat open. She wrapped her skirt hem around her finger and touched the trackpad. The screen lit up, showing a draft email to Cara Sparkle which was full of vicious abuse and threats.

'What are you doing?'

Tina jumped and backed away as he stomped towards her. He glanced at the laptop as he passed the desk, then focused back on her with a frown.

'What? Don't you like the love letters that I'm writing to that woman?'

He lunged forward and grabbed Tina by the upper arm. 'No need to be jealous,' he said as he squeezed her bicep.

He wrapped his other arm around her and grasped her hair, tugging the pins that held her black wig in place and making her wince. He twisted his fingers within the strands and pulled her head backwards as he leaned over her.

'She's a whore. Just like you're a whore, and all you women! Whores!' he snarled. 'Dressing in next to nothing and manipulating men into doing what you want, then throwing them away like garbage. But no, not me. You'll do what *I* want.'

Tina reached behind her back, trying to grasp the small stiletto that was hidden in her top. She managed to loosen the catch on the small pocket, but he pulled his own knife on her. Instinctively, she grabbed his wrist and twisted, pushing it away from her body and back towards him. The blade sliced upward into his belly, he jerked, then collapsed to the floor. She staggered back from him and looked down at where he lay with the dagger lodged up under his ribs, his fingers clasped around the handle.

He glared at her, ignoring the wig which was still clutched in his left hand.

'What … why …'

'You know why, you fucker,' she said, drawing deep breaths.

She ripped her wig from his hand and wagged it at him as she spoke, her hoarse voice gradually rising in pitch. 'Arsehole! What did you expect when you threatened someone like Cara Sparkle? You've upset all her fans … fans like me. Did you think that you could be such a condescending, misogynistic … *arsehole*, and get away with it? You made this job soooo easy to do—not a flinch, not a moment of doubt. This was a real pleasure!'

He twitched and coughed.

'Will you hurry up and die already? I'd like to get cleaned up and leave—geez, I have so much to do and so little time.' She nudged him with her toe. 'Are you done?'

She pulled latex gloves and a folded plastic bag from a pocket in her skirt and placed the wig inside the bag. She washed up in the small bathroom, checking her clothes for bloodstains. Wearing the gloves, she scoured the room for any sign of her presence and eliminated it, including strands of her wig from his fingers. She picked up his phone and held it to his lifeless face, then found his music app to select a playlist for Cara Sparkle. With a smile, she set it on shuffle and left the room, heading for Effig to wait for the man who would never show up.

No Tengan Miedo. *Be Not Afraid.*

Rayne Wilson

"Behold, the day of the LORD comes, cruel, with wrath and fierce anger, to make the land a desolation and to destroy its sinners from it."

— Isaiah 13:9

Borne from the cinders of the planets burnt crust we are shaped anew.

Él se eleva.
He rises.

The sky buzzes with the static of a dead channel, grey and glitching beyond the cathedrals broken façade. It hums just like everything below the Ether, a constant noise like the drone of flies. Curious how flies have survived when most else perished from Earth.

The boy rests his head on the ledge, his pale face raised to the crumbling canopy of cracked stone and rotting timber.

His jade eyes don't twitch as shiny black beetles swarm over his pupils. He does not see the miasma of neon light through the dust warped windows. In his faith he has found the beauty of submission.

The flesh of his eye squelches as he drives a blade deep within his skull.

Whispered prayers echo through the ancient hall. Chains chime like bells as they brush amongst the bodies of the congregation. Screams of delight dance on clouds of ceremonial incense as our followers succumb to the bliss of true faith.

A pale hand stretches from below, nails broken and bleeding. It reaches out, searching for reassurance the congregation will save them as they are dragged down to their salvation. Their screams echo the loudest.

I grab my whip from the wall, dried blood clings to the strands of leather from yesterday's prayer and sink to my knees before the altar.

'Beloved seguidores!'

'Beloved followers!'

I beg for their attention. 'In a world glittering with potential and crumbling under the weight of neglect, we float above the wasteland of our forefathers.'

CRACK.

'We suck in the fumes of death! Our masks of artificial health dig into the hollows of our cheeks and force their recycled air down our throats, forcing our compliance, our gratitude as we claw our way into the gaping maw of servitude. We raise our beaten faces to the heavens, only to be shoved down. Their manicured nails pierce the soft flesh of our necks as they choke the life from our bodies.'

CRACK.

'The new God was borne from the chaos of destruction. He was borne of misery, death and the ultimate truth behind infinity. The molecules forming our lives are as meaningful as the grains of sand crashing together in the tumbling oceans far below us; worthless. We will be consumed by the force of His waves and His currents shall break us to His will.'

'Anciano Malphas ...'

'Elder Malphas ...'

Seguidor Darmont pauses at the bottom of the dais. 'I am sorry to interrupt ... Maria is not progressing as you would like.'

'I see. Take me to her.'

I descend the dais as he moves towards the stairwell leading down to the cathedral's conversion clinic. As we descend into our holiest sanctum, I note the claw marks lined with traces of dried blood embedded within the pale wood of the stairs. I admit not all come willingly to the faith, however, the bliss of His glory is realised in darkness and felt in the burn of endless agony.

As we enter the clinic my whip caresses the low ceiling before cracking against my wet flesh. My senses are flooded with the smell of sterility and the bliss of His presence washes over me. It burns in the marrow of my bones. The fluorescent lights buzz and metal groans down the hall as Seguidor Darmont sweeps open Maria's door. Before I breach the small room, I am greeted by the high-pitched whine of the child's begging and the acidic smell of piss and vomit.

'Please, please, please. Let me go! I've been so good. ¡Por favor favor! I beg for mercy, please!' Her words are muffled by the gag in her mouth and drool slides down her chin. Exquisite. The chains binding her to the wall rattle as she shakes her head. Her small frame thrashing against her straight jacket.

'Now, now, Maria,' I chide her. 'Let us try another lesson, shall we? "Satanás, el Dios de este mundo, ha cegado la mente de los que no creen. Son incapaces de ver la gloriosa luz de la Buena Noticia. No entienden este mensaje acerca de la gloria de … Dios." – 2 Conitios 4:4.'

"In their case the god of this world has blinded the minds of the unbelievers, to keep them from seeing the light of the gospel of the glory of … God."
— *2 Corinthians 4:4.'*

The last edge of defiance shines in her eyes. 'No?'

CRACK.

She whimpers at the noise, flinching away from my penitence, petrified of the pain I willingly submit to.

'Oh, my sweet, be not afraid of my ministrations. No tengas miedo. Soon you shall bear our marks of your own volition. But for now, I shall ease your worry. Seguidor Darmont!' I hold out my whip. 'Would you kindly take my family and bathe them whilst I talk with our dearest Maria?' Her name caresses my tongue, rolling with euphoric sweetness over every sacred syllable as Seguidor Darmont graciously removes my whip from my grasp.

'Family?' Her tone stops Seguidor Darmont from leaving.

'Sí, mi familia.

'Yes, my family.

'You remind me of my own daughter, Maria. She had skin just like yours, see?' I reclaim my whip and hold it out for her inspection. 'Though it has now been anointed by my blood, I can still feel her warmth radiating through my soul as I conduct my prayers with her body.'

'You made your whip from the skin of your daughter?' She quickly turns and vomits in the corner.

'No, not just my daughter. My whole family. It was how I proved my devotion to God. As such He rewards me greatly.' I smile at the memory.

'Por favor. This is madness,' Maria whimpers.

'Silence, child!'

We embrace the chill of the room as blood drips down my exposed ribcage and pools on the floor.

'Seguidor Darmont,' I say. 'My whip.' He shuffles forward, accepts my family, and leaves the room.

Maria's steady tears cleave lines along her dirt smeared cheeks, the light beyond the door shines bright within each track of her damp solitude. Her filth has clearly not dissuaded her from the delusions of the old god. We must try something else.

I move to caress the shallow planes of her face. She flinches and huddles deeper into the corner.

'No tengas miedo. Te amamos, y Dios te ama, cariño mío. Su oscuridad calamará tu dolor.'

'Be not afraid. We love you and God loves you, my darling. His darkness will ease your pain.'

Stepping closer, I sweep a long line across her face. Blood pearls along the thin cut I make with my nail. 'You need not hold on to your suffering. Offer it to Him and it will serve His glory. These sacrilegious passages of old hold truth. They speak of the destruction and creation of worlds and how we so easily lose sight of the true path of God.' The tears rolling down her face come faster and turn into wails of disgust.

'I see you are not ready, my dear, but you will be soon … Seguidora Katris! Would you come here for a moment?' Seguidora Katris's frame fills the doorway. 'I believe darling Maria needs a breath of fresh air. The recycled oxygen seems to be making her quite unwell.'

'NO, PLEASE NOT THE AIR!' Maria's chains rattle and clang louder with every step I take towards the door. Her wails break into a scream that rips her throat raw.

'Of course, Anciano Malphas.' Seguidora Katris's soft voice is almost drowned by the terror within Maria's plea for release.

'Make sure she doesn't sleep. He will contact her soon.'

'Of course, Anciano Malphas.'

Amongst the rattling of chains and muffled screams of the clinic I sense a throbbing pocket of silence. It stretches beyond the open door of room 237, beckoning like a siren's song. I feel His talons sink into the weeping slabs of flesh that once was my back and push against my spine. Within this silence … I find a man. His image is one of an angel consumed in prayer, arms stretched to the sky, shackled to the ceiling. With the skin of his back peeled away, his ribs shattered to reveal pulsating lungs. The flesh is pinned to wooden posts like decomposing wings, heralding the blossoming of true faith.

'Beautiful,' I utter, unleashing a gasp. The man raises his head at my presence. 'My apologies for interrupting your prayer, child, but I find myself enthralled by your figure. May I ask, who composed such art?'

'I begged Seguidora Katris, Anciano Malphas.' His voice is raw and breaks with each word.

I wander closer to probe his wound. He does not flinch as I tug on the tendons which have been torn away from his shoulder blades. The edges of his wings bear the signs of mould as his blood feeds the bouquet of fungus growing along his spine. The purification has begun.

'I see.' Muttering to myself, I circle the man thrice before stopping to inspect his face. 'You have progressed much faster than I anticipated, child …

'Serás profesor.'
'You will be a teacher.'

ROT

J.L. Benkendorff

Stepping inside the motel lobby was like climbing inside a hot leather sack; humid air pressed down on James, making a bead of sweat trickle down his temple. 'Hello?' he called as he tentatively approached the vacant service desk. 'Is anyone here?'

Silence.

Setting his duffel down, James rang the bell beside a plastic pamphlet display and turned to survey his surroundings. Aside from the service desk, there were a few upholstered chairs lining the wall like in a doctor's surgery, their fabric stained and fraying. A flatscreen was mounted in the far corner, the garbled laughter of some '90s sitcom harmonising with the hum of the heater. The stale stench of incense and outdated wallpaper, which was pocked with mould and peeling from the walls like strips of lacerated flesh, reminded James of Thorngrave. Although, according to a news broadcast he'd managed to glimpse at a gas station a few days ago, all that remained of the orphanage—his home for the past sixteen years—was cinders, the building's foundations poking up from the earth like the bones of an ancient beast.

'Hellooo!' a voice sang, catching James off guard. It belonged to a plump woman with curly black hair and almond skin. 'Sorry for keeping you waiting, love,' she said, striding over to the service desk. 'I wasn't expecting guests at this hour. What can I help you with?'

'I'd like to book a room for the night.'

The woman began typing away at the computer, keyboard clacking; James winced at the sound. For a while, he had almost forgotten about the stitches in his abdomen and the tenderness at the base of his skull. But nothing, not even days spent on open road, travelling from town to town in fear of being recognised by police and civilians alike, could erase the memories of Thorngrave. Of the kids wrenching him from his bed and marching him into the orphanage's run-down church. Even now, he could still see the rich floral arrangements winding up the pillars and trailing from the ceiling, the altar engulfed in an explosion of white lilies and baby's breath; see Father Michael, face basked in candlelight, walking down the aisle, relishing the demands to *release Him from his mortal flesh!* See himself stumbling through woods, a column of smoke rising from the inferno behind him while he clutched his stomach, keeping his intestines from spilling out.

James squeezed his eyes shut. *You're fine*, he reassured. *You're safe here. No one can hurt you. No one can hurt you. No one can—*

'Single or double?'

James blinked. The woman stared at him, the computer screen casting a kaleidoscope of silvery light across her face. 'Sorry, what did you say?' he asked.

'Would you like a single or double? We've got plenty of both rooms available. Of course, the double will cost more—'

'Single,' James answered, sliding a few crumpled notes across the desk: the last of the money he'd found in the glovebox of the car he'd stolen. 'I'd like a single, thank you.'

A frown. 'Aren't you a little young to be on your own? Where are your parents?'

James's heart lurched, but his face remained impassive, a trick he'd learned to avoid Anya Thorngrave's wrath whenever he snuck out of the dorms at night to explore the woods—something he had come to regret doing. 'I've been on my own for some time now.'

Truthfully, he had only been alone for four days, but it might as well have been an eternity.

'Oh, I'm sorry. I just assumed …' The woman retrieved a small object from under the desk. It was a key, the brass smooth from years of use. When James made no move to take it, she pried his furled hand open and pressed the key into his palm. The cold kiss of metal soothed his scorching skin. 'You're on the second floor,' she said, offering him a small smile.

James had seen that look before, knew all too well what the glimmer in her eyes meant. The thought made something inside him curdle, threatening to ferment his expression.

If anyone deserved to be pitied, it wasn't James. Not after what he'd done, the lives he'd destroyed, the people he'd killed by knocking over those candles in his escape …

'Enjoy your stay, love,' the woman added, patting his hand. 'And take care of yourself, ok? This world, as beautiful as it may be, can be especially cruel at times.'

If only she knew.

James curled his fingers around the key, relishing the feel of its teeth biting into his skin. Not trusting himself to speak, he nodded and turned to retrieve his duffle …

But the woman gripped his wrist. Her pupils, he noticed, were black pools, her breath stinking of rotting wood and honey. Panic trilled through James.

It was happening again.

'Let go,' he urged, struggling against the woman's grasp.

'I-I can't.'

'Please,' James tried again, desperation tinging his voice. *I don't want to hurt you.*

She shook her head. 'I don't know what's happening. I can't … I can't m-move my—my—my—mmmmm—' The woman's voice shuddered and broke, spiralling into gibberish.

Unable to pull away, James watched helplessly as whatever rot dwelled inside him, whatever ancient power he'd stumbled across in the woods, seeped into the woman, changing her. Carrion flowers sprouted from her eyeballs, root systems spreading and multiplying in a red-black latticework across her temples. Vines slithered out from blackened fingernails, coiling around her arms and wrists like barbed wire, while fissures weeping ants and amber liquid opened along her face. A foul stench undercut with a cloying sweetness exploded throughout the room. Bile flooded James's mouth.

For a moment, he said nothing, his heart a furious drum.

'Ma'am?' he finally murmured, voice strangled as if he were choking on the guilt and shame gathering in his heart. 'Can you hear me?'

The woman's head lolled towards James. 'He sent you, didn't he?' she cooed, releasing a cloud of sugary breath into his face. 'The Angel?'

No … No, no, no. Not again. Please …

'You're mistaken,' said James, ignoring the tremor in his voice. Her euphoric expression reminded him of Father Michael, of the way he'd followed James that night and found the younger cowering, naked and covered in insects, beside what James could only describe as a crack in the world—a place frozen between life and death. Of the way Father Michael rushed to his side, only to freeze as soon he touched James's clammy skin, necklaces of saliva sagging from his mouth: a sign he was infected with the heady power that'd latched itself onto James. That'd quickly spread to the rest of Thorngrave, destroying the only home James had ever known. 'No one sent me.'

'H-He did—He did!' the woman cried. 'He sent you here to save us all!' At the corner of her mouth, something unfurled from a ruptured pustule. Tiny legs. Shellacked black body.

A beetle.

James watched as it crawled out of the wound and into the anaemic white flowers growing from the softening remains of her eyeballs. 'O-Or maybe,' she continued, 'maybe you are but a mere vessel. Yes! A vessel! Yes, yes, yes. He meant for us to release him, free him from his mortal binds! I must free the Angel … shed his human form. Free the Angel—I must cut—mortal flesh—Angel—!' The woman began rummaging through the service desk, batting aside stationery and stacks of paper in her haste. An image of Anya Thorngrave, dagger in hand, appeared in James's mind. He shut his eyes, fighting against the sob building in his chest.

If only he'd never discovered that place in the woods. Never snuck out that night. James would still be at Thorngrave, sleeping in the dorm he shared with fifteen other kids, eating stale bread and stew every night, and soaking up the sun in the rose garden instead of doing his chores, a book resting open on his face. Not living in fear of infecting people, just as he had this woman, or wanted for the murder of the only family he'd ever known.

Even now, he could hear them calling to him from the ashy remains of Thorngrave: *You did this. It's all your fault. Look at us. Look at—!*

'I'm sorry,' James whispered before pressing his lips against the woman's mouth. It was a soft, fairy tale kiss, one made gruesome by the blood and puss on her lips. She shuddered under his touch and then … stopped, limbs going boneless. Just like when James kissed Father Michael that night in the church, corruption began spreading through the woman's body, fissures widening, vines coiling tighter and tighter and tighter—

Until she burst, leaving behind a writhing mass of flesh, rot, and carrion flowers.

I'm sorry. Tears slipped down James's cheeks. *I'm so, so sorry.*

Slipping into the parking lot, he threw himself into the driver's seat and, with the woman's blood coating his hands, disappeared into the night.

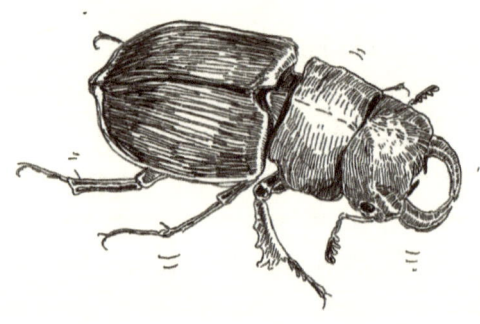

Setting Moon

Kaide Voltz

I wake to the sound of banging at my door. I think, *It's 7am on a Saturday for God's sake, what could be so important?* Grumbling, I stomp to the front door and pull it open to be greeted by a very enthusiastic delivery driver.

He hands me an envelope. 'Here you go! Have a good day!' He walks back down my front steps before I can even say a word.

I shut the door, feeling very confused, and examine the envelope. There's no postal stamp or return address. Curiosity gets the better of me and I tear it open to find a ticket and a letter.

Congratulations Della Albright!

You are one of the major prize winners of this year's Snapshot competition!

Details below for your all-expenses paid trip to Setting Moon.

I look at the letter in shock. I never entered a competition, I don't think. And Setting Moon? That's an exclusive campground, fenced off from the public for preservation in one of the most picturesque settings in the country. I look at the ticket and it's indeed my name on it. And the date of entry is today! My heart pounds. I quickly pack a bag with everything I need for a weekend away and rush out the door.

As I get in my car, I wonder who could have entered me into the competition. I decide to call the number on the letter to find out more information.

Talking with a representative, I learn that the competition was open to anyone who had taken a photo in the last year and submitted it online. Someone had submitted one of my photos without my knowledge. Though I'm sceptical about the whole thing, I can't resist the opportunity to visit Setting Moon.

As I drive towards the exclusive campground, I can't help but notice how remote the area is. The road leading up to it is winding and narrow, with thick trees lining the sides. It's a beautiful drive, but also unnerving.

I finally pull up to the campgrounds and am greeted by a small group of people who are also winners of the competition. People I assume are staff usher us to our individual cabins and I'm handed my schedule of the weekend's events.

The first event is a photography workshop where we learn from some of the best photographers in the industry. They teach us about lighting, angles and composition. After the workshop, we're given free time to explore the campground and take pictures. It's then that I realise there's something strange about this place. The other winners all know each other, as if they're all good friends from before. The events are all silent, so how would they know each other so well, so quickly?

I shake off the weird feeling and go to take some pictures around the lake.

As I approach, I am greeted by a woman. She's beautiful and tall and introduces herself as the camp mother. She smiles warmly at me and invites me to sit with her by the lakeside. I oblige and she talks about how much she's been looking forward to meeting me. *Wow, she's very direct,* I think but brush it off as her just being friendly.

As we chat, I notice how intently she's staring at me. It makes me uncomfortable, but I don't want to be rude and break off the conversation.

Soon enough, the sun sets and the camp mother bids me goodnight, promising to see me at breakfast the next day.

I spend the night in my cabin, feeling uneasy about the whole experience. Something about the camp mother doesn't feel right to me.

The next day, we all gather for breakfast, and once again the camp mother is there, smiling at me and welcoming me with open arms. This time I can't ignore the nagging feeling of doom in the back of my mind, especially as it feels like she hugs me too tight and too long. I watch her as she moves about the room, talking to each of us individually, but keeping her focus on me. It's like she's studying me. Trying to figure me out. I can't help but feel like I'm being watched, even when she's not looking directly at me.

As the day progresses, the camp mother's behaviour becomes more and more concerning.

She seems to be everywhere I go, always within earshot or just out of sight. It's like I'm being followed and I can feel her eyes on me, even when I can't see her.

I try to stay with the other winners as much as possible, but they all seem to be in on it, like they're all part of some secret club. They all brush me off and they whisper when I get in earshot. I feel like they are staring at me as well. I start feeling like I'm trapped in a horror movie, and I'm the unwitting victim. But despite my growing paranoia, I can't resist the allure of the camp. The serene lake, the lush forests and the cool breeze are all too tempting to resist. So I force myself to push aside my worries and immerse myself in the activities of the day, despite my brain screaming at me to leave.

As the days go by, I feel like I'm slowly losing my grip on reality. The constant surveillance, the strange behaviour of the other winners, and the inexplicable occurrences around camp all add up to create a sense of dread that I can't shake. But no matter how hard I try to convince myself it's all in my head, the growing fear in the pit of my stomach refused to go away. For a moment I contemplate just going. Grabbing my things, getting in my car and just leaving, but I just can't seem to take the action. Like something is warning me that I am be in danger if I leave.

On the last night of the camp, after the long day of activities, we all gather around the bonfire for a celebration. A few of the other winners are not present, so I ask the camp mother where they've gone.

'Oh, they left early,' she says flippantly.

Strange. 'Oh, but they seemed really excited about the party? Seems odd that they would go without saying goodbye?' I say, watching the camp mother's face.

The camp mother stares me with a strange intensity, and I get an overwhelming feeling that something is very wrong.

I walk away when she busies herself, after realising she is staring and trying to make small talk with the other winners that have stayed, but they all seem distant and evasive. It's like they're hiding something from me, and I can't figure out what.

At the end of the evening, I return to my bunk to make sure I have packed all my things when I hear the door slam behind me. I spin around to look and see the camp mother. She's smiling at me. She steps forward. Her smile is not friendly, it's cold and calculating like that of a predator sizing up its prey. I take a step back, and she steps forward again, closing the gap between us. Panic sets in. I try to run but she grabs hold of my arm with a painfully tight grip.

'Where do you think you're going, dear?' she whispers in my ear. I struggle against her hold, but she only tightens her grip. 'You're not going anywhere.' Her voice is growing more menacing. 'You belong here now, and you'll do exactly as I say.'

I try to scream but she covers my mouth with a faintly sweet-smelling, wet cloth.

'Don't worry, dear,' she says in a sickly-sweet tone. 'You'll never want to leave, soon.'

She drags me towards the door, and I feel myself starting to sweat and shake. My throat tries to squeeze out a scream but there's no sound. *This can't be happening. It can't be real.* But as I'm passing out, I know it is. I know that I'm trapped.

When I wake, I'm in a room filled with photos plastered all over the walls, and I realise they are all photos of me. With growing horror, I think that this woman must be a stalker.

Camp mother walks through the door with a smile that makes my stomach flip in fear. Definitely a stalker.

'Finally awake? Good, you need to take your medicine.'

Another person walks in and I nearly vomit. It's the delivery driver who handed me the envelope saying I won the competition.

And I finally understand. The others didn't leave. And neither will I.

Colourless

Deaghlan Kealey

Clarice Hemmingway awoke at sunrise like clockwork. She dressed in her burgundy formal suit, finished the final chapter of her book with a nice coffee, and began—as always—by opening the many windows of the Blatherskite manor's many rooms; letting the big house breathe in the new day. Then, after cooking a lovely platter of eggs and crispy bacon, she ferried the feast up the twin staircase to the mayor's bedroom. The gears of her routine jammed as she rounded the last flank.

His door was open.

She could see the bed strewn with stray quilts and pillows from where she stood. He was never up before her …

Clarice, careful to not stain her suit with bacon grease, strode the last length and moseyed down the hall to the mayor's office. The door creaked open as her knuckles rapped against the dark wood.

All at once the breakfast crashed to the floor, mixing with a maze of crimson streaks strewn across the polished wood.

Her screams blared through the many windows in her sprint back through the house, for kind Mr. Blatherskite hung from his office wall—a band of bronze on his brow and magnificent red wings painted beside him.

*   *   *

Detective inspector Carmichael blinked his way back to reality and folded the *Hershley Times* into four even quarters before placing it on the table. His coffee had gone cold in the black paper cup, a pool of tourmaline liquid seeping from the cheap material's base. Rain tapped on the window beside him, pecking at his drowsy senses. He watched as the water bled gold pinpricks of lamp light into tiny swirls on the dark glass. Carmichael stretched in the red leather booth seat. The diner was empty. Behind the counter the red clock showed 7:37.

'Three hours,' he mumbled. 'How'd that happen?'

Rubbing his eyes, the detective brushed pie crumbs from his grey suit-pants and re-fastened the buttons on his long sleeves—folding them three equal lengths back up to his elbow. He raked his grey coat from the bright booth, ruffling his salt and pepper hair before adjusting his dusty grey hat—stretching again as he stood up. He was a tall man, slim for his age, too—something *she* would have been proud of. The detective drew in a deep breath, ignoring the sliver of ice in his heart. As he slipped on the coat, he fished out a handful of coins from one of its many pockets, piling them on the table beside his perfectly folded paper.

'Thanks, Melanie,' he said quietly, knowing full well the young waitress had flipped the sign on the door to closed and left some time ago. 'Coffee needs a little work, though ...'

The words drifted away, unimportant. What had he seen just now? He rubbed his prickly chin with his cold hand, eyes scouring the table, the paper, the folded back page. He nudged the crease over, half the paper slapping into the pool of cold black sludge. The words revealed themselves like parting theatre curtains.

Hershley's Angel Maker back from hell

Mayor Blatherskite has been found massacred in his home by authorities earlier this morning in what officials are calling the return of the notorious 'Angel Maker'.

Detective Carmichael leaned over the now messy article, veins bulging across his pale hands as he gripped the table. Coffee stains swallowed the words as he tried to read more. How could they leave him out of this? He should have been the first to know! Damn Parker, like hell they knew what was best for him. His heartbeat drummed in his ears, every deafening pulse pushing him closer to an edge he could feel building inside him. He closed his eyes.

'One,' he whispered, taking a shuddered breath and standing up straight. He could see her pale face, the shape of her nose, her smile, those faded grey eyes like twin moons. The drumming slowed.

'Two.' He watched her dance in the blackness of his mind's eye, her ethereal movements delicate and slowed— arms flowing like wing beats. He gently unruffled his coat sleeves, feeling out the creases. Next, he re-folded his shirt collar, tracing the sharp fold with his long middle fingers, watching as she glided in black silence.

'Three …' She was right before him now; he could almost feel her cold hands holding his face. She mouthed something to him, her silent words a blessed memory.

Find me, my love.

He opened his eyes. The diner still empty. The banging in his chest was slow again. He needed to see the body for himself. If his Angel was back, then retirement would have to wait.

Carmichael pulled his coat tight and held his hat down as he stepped onto the street. The rain soaked him in the short distance to his sleek black car. He slammed the door behind him, flicking the lock and shaking out his hat. He tugged off his wet coat and folded it neatly with his hat on the passenger seat. The mayor's house was a ten-minute drive.

With no traffic, he could be there in seven.

The detective fiddled with a small holster hidden at his side, producing a sleek silver wand. It was an older model, only two glyphs etched into its black and brown Hawthorne handle, an antique to the police force nowadays—but just as powerful. He tapped it twice against the steering wheel and the car rumbled to life, the broad beam of the headlights suddenly piercing the rain-misted street. He brought the wand to his mouth and tapped one of the glyphs.

'Destination: Blatherskite residence. Sanction: official practice. Speed: special access,' he said, speaking into the silver wand. The Detective then deftly traced a symbol in the air. The car revved loudly in response, jerking out onto the street before shooting forward into the rainy dark.

The car pulled up and swiftly parked along the street out front of Blatherskite Manor, an impressive two-storey brick building surrounded by a sprawling wrought iron fence. From his car, he could see lights gleaming through the rain from the second story windows. One officer, dressed in their crisp green and silver uniform, stood before the doorway—his wand out, an umbrella of faint blue energy keeping him dry in the dark and damp street. Carmichael couldn't see Parker, but he knew they'd still be inside somewhere—this was the *Angel Maker* after all. He put on his coat and hat and slammed the door behind him.

The officer looked his way at the noise, squaring his shoulders as the detective strode toward him from the darkness. The detective kept his hands in his pockets, wand tucked in his right sleeve.

'Detective Inspector,' said the officer. 'The situation is being handled by our best, sir.'

This one was a younger man, mid-twenties by the chin scruff and too-sure voice. He knew his type immediately: all training and no field work. He stared at the young officer and smirked.

'It can't be, son,' he said, rain dripping from his soaked hat. 'I only just arrived.'

The young officer gripped his wand ever so tighter, brushing a faint blue glyph on his wand. He wouldn't have to wait long.

'I'm afraid this area is off limits to the public, Mr. Carmichael,' said the young officer. 'You can be right on your way now.'

One. The detective looked down, hiding the twitch in his smile beneath his wet hat. The drumming crept back into his ears as his fingers tightened around the wand in his pocket. Her pale face flashed behind his eyes.

Two. He met the young officer's eyes again and smiled, gritting his teeth. She flew higher against the inky dark with every violent pulse. He swallowed his next words as the door behind the young officer yawned open, washing the space in a sliver of yellow light. The silhouette of a tall figure divided the light of the doorway, like a slit pupil in a great yellow eye.

Three. The drumming faded, and his grip relaxed.

'He, Officer Cayde, is not public,' said the figure, stepping out from the doorway. They gave a nod and beckoned the detective inside.

'Thank you, Parker,' said Carmichael, stepping past the red-faced officer Cayde into the well-furnished foyer. Parker, dressed in their juniper-green suit and officer cap, closed the door behind them—a polite smile fading on their wrinkled face.

The foyer was an open and well-lit space with tiled orange floors and dark wooden walls. A split set of heavy wooden stairs lay ahead, a crystal chandelier lighting the carpeted landing between them. Twin halls either side of the room lay dark, closed doors hiding in their shadows.

'Why didn't you commune with me, Parker? I should have been the first to know,' said Carmichael, swiftly tucking his wand back in its holster.

'Didn't want to ruin your retirement party, Detective,' said Parker, folding their hands behind their back. 'Hoped you'd trust us to sort this one.'

Carmichael looked back at Parker, streaks of water pattering onto the cold tile around the detective. In the foyer's splendour, Carmichael stood as a streak of ash. He stalked slowly back towards Parker, his damp footfalls echoing in the large space. He stopped face-to-face with them and carefully dropped his heavy coat from his shoulders, draping it neatly onto a rack beside the door.

'Show me,' said the detective.

Parker's face was stoic, experience etched in their wrinkles and scars. For a long moment they stared right back at Carmichael, their eyes pleading, before a sigh broke the silence.

'Follow me.'

Parker led him upstairs to the mayor's office. The drumbeat erupted once more; he knew it was her instantly. The mayor's body had been moved off site, but the bloodied metal stakes that had pinned him to the dark wood wall lay in evidence bags on his heavy oak desk. A simple bronze circlet lay beside them, its elysian surface reflecting wild eyes. He didn't need to see the photos, didn't need to look at the report in Parker's hands.

The world drained away beneath the beating. Not of drums, but of wings. He'd followed her career closely; watched her grow with every file, every call-out, every breakthrough.

She was back. His angel was back.

He couldn't help but smile.

Blue Fountain Pen

Lauren Pitt

The semi-detached house had its garage wide open. A table of trinkets was centred in the driveway, a garment rail bursting with clothes to the right and old gardening equipment to the left. A scribbled sign read: 'Garage Sale. Deceased Estate. All Must Go.'

An old woman was haggling with the man behind the table over a blue teapot. A young mother and her toddler were admiring a knitted rabbit. I wasn't going to stop. I continued along the path without hesitation. We were going to the beach. It was sunny for the first time in weeks and my arms felt hot with the glow.

It was Peggy who was interested. She made a beeline for the driveway and sniffed at the cardboard boxes under the table until she stopped and snorted at one labelled: 'Dog Toys.'

While Peggy chose a strange, discoloured chicken, I fumbled through a box of thick paperbacks. Most were old, yellowed and torn; mainly tattered romance novels with questionable covers.

It was here that I found it. A small, weathered paperback flattened under a heavy short story collection. The cover was a musty sulphur colour, and the edges were creased, but it was the title that alerted me: *The Killer in the Glass*.

I opened the cover to read the copyright page but instead landed on the title, where written messily in blue fountain pen were the words: *And so the case begins …*

It made me chuckle; this odd, patchy, scribbled writing, written so hastily under the book's title. I turned the page:

'Chapter One: Glass shattered, shards skidding across the floor …'

This sentence was underlined, an arrow drawn to the margin where the blue fountain pen had written, *I guess that's the end of the killer!*

I flicked through the rest of the book. Blue ink marked every page, underlining quotes, writing quips in the margins.

I was intrigued. I liked to read, but reading was solitary. I had no friends or a book club to share my hobby with, no one to discuss favourite novels or authors. But this person—existing only in their blue scribbles—had a shared interest. And it was the blue writing inside—not the title or the cover—that made me choose this particular book.

I carried that book with me everywhere. Read short lines while in queues, long chapters on the bus. And on every page, Blue Fountain Pen had something to say. The margins screamed, *Codswallop!* and whispered, *Utter drivel.* Descriptions were underlined and labelled, *Beautiful.* Quotes were highlighted in faded blue and marked, *Save for later.*

The title's all wrong, Blue Fountain Pen wrote on the second page. *The murderer kills their victims with glass. They're not in the glass. Who vetted this?*

It was like reading a diary. Their personality infused into the fevered handwriting. Questions, thoughts and comments scribbled between the margins; shopping lists in the headers (at the top of page 10 was written, *Buy dog food!*)

Blue Fountain Pen's own life seeped into the pages, entangling with the words until they were one book. Certain characters were circled and related to real people. The pompous arrogant suspect was labelled, *Like Sally* and, *I can relate* was written beside the scene when the detective drank his sorrows.

Yet, they were humorous too. Even in a crime novel, Blue Fountain Pen made me laugh. *Don't try this at home*, was written beside the murder scene and, *Clearly this is a waste of time!* was written about the detective's pursuit of an empty lead.

I was anxious to know what Blue Fountain Pen had to say, desperate to know their opinions. It was like reading a book with a friend, internally responding to their comments, reading parallel across time.

It made me wonder who Blue Fountain Pen was, where they lived, what they did. Could they be the lady on the bus? The one who always had her nose in a book. Her white hair desperately dyed orange, clutching onto her youth like the handbag clasped to her chest. Or maybe the man down the road? In his perpetual uniform, his proud badge shining. Were crime novels his secret vice? Did he confidently accuse suspects like Blue Fountain Pen accused theirs?

I flicked through every page, read every note, but Blue Fountain Pen never named themselves.

I think he's the murderer ...

Blue Fountain Pen was very certain in their predictions. They thought themself a very good detective—in fact, *I'm a very good detective*, was inked on multiple pages. Not once did they waver in their suspicions. The wealthy patriarch was Blue Fountain Pen's murderer of choice.

It's the way he talks, they wrote. *He's hiding something. I can tell.*

Our detective fit the standard tropes: intelligent, troubled, hard-drinking. But he had a dog, a small English Cocker Spaniel—like Peggy—which Blue Fountain Pen said was, *The best breed of dog.*

When our detective clattered through the door late at night, Rover was there to greet him. With his droopy eyes, floppy ears and wagging tail, he was the only one who made our detective happy.

In chapter 12, the detective returned home from work as normal. But Rover wasn't by the door. Or in the kitchen. Or in the bedroom. He was lying still in the garden, his golden coat flat on the damp grass, his snout in the dirt. A warning from the murderer.

No! Not Rover, Blue Fountain Pen wrote.

With tears, I looked down at Peggy, sitting by my feet and chewing on her strange chicken. She looked up at me, with big droopy eyes and floppy ears.

They killed the dog! Blue Fountain Pen went on. *That's it. I'm done.*

In a panic, I flipped to the next page, only to see—in relief—a sad face drawn in the margin with that familiar blue ink.

The murderer's reveal. The moment I—and Blue Fountain Pen—had been waiting for. Our brilliant detective had cracked the case and gathered the suspects.

The victim: a rich heiress out late one night.

The suspects: her artist boyfriend, her arrogant friend, and her father (the patriarch of the family and Blue Fountain Pen's murderer of choice).

Our detective paced, detailed his method of investigation, his original suspect, and marvelled at how difficult the case was, then—finally—revealed the killer.

I knew it! Blue Fountain Pen wrote, and I revelled in the fact that I knew it too.

I sped through the remaining pages, then sank into a slump when the book closed. Blue Fountain Pen inscribed on the last page, *The end. Goodbye.*

But it really felt like I was saying goodbye. I'd walked with Blue Fountain Pen for days, glimpsed into their mind and grasped their personality, and then suddenly the story was over, the book closed and they didn't exist anymore. Their humanity preserved only in ink. A time capsule of a person gone.

Reading wasn't solitary with Blue Fountain Pen. We bonded over a shared interest, loops of blue ink projecting feelings through paper. Connecting only through scribbles.

I had to pass Blue Fountain Pen on. I couldn't keep them to myself, dusting alone on a bookshelf, when they had so much to say.

I found my next book in a street library. Left Blue Fountain Pen on the shelf in exchange for the book I chose. Another mystery; a new murder waiting to be solved. But no blue ink; a blank canvas.

I opened the book, turned to the title page and wrote in black Biro, *And so the case begins …*

www.ingramcontent.com/pod-product-compliance
Lightning Source LLC
Chambersburg PA
CBHW050110120726
47904CB00004B/1286